NEW YORK TIMES & USA TODAY BESTSELLING AUTHOR

SHANNON McKENNA

EDGE OF *Whispers*

OLIVER-HEBER BOOKS

Prologue

John was stoked. Finally, he was closing in on his prey.

He pulled into a parking place in the shadow of a large tree, not that his quarry could see him, parked around the corner. That shriveled old fop was probably congratulating himself for being so smart. Marco Barbieri's plane from Italy had landed six hours ago, and the old coot had been cruising in big circles around the boroughs of New York City in a taxi ever since he emerged from the airport. He'd changed cabs several times, but he always carried that traitorous RF trace with him, the one that John had arranged to have planted deep in the wheel mechanism of his trolley.

That trace had led John right to the small upstate town of Hempton, New York.

It was the asshole's own fucking fault for trusting his domestic staff back at the ancient palazzo in Castiglione Santangelo. All it had taken was some money to get the device planted in Barbieri's suitcase. And not even that much.

John slunk along the spiked wrought-iron fence that lined the street, staying in the shadows of overhanging shrubs, wary of ubiquitous security cameras. The taxi was pulling away now. Turning the corner.

Barbieri climbed the steps slowly and stood outside the door. His movements seemed nervous and hesitant.

John was flushed with triumph. He'd found the elusive, long-lost Contessa at last. Marco Barbieri's long-ago runaway bride. Of course, she'd be a shriveled hag now, which was a big shame when one calculated the job's basic fun factor. But even so, she was still the key to the treasure.

Marco Barbieri himself knew jack-shit about that treasure. Barbieri was all played out. Ripe for the coroner's slab. But the Contessa was another story.

The Contessa would know what John's boss needed to know. Why else would she have run away so far, and stayed away so long? She'd been gone for more than half a lifetime from Castiglione Santangelo, which was widely considered to be an earthly paradise. It certainly was compared to a nowhere little town in upstate New York.

Nobody did that without a good reason. His hands twitched with eagerness to pry the knowledge out of her by force. That was his gift. His happy place.

The door opened. He saw a rectangle of light, a tall, narrow female form silhouetted against it. The two figures stared at each other, motionless. John squinted in the dark. It was too far to be sure, but saliva still pumped into his mouth.

They were speaking in low tones. John wished he'd been able to plant a listening device in that suitcase, but chances were good that they were speaking Italian anyhow. He'd get the Contessa to give him a detailed transcript of their entire conversation in English, word for word. After a few minutes of John's special talents, and the old bitch would walk on her hands and bark like a dog if he said so.

He enjoyed that part of his work perhaps a little more than

he should, but no one had to know how much he enjoyed himself on the job except for his victims.

God knows, they weren't telling.

He steeled himself to wait. Killing Barbieri in front of the Contessa would put her in just the right mind-set for his interrogation, but it would make a hell of a mess. John was capable of patience when the situation warranted it. Still, his employer had been waiting for decades. He was cranky and bad-tempered from waiting.

Both of them were eager to pick up the pace.

John drifted like a big ghost up the stairs, pulling on his mask. It was unnecessary, since the Contessa would not live out the night, but John had found over time that the mask unleashed him, in some obscure and pleasurable way. While masked, he abandoned his mortal self and became Death itself. He was the Grim Reaper, in flesh and blood. It made him buzz with almost sexual anticipation.

He heard voices behind the door and the soft click of locks disengaging. John slunk to put his back to the wall, reining in the blood-drinking beast inside him. No knives or guns tonight. If Barbieri's blood was spilled here, it would narrow John's options afterward.

The instant the old man stepped out the door, John seized him. A sharp wrench, a strangled grunt, the wet crunch of a spine snapping—like a neck-wrung chicken.

"Marco!" The old woman sprang out the door. "No!" she shrieked. *"Assassino! Aiuto!* Help!" She lunged at him, clawing at his face.

He jerked back, startled at her attack, and dropped Barbieri's limp body. The Contessa's shrill cry broke off as he batted her back into her house. She lost her balance, fell to the floor, and scrambled back, crablike. She huffed as he landed heavily on top of her, knocking the wind out of her.

He clapped his hand over her trembling mouth. Feeling her ribcage hitch and jerk, desperate for oxygen. Soft, wrinkled skin beneath his hot, wet palm. He pinned her flailing hands. Her long white hair had come loose. Her frail body vibrated with terror.

He was grinning widely beneath the mask, heart thudding. He couldn't get enough of it.

"Not as fresh as I like," he mused aloud. "You must've been good-looking about a century ago, eh? But I'm a professional. I find my inspiration where I need to." He yanked out the first implement that came to hand, a hooked blade, and waved it in front of her eyes. "So, Contessa. Let's talk about those sketches."

Her eyes widened in horror. "What...what sketches?" She had a faint accent.

He narrowed his eyes. "Don't play dumb. You'll tell, Contessa. You'll tell."

Something flashed in her eyes, despite her fear. Something ironic—almost like amusement. She gave him a firm, resigned little head shake. *No.*

Laughing at him. That uppity dago bitch actually dared to laugh at him. Like she thought she was smarter than him. Better than him.

Killing rage was like rocket fuel. It went beyond inspiration now. He would carve every last bit of knowledge out of the uppity old whore, piece by piece. He lunged close, digging the blade into the flesh beneath her eye—and realized that she was no longer looking at him. She seemed to have forgotten that he existed entirely.

She was staring at the ceiling now, gasping for air. Her lips purple.

He rolled off her, and her hand flew to her chest. Clutching, rubbing. Pounding, weakly against her heart.

Oh, Christ. A fucking heart attack? Now? No fucking way.

He leaned over and slapped her face to get her attention. "You useless, troublesome bitch," he said.

Her eyes focused on him with some difficulty. His heightened predator senses felt her slipping away to someplace where he could not follow. He sensed rather than saw the hint of triumph in her eyes before they rolled up, went blank and empty. Gone.

She'd croaked, just to spite him. And now old Barbieri was dead, too.

The boss was not going to be happy. He did not feel like the embodiment of Death now. He felt like a dumb, clumsy dickhead who'd been brutally fucked with.

He touched the Contessa's throat. No pulse. Stone dead.

He suppressed the intense urge to mutilate their corpses. That would be undisciplined. A tantrum. He didn't allow himself tantrums anymore. Too risky.

He got up, panting, and looked around. He needed a plan of action, another lead.

A swift search of Barbieri's suitcase and briefcase yielded no insights. They'd fucked him good. The room was empty but for a writing table, a few carefully lit art pieces, and three envelopes on the table—stamped and ready. The one he picked up was addressed to Nancy D'Onofrio. He ripped it open and squinted at the antique cursive script.

> *My dearest Nancy,*
>
> *I'm afraid what I have to tell you will come as a shock. I'm sorry to have to tell you in a letter. I wanted to speak to all three of you in person, but after my cardiologist appointment last week, I decided I can't risk waiting until I have all three of my precious girls together in one room...*

Girls? His head lifted like an animal scenting prey. His eyes lit on a shelf crowded with photographs.

He went over to study them more closely. Sure enough. Three young women smiled out of the picture frames. Pretty young women. Too young to be the dead bitch's daughters. Granddaughters, maybe.

Fresh meat. And their addresses, written right there on the letters. Sweet detail.

He stared at the images. He was breathing hard. In one photo, a luscious girl with big dark eyes and long, curly dark hair was curled up in a window seat, reading. Another picture featured a tall, smiling girl with auburn hair who held a calico cat up beneath her chin. A slim waif with red hair wearing a slinky evening gown gestured proudly toward a huge abstract sculpture that towered behind her.

All three had bright, sparkling eyes, rosy lips, expanses of smooth, unmarked skin. Curves and hollows, for him to pinch and squeeze.

Those girls would walk on their hands and bark like dogs for him, too. He'd find the old man's long-sought prize, earn his fee, and have a fine, juicy time doing it.

So much saliva exploded into his mouth, he started to dribble. He licked his lips and wiped his chin. He knew better than to leave genetic material for the forensic types to test.

Finally, this job was starting to get interesting.

Chapter One

Nancy

"Are you girls going to be all right, Nancy?" Elsie's white brows knitted anxiously above her faded blue eyes. "I can stay longer, you know. As long as you need."

I manufactured what I hoped was a calm and reassuring look as I herded the old lady gently toward the door. I hugged Elsie warmly and gave her wrinkled cheek a kiss. "We'll be fine," I assured her. "We're exhausted, that's all. We need a little down time."

"But Lucia wouldn't have wanted you girls to be all alone," Elsie fussed.

My younger sister Nell seized the elderly neighbor's hand and patted it. "We'll be okay," she said gently. "Thanks so much for the casserole, Aunt Elsie. You've been wonderful to us. Lucia was so lucky to have you for a neighbor. We all feel lucky. It meant so much to her, and to us. Really."

After Elsie was finally nudged and flattered out the door, I locked it, deadbolted it, and collapsed against it, sliding down its length until my butt hit the floor.

"My God," I muttered. "That took forever. I think Lucia must've known everyone in town."

Nell sank down beside me. Vivi, our youngest sister, flopped onto her back on the scratched floorboards. She put her hand over her eyes to block a bolt of late afternoon sunlight coming through the panes in the door.

We were all in black for the graveside service. Vivi's fiery locks, spread across the floor and lit by the golden rays of the sun, seemed like the only bright color in the room. Everything else was drained of color.

I felt colorless, too—flavorless and used up, like gum that had already been chewed. Our foster mother Lucia's graceful, shabby old house had always felt like a benevolent entity in its own right, one that enveloped and protected its people.

Now, it just felt sad, tired, and empty. Robbed of its very heart.

Well. It had been. Literally. Figuratively too, I guessed. The warmth, the benevolence, that had been Lucia herself. Now it was just an old house—faded, creaking, and slightly shabby. For the first time, I saw the marks and scars, the stains and cracks I'd never noticed before, even though I'd lived there through all of my teenage years.

With Lucia in residence, the place had been graced with a flattering filter that obscured all its flaws. Lucia had that kind of magic. She cast it onto people, too. She had always made us feel somehow bigger, better, finer than we actually were.

In her eyes, we were already our best, ideal potential selves. And we could accomplish any fabulous, improbable thing. In her mind, it was just a matter of time.

But she was gone, and the faith she'd had in us vanished with her.

So much for my best self. Right now, I couldn't even remember what was so damn great about it—not without Lucia to remind me.

She used to tell us she had an eye for treasure. That was her special gift—recognizing hidden treasure, whether it was art, antiques, books, or people. That was why she'd fostered and then adopted the three of us. It made us all feel so special. We'd needed that so badly, back in the old days. Being chosen had been so healing.

And now the chooser was gone.

It was a good thing Vivi and Nell were here with me, because if I'd been alone with these feelings, I would've slid down into a very dark place.

As it was, I was hanging on by my fingernails.

"I hadn't been up here to see her for over a month." Nell's voice was bleak and small. "I just kept thinking, well, we'll be celebrating her birthday soon enough, so I kept on taking extra shifts. Putting it off. Like I had all the time in the world."

"Same," I said wearily. "Same thoughts. Same regrets. I've been so swamped lately. Two albums to cut. Mandrake about to go on tour. Blah blah blah. I thought it was all so goddamn important."

"Lucia's birthday was today," Vivi said. "We should have been drinking port wine, eating *schiacciata all'uva*. Remember how I used to tease her to get with the new millennium and make fudge brownies or Rice Krispies treats like a normal, red-blooded American? But right now, I'd give anything to crunch that weird grape focaccia and get the lecture about the sacred importance of tradition."

"Oh God, Vivi," I pleaded. "Don't do that. Don't get us going again."

The warning came too late. Lucia's *schiacciata all'uva* set us all off.

The three of us didn't have family traditions of our own. We'd lost our families of origin a long time ago. Lucia had plucked us out of the system and given us all the noise and mess of a real family—and with it, the weight and ballast of the past.

She'd even given us her name—D'Onofrio. It was a precious gift for all of us.

We avoided each other's eyes once the sobbing eased. At this point, my sob muscles ached like they'd been beaten black and blue. Enough already.

Nell's fingers found mine and squeezed. "I'm so sorry you had to find her all alone," she whispered. "I don't know what I would've done if it had been me."

I sucked in a big breath and let it out slowly, trying not to see it—but the image of Lucia crumpled on the floor would stay with me forever. "You would have done the same as me," I said. "I was nervous already. I'd called her two evenings in a row and she didn't pick up. That's not like her. So I guess I was braced for it. Kind of, I suppose. Not that being braced makes any damn difference in the end."

"That sick bastard could have called an ambulance when he saw she was having a heart attack," Vivi said. "It would have cost him nothing. He murdered her, even if the coroner called it natural causes. Since when is being scared to death a natural cause?"

"The thief certainly was an idiot and a dickhead, aside from being a sick bastard," Nell said. "He takes her jewelry, her computer and her TV, and leaves her Fabergé picture frame and her Cellini bronze? Wow."

"Speaking of which, we can't leave Lucia's fine art in an empty house," I said. "You're the sculptor, Vivi. Why don't you take the bronze?"

Vivi slanted me an ironic look, upside down. "Right," she

said. "A bronze Cellini satyr would look perfect on the dashboard of my van. Right next to the air freshener and the plastic Madonna."

"But I thought you were winding down from your time on the crafts fair circuit," I said. "Didn't you say you wanted to try being in one place for a while?"

Vivi shrugged. "Sure, I'd like to. But there's a big gap between saying it and doing it. I still have stock to sell, and I don't have a place to land yet. It makes no sense to settle unless it's in a place I can have a big studio, and that's expensive. So no. Not quite yet." My sister twisted, sinuous as a cat, and rolled over to face us, still lying on the ground. "I'm guessing that studio apartments in Alphabet City and Williamsburg aren't much better than a Volkswagen van when it comes to museum-quality art exposition, huh?"

"They most certainly are not," Nell said fervently. "I would never sleep again."

I bit my lip as I chewed on the problem. "What do we do? Rent a safe-deposit box?"

Vivi looked dubious. "Well, possibly. But we certainly can't put Lucia's *intaglio* writing table in a safety-deposit box."

The three of us regarded the graceful and ancient little table in question for a thoughtful moment.

"Should we just leave it here for now? And get an alarm?" Nell suggested.

Vivi shrugged. "Seems pointless. The house is empty. The whole town knows it."

"Let's at least buy a plastic tablecloth," I said. "Something truly hideous. I'll take the bronze. You take the picture frame, Nell, at least until we come up with a better plan. Put it up on your wall with a photo of all of us with Lucia in it. Let it hide in plain sight. Lucia can help protect it for us."

That attempt at brisk practicality petered out quickly into

another sad silence. Vivi rolled onto her back again. I slid my hand into my sister's long, silky mane.

"She was our bedrock," Vivi said softly.

"No, she gave us our bedrock. We can't ever lose it," I told her, trying to believe it. "We always will. We'll build our lives on it. That was her gift to us. And we've got each other. Another gift. Sisters."

Predictably, that set us all off once again

The doorbell jangled in the middle of the fresh sobfest, making us all jump and sniffle anxiously into our soggy tissues.

"Oh God, no," Nell whispered. "Not another condolence call. Please, no. I just can't. Check out the peephole, but don't make a sound. We're not even here."

I slowly rose to my feet and peeked out the peephole. A young man in a uniform stood there, holding a box and an electronic signing tablet.

"It's a delivery guy," I told my sisters, mystified.

"More flowers?" Vivi asked.

"No, it's a smallish box." I pulled the door open. "Yes?"

"Special hand delivery," the guy said, in a bored voice. "From Baruchin's Fine Jewelers. For Lucia D'Onofrio."

"She died a few days ago," I told him. "Today was her funeral."

The guy blinked, his mouth dangling, his eyes blank. This scenario was not covered by the set of simple and limited flowcharts in his head.

I took pity on him. "I'm her daughter," I told him. "I'll sign for it, if you want."

"Just a second. Lemme call my boss." He turned away as he made the call, and muttered into his phone. He turned back and passed me the tablet, eyes downcast. "Sorry for your loss," he mumbled as I signed my name.

I nodded and shut the door, examining the small box.

"Baruchin's Fine Jewelers since nineteen thirty-eight," I read off the front. "Weird. Who wants to do the honors?"

Vivi and Nell exchanged nervous glances.

"I'm not in the mood for surprises right now," Vivi said, her voice small.

Nell let out a shaky breath. "Go for it, Nance," she said. "Open it up."

I pried open the seals. Inside the box were three small identical leather boxes. I flipped open each box, laid them out in a row. We leaned over and gazed at their contents, awestruck.

A gorgeous Renaissance-style pendant was inside each box —each one unique, each one adorned with different gemstones. One featured sapphires, one rubies, and one emeralds. They were luscious. Extravagant. Exquisite.

The three of us turned away and sobbed for several minutes.

Vivi dragged a crumpled tissue out of her pocket and honked into it. "She was going to give them to us on her birthday," she said, her voice thick with tears.

"Our birthstones," Nell whispered. "Like when she gave us the earrings, that Christmas two years ago. I would bet money that those gems are absolutely real. They look like Renaissance jewelry. Something Lucretia Borgia might have worn."

Vivi pulled out her phone, plugging in the info from the delivery. "Baruchin's," she said, frowning down as she scrolled. "Yes. This jeweler specializes in reproductions of historical jewelry, among other things."

I loosened the emerald necklace from its velvet nest, reached around Vivi's slender neck and fastened the clasp. I dropped a kiss onto my sister's tear-dampened, freckled cheek. I did the same for Nell with the ruby pendant, struggling a bit to push my sister's thick mass of curly dark hair out of the way.

Then I pressed a kiss to my own sapphire pendant before reaching behind my neck to fasten it.

The necklace felt heavy, significant, full of portent around my neck. We stood there silently, our hearts full, holding Lucia's final, lovely gifts to us in our hands.

"Let's wear them always," I said, my voice a shaky croak. "Whenever we can. In Lucia's memory."

Vivi made a choked sound and ran toward the kitchen.

Nell rubbed her own pendant gently between her fingers, blinking tears from her long, dark lashes. "She saved our asses, you know," she said. "At least mine and Vivi's. Maybe not yours, Nance. You were born already grown up. I bet you could have saved yourself from the cradle."

I rolled my eyes. "Oh, please. Hardly. I needed just as much saving as anybody."

"I swear to God, it's a compliment," Nell insisted, her dark eyes indignant. "Really! I respect and admire you for it. In what universe is that not a compliment?"

"Stolid old Nancy," I said sourly. "Hit me with a brick, bam. I don't even blink."

"No, no. That's not it at all. You're not stolid, Nance. Stolid is thick, insensitive, dull. You're solid. A qualitative difference. You're tough, Nance. Strong. Not flaky. Tough and strong is a sexy combo."

I grunted. "Like boot leather? Useful, maybe. Not sexy. Ask any of my ex-fiancés."

Nell pantomimed spitting on the ground. "Not unless you want me to slug them out for you," she said tartly. "I admire many things about you, but your choice in men is not among them. Not that I'm in any position to criticize."

Vivi burst out of the kitchen, her eyes lit up with excitement. "I found it!" she said, waving a limp, yellowed scrap of paper. She hefted a wine bottle in the other hand.

"Found what?" Nancy asked.

"The recipe for that grape thing! *Schiacciata all'uva!* We even have the grapes! Elsie left some with the casserole. The recipe's in Italian, but you read Italian, right, Nell?"

Nell adjusted her glasses, took the paper out of Vivi's hand, and peered at it. "Sure. The measurements are metric, though. We can find a conversion table online, I guess."

I was baffled at Vivi's enthusiasm. "I thought you hated Lucia's *schiacciata!*"

"Oh, I do," Vivi assured me. "With a passion. But it's the perfect thing for Lucia's wake. Just us three sniveling together, a couple of bottles of port, and a panful of Lucia's weird Tuscan grape focaccia. In her honor. For tradition. For family. For her."

I pulled my sister into my arms and held her. Vivi felt so delicate to me, vibrating with emotion. She'd always felt that way—like a baby bird. I wished I had Lucia's easy skill to comfort my sensitive little sister. Lucia had pulled it off with effortless grace, perfectly chosen words. I'd always marveled at the way she could make anything feel meaningful and magical just by looking at it in just the right way and saying not too much, not too little. Just what was needed. The perfect thing, reverberating like a gong.

But I would do my best. Maybe I wasn't as good as Lucia had been, but it wouldn't be for lack of trying, or lack of caring. That I could promise.

None of us were good cooks, but we did our best for Lucia's sake. Our raggedy-ass *schiacchiata all'uva* was a far cry from Lucia's elegant traditional Tuscan sweet. The oven timer did not go off. The smoke detector did. But the port we guzzled made us indiscriminate enough to actually eat some of it.

It was wonderfully awful, especially burned.

Chapter Two

Nancy

The first thin blade of light that pierced between my gummy eyelids jabbed into the center of my brain.

Ouch. That got my attention. I rubbed my eyes as my belly did a slow, queasy flop. It took a second to orient myself in time and space.

It appeared that at some point we had migrated into the living room, bringing the last bottle of port with us. The bottle lay on its side, conspicuously empty. Three of Lucia's beautiful cut-crystal liquor glasses were tipped over on the floor, each stuck in its own small, dark puddle of port.

I had slept sitting up and had that resulting stiff, scrunched-neck feeling. Vivi's head was on my lap, and Nell was curled up on the love seat across from us, her thick dark hair draped across her face. I patted Vivi's shoulder, and she stirred, murmuring in a questioning tone. "Wha...?"

"Morning," I said, my voice thick and froggy. "Unfortunately."

Vivi struggled up into a sitting position with a hiss of pain, putting her hand to her head. "Oh boy," she croaked. "I don't even remember making it into this room."

Nell stretched, yawned, and winced. "Ow," she murmured. "I vaguely remember half-carrying you. We did a lot of toasting. Now we pay the price. Yay, us."

"It's worth it," I said. "You embrace both sides, right? Like Lucia says—said. The dark and the light. *Il dolce e l'amaro.* The bitter and the sweet."

"Don't you dare, Nance." Nell gave me a dark look. "Don't start up with the sentimental stuff and get us all wound up again. Did Lucia keep any painkillers?"

"As I recall, she disapproved of them on principle, but I have you covered," I assured her. "I have a witch's brew of Tylenol, aspirin and caffeine in my purse that'll put hair on your chest."

"Yum," Vivi said. "Bring it on."

We took turns in the bathroom, washing up. I swabbed off the ill-fated remnants of yesterday's makeup and wound my hair back tight enough to make my forehead hurt. When I got downstairs, coffee was ready and Nell was gazing in dismay at the total wreck of the kitchen.

She poured me a cup. "It looks just terrible in here," she said, handing it to me. "I would clean it up right now, but I have to proctor an exam today, and Vivi has to drive me back to the city to get there in time. But we're not dumping this all on you, understand? We'll come back here and deal with it. Don't you dare do it yourself. You've done enough."

Hah. Like I was constitutionally capable of leaving Lucia's kitchen looking like that, knowing how Lucia would have felt about it. Lucia had been a passionate neatnik, and she'd passed the quality on to me, and only me, of the three of us. It got lonely and frustrating, being the only neat-freak sibling.

I waved a vague hand. "Don't worry about it."

"No way!" Nell said forcefully. "Don't do it alone, or we'll writhe in guilt. You always do that. Stop that shit. Don't be the martyr. It's not good for any of us."

"Okay, okay," I lied, holding up my hands. "We'll all do it together later."

My sisters gathered up their things, and I followed them out to Vivi's gaudily painted Volkswagen van, which was parked in the driveway. I gave them both long tight hugs.

After they got in, Nell leaned out of the passenger-side window and shook her finger at me. "We'll hook up after I finish that exam. Don't clean up yet, or I'll make you sorry you did. Take it easy. Rest. Recover."

"I can't rest, Nell. I've got a million things to—"

"Yes, yes. Of course you do. But you need to take care of yourself first of all," Vivi was scolding me now, leaning over Nell's lap from the driver's side.

Take care of me? I didn't even know what that would mean. I watched Vivi's taillights glow in the morning mist until she turned the corner and was gone.

The sky had a heavy, bruised look, altogether appropriate for my mood. Sunlight would have been discordant and painful. Our drunken revels had been cathartic at the time, but in the moment, I felt as if I'd been scraped off the bottom of a shoe.

Time to get busy. My frantic schedule would save me. All the things that I'd put off last week because of Lucia's death and funeral would keep me too busy to think, or hopefully, feel. Constant activity was my number one coping mechanism, and lucky for me, my career choice—managing an eclectic bunch of singer-songwriters and folk bands—involved ceaseless admin.

Back in the day, I'd dreamed of being a musician myself.

Eventually, I grew up and accepted the fact that I didn't really have the musical chops, practice as I might.

I had, however, identified other talents while helping my musical friends get gigs in college. I was good behind the scenes. I figured out how to make myself indispensable. Got hooked on the feeling of being in the middle of it all. The one who made it happen.

Everyone had their gifts. When it came to niggling, detail-minded, dogged, tenacious determination, I was unbeatable. It was good to identify one's strengths, even if they weren't the glamorous, shiny ones that most of the world noticed and admired.

I'd steadily nudged my handpicked group of folk artists and ensembles out of the pub and coffeehouse concert series circuits and into bigger theaters and more prestigious folk festivals. I'd been getting more airtime on radio stations, marketing them hard on all of the social media platforms, and my efforts seemed to be paying off. A few of them were actually poised to break into the big time.

If that finally happened, I would be able to call this activity an actual career, and not just an extremely expensive, time-consuming, more-or-less delusional hobby. I just had to slog onward, toward that glorious day when I could hire a staff, instead of being a one-woman outfit. I would break through that brick wall eventually.

But today, a long 'to-do' list suited me fine. If I was zipping around at high speed, all hands waving like a dancing Shiva, with a phone in every one of them, I wouldn't have time or space to feel that black hole of grief at my core. Or if I did feel it, it would be on the periphery of my consciousness. Not smack-dab in the center.

Coping mechanisms got a bad rap, but damn, they kept the world duct-taped together. I was a big fan.

I pressed my hand against the sucking pain in my midriff and tried to breathe. I had never put my coping mechanisms to the test like this.

First things first. I needed an appropriate hideous table-cloth to cover the precious *intaglio* writing table. I drove down to the dollar store and stood in the aisle pondering the relative merits of hideous florals or plastic plaid in dull hues of beige and taupe.

I concluded that in the context of the understated elegance of Lucia's front room, the beige and taupe plaid mumbled "Please don't notice me," while the hideous floral squawked "What's wrong with this picture?"

I was probably giving mouth-breathing burglars too much credit. As if those bottom-feeders were going to listen to what the plastic tablecloths whispered to them.

It was starting to rain when I got back, and I darted up Lucia's steps, holding the plastic bag that held the tablecloth over my head.

"Excuse me?"

The deep, resonant masculine voice startled me into dropping the bag. It slid down the porch stairs, coming to a stop at the feet of the man who stood there, looking up at me. He stooped to pick it up. Rain sparkled on the spiky tips of his dark hair. His eyes met mine, and my breathing stopped. Everything stopped. Including time.

"Sorry. Didn't mean to startle you," he said.

His words started the clock again. *That's okay,* I tried to say, but no words would form in my mouth. I gave him a jerky little nod. My glasses were spotted with rain, so I dried them on my sweater, or at least smeared the drops around some. Even out of focus, he looked amazing.

I couldn't focus on any particular detail that stood out amid the general excellence. His face was wet with rain. A sexy shadow of beard stubble accented all the sculpted planes and angles of his strong jaw. He had a bump on his nose. His eyes were pale green. Dark brows, long thick lashes. Broad shoulders, a barrel chest, and muscular legs in faded work jeans. I was willing to bet he had a stellar ass to match. I was definitely going to verify that hypothesis at my earliest opportunity. Discreetly, of course.

And I horrified myself that I could be knocked on my ass by something so frivolous today, of all days. I had to shut this down right now, before I lost all respect for myself.

He observed me keenly as the rain pattered down. It gave me the uncomfortable sensation that everything noteworthy about me was written all over me, in a language that he could read in one sweeping glance. Which was unfortunate today, since God knows, I was not at my best.

I put my glasses back on. In that moment of grace before they got spotted up again, and before I could forbid my brain to do it, I flash-memorized every detail of him. The winged sweep of his thick brows, the grooves that bracketed his mouth. The smile lines. But he wasn't smiling at the moment.

He wiped rain off his forehead with his sleeve. "Are you Nancy D'Onofrio?"

This epitome of hot manhood knew my name? I nodded, wishing I'd opted to wash my hair this morning. The tight bun was a lazy, deal-with-it-later choice. A peeled-onion, tight-lipped schoolmarm still in yesterday's stale funeral black, eyes swollen up, breath reeking of alcohol. I looked like a walking cluster of big red flags.

This guy, by contrast, looked clear-eyed and clean-living. He probably went to bed at ten and got up at five to stand on his head for ten minutes, or run ten miles, or something insane like that. He probably drank green tea, not espresso.

I saw him in my mind's eye, shirtless. Moving smoothly from yoga pose to yoga pose.

Whoa. How shallow was I?

It's just distraction. The answer bubbled up from a calmer place inside my head. He was eye candy, and my eyes were hungry. Gawking at a beautiful man was a way not to think about the piece that had been torn from my life. And the ragged hole left behind.

Oh shit. Now my eyes were fogging up. The guy's mouth was moving, and I'd just been staring. Mouth open, no doubt. I hadn't followed him at all.

"... Mrs. D'Onofrio here? I had an appointment with her this morning."

Oh, God, not again. Irrational anger flared inside me. Why was it my goddamn job to announce this catastrophe to the whole world? I'd been the one to find Lucia's body. I'd been the one to call the cops. I'd been the one to call my sisters. I'd gone up and down the block, telling neighbors, activating their community phone trees. I'd told the delivery people, I'd dealt with the funeral home, I'd written the obit. Could somebody else please take a fucking turn?

Not his fault, I reminded myself. I shook my head. "Lucia's dead." My voice was colorless.

His face went blank with shock. "Oh, my God. When?"

I rubbed my wet eyes under my glasses, took a deep breath, and tried again. "A few days ago," I said. "The funeral was yesterday."

He was silent for a long moment. "I am so sorry," he said gently.

There was no good response to that. I'd learned that this week, to my great cost. I just nodded. "Yeah. Me, too. So who are you?"

"I'm Liam Knightly. I'm the carpenter. I'm here to start the work on the house."

"Work? On the house? What work?"

"She didn't tell you about the renovations she was planning?"

I shook my head. "I hadn't spoken to her for a couple of weeks before she died."

"Neither did I," he said. "We set this date weeks ago."

I shook my head. No clue what to do about him and his plans for Lucia's house. He was an ambassador from that alternate timeline, the wonderful one that would have existed if Lucia hadn't been ... no. I had to stop the what-if thinking. It didn't help.

Liam Knightly wiped the rain off his face. "Would it make you nervous if I stood under the porch roof with you? I'm getting drenched."

"Uh, that's fine," I said distractedly. "I'm sorry I didn't ask you before. Do you want to come in? For a cup of coffee, or tea? If Lucia has tea. Or had, I guess I should say." Damn. Babbling again. I did that when I got nervous.

Knightly's eyes showed the subtle gleam of a smile. "Thank you, yes. Wait just one moment. I'll go tell Eoin to wait."

I watched him run lightly down the walk and concluded that his ass was as fine as his quadriceps had suggested that it might be. "You could both come in," I called.

"No, he's shy. He'll be fine in the truck." Knightly jerked open the driver's side door and exchanged a few words with whoever sat on the passenger side. A few long, loping strides brought him back up to the porch.

It took me forever to get the locks open. My hands felt clumsy and thick. When the door finally swung wide, the smell of the funeral flowers was intensely strong.

Knightly followed me through the house. His footsteps

were weirdly quiet for such a big man walking on such old, creaky floors. I snapped on the kitchen light and had a bad moment when I remembered how we'd trashed the place last night. Every surface was covered with spilled flour, shreds of dough, and the odd grape here and there, squished on the floor and the countertop. The scorched crusts of the *schiacciata* looked sad and unkempt on the fine china serving plate. Sticky port bottles lay empty and forlorn, both on and under the table.

He must think I was a total lush. A slob, too.

"We had a wake for her last night," I felt compelled to explain. "Me and my sisters. Up all night with port wine and Tuscan pastry."

Knightly nodded. "Sounds like an appropriate thing to do."

I touched my aching head with my fingertips. "It seemed that way at the time," I said dully. "So what was I... oh, yes. Coffee. Or tea." I started rummaging in the kitchen drawers, feeling shaky and rattled. "Which do you prefer?"

"Tea, please. If Lucia has it. Had it."

"I thought you'd pick tea," I told him. "What kind? Green? Herbal?"

"Black tea if you have it," he said. "With sugar. And milk if possible. I'm Irish. I get the tea thing from my folks."

"I'm Irish, too," I confessed.

His eyebrows lifted. "Really? With a name like D'Onofrio? Wasn't Lucia ..."

"Italian? God, yes. Down to her toenails." Nancy yanked a green canister of Irish Breakfast tea out of the drawer. "Will this do?"

"That'll be fine."

"She adopted us," I went on, rummaging for the teakettle. "She took us in when we were foster kids. I was the first one she found. I was thirteen. Nell and Vivi came later. My name was O'Sullivan, then." Pans rattled and clanked as I shoved them around. "O'Sullivan was my mother's name. I don't know about my father. He could have been Italian, for all I know. The way things went, I was lucky to have a surname at all."

"Hey," he said gently. "You seem upset. You don't have to tell me all this—"

"I was so glad when Lucia finally adopted me." I couldn't stop talking, although there was a tight quaver in my voice. "It was a dream come true. I was so proud she wanted me. I've been a D'Onofrio for more than half my life now, so I guess that means I'm Italian now too, whether the Italians want to claim me or not." I yanked out a kettle that was nested in some other pans and ended up pulling the whole cluster out of the cupboard. They hit the floor with an ear-splitting clatter.

I stared down, the kettle clutched in my hand. I felt Liam Knightly's big, warm hand at my elbow, gently steering me toward a kitchen chair, turning me around, then nudging me steadily backward until I lost my balance and was forced to sit down on it.

"Let me." He took the kettle from my numb fingers.

I just sat there, speechless, and let him do it. He ran water into the kettle, set it on the stove, lit the gas. He gathered the pans and slid them back into the cupboard without so much as a sound. Without seeming to search for anything, he assembled sugar, mugs, spoons, milk. Damn, he was smooth.

He gently pushed the clutter aside on the table and draped a tea bag in each mug. Hot water gurgled pleasantly as he filled them. Steam rose.

Knightly put the kettle down and sat, waiting patiently. I was so embarrassed at my little freak-out. When I made no move to drink, he finally stirred some sugar and milk into both cups and nudged one toward me.

"Go on," he urged. "Tea helps with everything. My mom always used to say that."

I tried to smile. Took a cautious sip. It must have been the hot steam against my face, but suddenly tears were slipping down. They tickled my face, dangled from my chin, filled my nose. Damn that nose. Already puffy and red from yesterday's tears.

"She was a wonderful lady," Knightly said. "Pure quality."

Right then, I wished desperately that I'd left my hair down, unwashed or not. I would have loved to tilt my head forward and have curtain of hair to hide behind.

But it was not to be. My hair was slicked back cruelly tight, every wisp smoothed, with my pale, wet face naked and exposed in the cold, gray light of morning.

"Yes," I said. "She was. The best. In every way."

The sounds of the morning smoothly shifted into the foreground as the silence lengthened—cars passing by, rain sluicing down the window glass. Steam curled up from the two cups.

Liam Knightly reached out and took my hand.

My first instinct was to yank it back, but I didn't want to be rude, and he'd been so nice about the tea. Besides, he had a nice hand. Big, warm, callused. His gentle, careful grip made my own hand tingle.

"I lost my mother six years ago," he offered. "I couldn't breathe for weeks afterward."

"Oh. So, um. You know," I mumbled. "How it is."

"Yes, I know."

Tears blinded me again. He just sat there, sipping tea, clasping my hand. In my usual tense and anxious state, any kind of silence felt like dangerous emptiness that needed to be filled.

But Knightly's silence was different. It made space for me. He didn't seem embarrassed or put off by my little breakdown. He was in no hurry. He didn't seem to be wondering how quickly he could get away from the whacked-out, grieving girl.

My hand felt good in his. Warm.

It occurred to me suddenly that this was the most inti-macy I'd had—besides hugs from my sisters—since my last fiancé's defection. And maybe a good long time before that, if I was honest. Maybe he was just being nice, but the patient way Liam Knightly held my hand, witnessing my tears without flinching, was more subtly erotic than anything I'd ever shared with Freedy. Or any of the others either, for that matter.

I mopped my eyes with a crumpled napkin, then felt a soft square of cloth tucked into my hand. A handkerchief, of all things. I looked at it, bemused. "Wow," I said. "I didn't know people still used these."

"I'm old-fashioned," he said. "My father liked them. It's an artifact from a bygone age. One I happen to like."

I dabbed my eyes with the crisply ironed cotton, wishing I looked prettier, and feeling stupid and childish for wishing it.

He squeezed my hand gently. "I don't mean to touch anything painful, but could you tell me what actually happened to Lucia?"

The question jolted me out of my self-absorption. "Oh. Yeah. A thief broke into the house while she was here alone. The shock and fear must have provoked a heart attack."

His mouth tightened. "That must have been so terrible for you."

I nodded. "I was the one who found her, about two days later. I'd been calling her, but she hadn't been answering. So I came to check on her. I was already scared for her."

"Christ, that must've been hell." His hand tightened. "Did he ..." He hesitated, clearly afraid to ask. "Had the burglar hurt her?"

"Not as far as they could tell," I told him. "The chain on the door was broken. The TV, computer, and stereo were gone.

And Lucia's jewelry. Just a petty thief, I guess." I tugged my hand away. "Let's get back to practical matters, okay?"

His smile flickered. "Whenever you like. There's no rush."

"I imagine you're losing money right and left as the clock ticks," I said.

"Not really," he said. "I'm self-employed. And I choose not to see my time in that way. There's always time for a cup of tea and condolences for a lost friend."

"Ah." Well. Just call me brittle, shallow, and uptight then, why didn't he. "Okay. Anyhow, I have no idea what kind of arrangement you made with Lucia, but—"

"How about if I just tell you now?"

I retreated behind my tea mug. "Ah, okay."

He pulled a square of folded paper out of his pocket, which proved to be a floor plan of Lucia's ground floor. Several notes and edits had been made in Lucia's distinctive, elegant script. It hurt to look at it.

"We chose this date to start the work," he said. "She was going to make the changes to the ground floor that you see on that plan—build a new deck, put in teak flooring, redo both bathrooms and the kitchen, update the stairs, enlarge the upstairs closets, finish the attic, and add skylights in the upstairs bedrooms."

"Ah ... wow." I stared at the plan, bemused. "I am so sorry that it all went up in smoke. I imagine that will create big problems for your work schedule."

He shook his head. "I'll be fine. I have plenty of work, and for this job, I'd only hired one assistant. But I do have a truck full of building materials parked outside, and another full load in my barn back home—bought and paid for. That stuff's not smoke."

I was startled. "Bought already? Lucia bought it?"

"Yes. Forty-two thousand dollars and change."

My jaw dropped. "Forty-two ... oh my God! Is it refundable?"

Knightly hesitated, gazing into his tea mug. "Ah, no," he said, reluctantly. "I knew a guy who was going out of business and liquidating stock, so I took Lucia there a few weeks ago. We picked out supplies at a quarter of the list price. No refunds. And the lumber's already been cut."

I blew out a shaky breath. "Oh, man. That's a kick in the ass. Forty-two thousand bucks' worth of lumber, flooring, tile, and bathroom and kitchen fixtures."

"I'm sorry," he offered. "I really liked her, so I was trying to save her money."

"Well, thanks for that," I muttered.

He drummed his fingers against the table thoughtfully. "You've got a couple of different choices here," he said thoughtfully. "You can try to sell the stuff on eBay or Craigslist and probably recoup at least a portion of what she spent. Or you can go ahead with the renovation. It'll definitely boost your property value. Though I have no idea who currently owns the house."

There was a delicate pause. "My sisters and I," I supplied. "In equal measure."

"Ah. Good, then. So all you'd have to pay for now is labor, and a few odds and ends for whatever comes up last minute. You'd recover that and more in the increased property value. That way, the investment won't be wasted. If you intend to sell the house, that is."

"We don't 'intend' anything." My voice came out more sharply than I meant it to. "The funeral was yesterday. We have no plans yet."

He lifted his hands. "Sorry. I didn't mean to seem like I was pressuring you."

His quiet tone shamed me. This was not his fault at all. It

was so hard to think clearly. I kept losing the thread, getting muddled and lost. "My sisters should know about this," I said. "Would you mind if I called them right now?"

He set his cup down and rose to his feet. "That's fine with me. I'll step outside while you make the call. To give you some privacy."

"Oh, no, it's fine. Please, sit down." I waved him back down and dialed Vivi's number. Nell, the impractical bookworm scholar, had a smartphone in her possession, but she may as well not have it, since she almost never turned it on or charged it up, and when she did, she never had the ringer on, or even kept it anywhere near her person. Nell considered smartphones evil in general; annoying, probably carcinogenic, and worst of all, a diabolical sinkhole for her precious attention. Chances are she was right about all of that, but in practical terms, this philosophical position drove Vivi and me nuts. Which Nell thought was hugely funny.

Or at least, she had thought so before what happened to Lucia.

"Yeah?" Vivi picked up immediately. "You okay?"

"I'm fine, but I've discovered a new wrinkle." I outlined the situation just as Knightly had described it, then waited while Vivi relayed it to Nell.

There was some muffled back-and-forth on the other end before Vivi came back with the verdict. "Our combined opinion is that if Lucia wanted it done and went to the trouble of buying all the supplies, we should respect her wishes. Problem is, I don't have any cash on hand to pay the crew." Nell said something emphatic in the background. "And neither does Nell," Vivi added.

"Okay. Maybe I can look into getting a loan. Later, babes." I ended the call and turned to him. "This is the situation as it stands," she said. "My sisters and I are disposed to proceed, so as not to waste Lucia's investment. But we don't have cash on hand to cover your labor—at least not yet. Lucia had some money tucked away, I assume, but we don't know how much or when we'll be able to access it. I can look into taking out a loan, but in the meantime—"

"Don't worry about it. I'll just go ahead and get started. Pay me later. When you sort it all out."

I was startled. "Are you sure that's wise? I don't even know when I can get the cash. I wouldn't want to put you in a bind."

His shrug was nonchalant. "I can cover costs for a couple of weeks. I only have Eoin to pay, for now. We'll just see how it goes."

"On just my word?"

His eyes gleamed over his cup. "I know your word's good."

"Ah ... you just met me fifteen minutes ago," I pointed out.

Knightly glanced at his watch. "Eighteen minutes. That's more than enough."

His gaze was so intense. It wiped my mind clear of coherent thought.

All thoughts but one.

No. Not today. I was grieving, wobbly, my judgment shot to hell, and I was probably imagining all these wildly inappropriate, ill-timed vibes. No, no, and no.

Or maybe I wasn't imagining them, and that was even worse. He was way too big for my tastes, for one thing. There was just too much of him. I steered around big men who gave off those commanding alpha-dog signals. I avoided them like the plague. And perfect though Knightly's manners might be, mellow though he might act, there was no mistaking a man like that. I could spot one disguised in any costume—a dress suit, a military uniform, or jeans and a T-shirt. The force field of Liam Knightly's natural machismo tickled my skin, all the more dangerous for how deliciously subtle it was.

It wasn't a bad thing. It was how he was, like having brown hair, or a nice ass. But even so. I had to run the show when it came to relationships, romance, sex. That detail was non-negotiable. And a guy like him would want to be on top.

Figuratively speaking.

My gaze skittered around and landed on the plastic tablecloth. Ah. Yes. Something to do. I grabbed the package, ripped open the wrapping and headed for the living room.

Knightly followed me, mug in hand, still sipping in that leisurely way of his. I'd long since nervously gulped down all of my own tea. He watched as I unfolded the tablecloth and shook it out. The stink of new, raw plastic overwhelmed even the scent of the funeral flowers. I positioned it carefully over Lucia's *intaglio* writing table.

"It's none of my business," Knightly said. "But why on earth are you covering that beautiful thing with that godawful plastic?"

"Camouflage," I said. "In case the burglars come back. My sister and I will take the smaller pieces of fine art home with us, for lack of a better plan, but none of us has a place for this table. Did Lucia tell you the table's history?"

"Yes, actually. She told me the SS officers used it during the Nazi occupation. That they used her father's palace for their headquarters."

I was startled. Lucia had not usually been so forthcoming about her family history. "Yes. The Nazi officers were the ones who made the graffiti," I said, tracing some of the brutal scratches carved into the delicately carved tangle of flowers.

"Bastards. But now that's part of its fascination. It's a piece of living history."

"Lucia's father was a count, you know? The Conte de Luca. So Lucia was technically a countess, even though she lived over half her life here in New York."

It felt good to talk about Lucia. Like a pressure valve releasing steam.

"I'm not surprised," Knightly said. "She looked the part. She was a class act."

I blinked back fresh tears and shook the tablecloth into place with an angry jerk. "Yes, she was." I positioned the jade plant in the center. "There. Who would guess?"

"Looks butt-ugly," he said judiciously.

"That's what I was going for," I said. "Thanks."

Knightly laid his hand gently on the table, as if he were stroking a living thing. "I'd love to study it someday. Figure out how the guy did it."

"Did what?"

"How he made something that's still intact and still beautiful after four hundred years of use, plus the vandalism and abuse," he said. "That's real talent. I'd love to learn from it." He turned away, taking his mug back into the kitchen.

My eyes fell on Lucia's shelf of photos as I gazed after him, and a thought occurred to me. I waited until he reappeared in the doorway.

"How did you know who I was, outside the house?" I asked.

That subtle smile lit his eyes again. "Lucia showed me pictures," he admitted. "She told me about you three. She bragged you up, actually. She was very proud."

A dark suspicion dawned in my mind. "Bragged me up?" I repeated. "Oh, no. What do you mean? What did she tell you?"

"That you work too hard," he said. "That you let everyone take advantage of you. That you live in a tiny Manhattan apartment surrounded by motorcycle gangs, crackheads, meth heads, and the criminally insane. That you come across as bossy and managing, but you'd give the shirt off your back to a stranger in need—"

I winced. "Oh, no. I see exactly where this is going."

"And that you're not married. She said you'd be here for her birthday. She wanted to introduce us."

"Oh, God." I felt myself turn a hot red. Lucia, for fuck's sake. Really?

Lucia would never have done this to me if this guy was taken. And a swift glance at Knightly's left hand confirmed that he wore no ring.

Of course, he intercepted the glance. His smile deepened, and my mortification deepened with it. "I'm so sorry," I babbled. "You being put on the spot, I mean. Lucia just couldn't stand it that I'm single."

"That was my impression, too. But I will admit, it is strange."

I covered my hot cheeks with my hands. "What's strange?"

"That you're single. You're not at all what I expected."

Don't ask it. Don't ask it. Just don't. "What did you expect?" I asked, helpless to stop myself.

"She told me you were beautiful. I could see from the pictures that it was true. She just didn't tell me how beautiful. Photos can't capture that."

Beautiful? Wild energy crackled through my nerves, as if he'd touched me.

Suddenly, I started to imagine how it would feel if he did.

I vibrated. Strange, that I was single? Hah. Little did he know. I forced my voice not to shake. "Don't flatter me."

"I'm not flattering anyone. I don't do that. Just the plain truth."

I looked away, flustered. No clue what to say.

A long, agonizing moment passed. "Ah. I'm so sorry," he said quietly. "That was totally wrong. I can't believe I just said that to you. Please forget I said it."

"It's okay," I murmured. Right. Like I would. Ever. In my life.

But the easy intimacy I'd felt with him before was gone. Knightly's face was closed and unreadable as we exchanged phone numbers. He and his assistant, Eoin, would unload supplies that day and start on the kitchen tomorrow, though I had to clean it first. We set a time to meet the next morning. All done. Just the facts, ma'am.

It gave me a pang to hand over Lucia's house keys to a man I'd just met, but the thought of having someone in the place was oddly comforting. I hated the thought of the house lying empty and bereft. This way, at least it was in a process of renewal. One that Lucia herself had set in motion.

Once he had the keys, there was no reason to not to let him and his assistant get on with their work. I shook his hand politely, gathered up my bag and the carefully bubble-wrapped bronze Cellini satyr, and took off.

I was pissed with Lucia for setting me up. At the same time, I missed her desperately. I felt raw and shaky, desperate to glom on to something else to think about. God knows, I'd been twitchy about dating and romance since long before Lucia's death.

It occurred to me that Lucia had probably filled Knightly in on my string of romantic disasters. The thought made me cringe.

The first time I'd been dumped at the altar by my fiancé was very bad. The second time had been worse. By the third time it happened, I was seriously starting to consider that maybe I was the problem.

Not that I had the faintest clue how to fix it.

So? Fine. I could resign myself to being a single woman. I would content myself with a series of cats. Or do what Lucia had done. If I experienced a great upwelling of motherly energy in my heart, and had the means and time, I could always adopt some half-grown kids who desperately needed a home.

There was more than one way to have a family. The center of a woman's life did not have to be a man.

Besides, men didn't seem to enjoy being at the center of my life. By all accounts, it was a prickly, uncomfortable place to be.

My sisters and Lucia had all politely despised Freedy, Ron, and Peter. But was it their fault they'd fallen out of love with me? A person either loved someone or they didn't. I wasn't about to marry a man who'd found out he didn't.

I wondered, not for the first time, if I lacked some innate womanly skill. Maybe I should've practiced gazing up through fluttering lashes more—hanging on their every word, puffing up their egos.

But that wasn't me. I'd always been too busy managing their careers, making them take their vitamins, wrangling their anxiety, making sure their socks matched.

Freedy told me I was too controlling. Ron said I was "driven." Peter told me I just was too prosaic. He said that I couldn't join him in that place full of dreams where he needed to go to make the magic happen.

But he sure hadn't minded me finding lucrative gigs for him from that prosaic other world. What a shame that watching me do all the scut work to support his precious career had been such a turnoff to him. Fussbudget Nancy, the detail freak. And that damn phone of mine—always ringing, shattering his precious creative trance. Aww. So sorry.

Not that I was bitter or anything.

The strange, raw mood I was in brought on a brutal kind of self-honesty. I stared, hot-eyed, out the windshield, and let myself ponder it. The real problem with my fiancés had been sex, above all. Sex had always been problematic for me. I didn't like feeling vulnerable, squished, crowded. Being overwhelmed in any way, physical or emotional, made me run away in my head. I became unreachable.

When that happened, the fun was definitely over. Everybody out of the pool.

My lovers, not surprisingly, had become impatient with this, and who could blame them.

The thought of having one of those uncomfortable, it's-not-you-it's-me conversations with Liam Knightly made me want to curl up and rock in the corner.

After Freedy's defection, I'd sworn off romance. Celibacy was easier, less embarrassing, and way cheaper. No bikini waxing, no scratchy lace push-up bras. It was comfy stretch cotton sports bras from here on out. Or better yet, no bras at all. Sweet, sweet freedom.

But Knightly's gaze made me feel as if he'd seen something in me that no one else had, not even me. I wanted to see him again, to find out if it was a fluke. A trick of the light. A passing spasm.

It was an experiment doomed to fail, however, because the guy was just too big. And he exuded that aura of controlled power that made me feel vulnerable, even fully clothed and a full table-length away. I could only imagine how that vibe would feel if we were naked. Skin to skin. And oh, *shit*—

I screeched to a stop at the red light, just in time. Face flushed, heart pounding.

I, Nancy D'Onofrio, hyper-efficient multitasker, couldn't even think about that man while driving.

Chapter Three

Liam

I hung onto the sight of Nancy D'Onofrio until her car turned the corner, suppressing the mad urge to sprint to the end of the block to catch another glimpse.

I didn't do it. I had that much self-control, at least. Which wasn't saying a hell of a lot.

I ran down the steps through the rain and got into the truck. Eoin, a distant cousin of mine fresh from County Wicklow, gave me a questioning glance as I wiped rain off my face.

"So?" Eoin asked. "What are we doing?"

"We're getting on with it."

Eoin's blue eyes widened. "Really? The daughters want to go ahead?"

I nodded, squeezing my hand around the sense memory of Nancy D'Onofrio's cool, slender fingers. Eoin caught the vibe, sensitive, curious little bastard that he was, and shot me a keen sidelong glance. "Daughter's a looker, eh?"

"She just put her mother in the ground yesterday," I snarled.

Eoin mumbled something apologetic that made me feel like a hypocritical piece of shit. Like I had any right to scold the kid. What the fuck was I thinking, coming on to a woman who'd just buried her mother? She was still in her funeral dress, red-eyed from crying. She probably took me for one of those slimy opportunists who preyed on grieving women. God. My tongue had probably dangled out like a slavering hound.

Lucia D'Onofrio had been a smart old lady—funny, elegant, with a sharp sense of humor. She'd reminded me of my own mom, which had made her feel precious to me. I'd only known Lucia a few weeks, but news of her death made me feel as if something had been taken from me personally.

A burglar? Jesus. It was so stupid. So fucking offensive. It made me furious.

"Ah ... is there a plan here, Liam?" Eoin asked cautiously.

"Yes, waiting for the goddamn rain to ease off," I retorted.

Eoin looked away without comment.

I sighed. "Shit. Sorry. It just winds me up. Mrs. D'Onofrio, getting attacked in a home invasion. She was a fine old lady, and it pisses me off. It's not your fault."

"I get it. Don't give it a thought." Eoin's voice was long-suffering.

I felt Nancy D'Onofrio's business card in my pocket and pulled it out. Her name was printed in bold, curvy letters that stood out sharply from the creamy paper. A name, a phone number, a QR code. Sleek, classy, minimalist. I was going to scan that code first chance I got and read everything there was to read about her.

I stuck the card in my pocket before Eoin noticed me fondling it.

I didn't usually admire black clothing on women, but

Nancy's tailored black dress made her skin look pearly and her mahogany hair gleam. That tight bun showed off every finely molded detail of her face. Only a woman with amazing bone structure could pull off that severe style and still look good. The oppressed-but-secretly-sensual governess look. I wanted to play the horny, unscrupulous lord of the manor. Sign me up for that.

I could have looked at her face for hours, always finding something new to admire. Her high cheekbone were striking, her skin impossibly soft. Her wide-set eyes were beautiful. She seemed elegant, smart, a person to be reckoned with. Sinuous. Tough-minded. Practical. And also like the perfectly formed but dangerous girl who undulates through the opening credits of a Bond movie. A fantasy woman.

And paying a crew out of my own pocket for an undetermined interval? That was a fucking fantasy, too. That was the little head talking.

But damn. I couldn't let a chance to see her again slip away. She was elusive, wary. Going after a girl like her would be like catching fish with my bare hands.

Christ, sometimes I scared myself. I flung the car door open. "Let's get started."

Eoin peered at the rain sliding down the windshield, started to say something, then thought better of it. He sighed and followed me out.

I ground through the whole internal mental lecture while we unloaded. Pursuing a woman like Nancy D'Onofrio would be a huge waste of time. I shouldn't even start. She was a hyper-focused, a workaholic. Lucia had told me how driven she was, and I'd regretfully written her off as soon as Lucia described her. She was the polar opposite of what I wanted in my life.

Over the years, after a few relationships went sour, I'd given some long, hard thought about what I really needed in a lover. No, in a *wife*. Enough dicking around. I was a grown-ass man. I wanted to take root. I wanted to have a family. I wanted someone who fit in my life. Who wanted what I wanted out of life, at least roughly.

I didn't need to look any further than my own parents to see what happened when you messed with that cardinal rule and tried to jam square pegs into round holes.

My mother's dream had been a big, noisy family, lots of kids. My father had been driven by professional ambition. He'd had no time to spend with me. He'd leave early in the morning for work, come home after my bedtime, never make it for meals. He'd always been working—holidays, birthdays, anniversaries, ball games, recitals. It was almost comical how consistent he was.

Mom had begged, schemed, and nagged for years. She finally accepted that he would never change and told him to leave. I hadn't seen my father since that day.

Not that I'd seen much of him before. I was eleven when that happened.

Mom eventually found the kind of man she wanted, but at that point, she couldn't have more kids. She'd wasted too much time waiting for Dad. She'd missed her window.

I'd taken the lesson to heart. When my time came, I knew what to look for, and what to avoid. I was plenty ambitious too, in my own low-key way, but I liked my life. Living on my land in the countryside, running my own business, keeping my own hours. I liked playing the occasional seisiún in the Irish pubs with my fiddle, whistles, and flutes, downing a few pints with friends now and then. I liked growing my garden, tending my small orchard of walnuts, apples, and pears. Someday, I hoped to buy a couple of horses, when I could afford a bigger pasture and had some kids to ride them.

I wanted to build my own house on that land, from the

ground up. A big, beautiful, comfortable, rambling place, made exactly to order. Full of kids, noise, color. Life.

I'd tried to picture the woman who might fit into that fantasy. She didn't have to be a raving beauty. I wasn't all hung up on that. It was more important that she be kind, good-natured, have a sense of humor. That she like gardening, canning, baking her own bread, that kind of thing.

But my body wasn't thinking about my long-term contentment. It wanted what it wanted, and it wanted that slim girl with big, mysterious eyes behind her trendy glasses and the high-heeled, pointy-toed boots on her tiny feet.

Nancy D'Onofrio definitely didn't make her own bread. Her type lived on yogurt, carrot sticks and take-out sushi.

The results were nice, though. I loved how her back stayed so straight, her head high, chin up. I liked the jut of her shoulder blades, the smart, nipped-in fit of her short black jacket. The delicate shape of her upper lip, the lush swell of the lower one.

I wanted to smooth away the anxious crease between her dark brows. Those shadowy hazel eyes were full of sadness. Secrets.

Problems. Sadness, shadows, secrets. Those were synonyms for problems. Always.

The voice of reason shouted at me from a far, echoing distance, but I was too lost in my fantasy to listen. I wanted to pamper her. Scramble her eggs. Butter her toast. Pour cream into her tea.

Crash. Thud. I'd knocked over a flower arrangement with my boot. Bruised white lilies scattered across the floorboards.

I laid my boxes down on the pile forming in the middle of the floor, gathered the flower heads up, and threw them away. The sweet, heavy smell of lilies reminded me of my mother's funeral, and the memory still made my belly clench, after all these years.

It didn't matter how attractive Nancy D'Onofrio was. By her own mother's admission, she was a compulsive workaholic. She would make me frustrated and miserable. But I kept visualizing her ass in that tight skirt. Her breasts were nice, too—small, but perky and firm, with a brash, in-your-face personality all their own. Taut nipples that poked audaciously through the fabric of her dress. No bra. No need.

God, enough. I was thirty-six and I still hadn't found my earth mother type. I was looking around in a relaxed sort of way, hoping destiny would kick in and help me out. I didn't want to force it, but damn. I didn't do casual affairs anymore. I hated that flat, feeling when one of those scratch-the-itch things had to end. It was just too depressing.

The morning passed in grim, sweaty silence. Two trips to Latham, loading, unloading, loading and unloading. It was late afternoon by the time we were done.

When we got back to my place, we were ravenous, having worked through lunch.

I put on the kettle to make a pot of tea for me and Eoin, who was currently boarding in my basement. Eoin cooked some hamburgers, or charred them, rather. I lunged for the gas and turned it off. "Making lunch?"

"I made one for you, too, if you fancy it," Eoin said timidly.

"Keep the flame a bit lower," I advised.

Eoin's freckled face flushed. "Sorry."

"Speaking of stoves, I found you a secondhand electric range. After we eat, maybe you can help me haul it down into the basement."

"Great," Eoin said. "Now I can make myself a cup of tea without bothering you."

I grunted. "It was never a bother."

"Thanks anyway," Eoin said earnestly. "For the place, the work, the stove." He laid the burgers on the table. "Are you going to the seisiún at Malloy's Saturday night?"

"I might. You going?"

"God, yes," Eoin said. "I've been working on that new tune of yours all week. I want to try it out with the lads."

"Fine, then. Malloy's on Saturday," I promised.

Malloy's was a good seisiún, from ten to two every Saturday night in an Irish pub in Queens. A motley but talented group of regulars gathered each week to mainline Irish tunes. I almost always went with my fiddle and flutes, unless I was too worn out from work, but young Eoin was religious in his zeal. And he was damn good on those Uilleann pipes. I'd never heard anyone better. The kid should go pro.

But work was work, so the tunes and the Guinness had to wait. Which reminded me that Saturday followed Friday, the day I was starting work on the D'Onofrio house.

Which meant that I would see her again tomorrow.

Through the buzzing zing of excitement, it occurred to me that I could go early. Help her get the kitchen ready for the reno. I could lift boxes. Wrap dishes in newspapers. Box up pots and pans. Eoin could come by later. Excitement swelled inside me, at the idea of being alone with her. And that wasn't the only thing that swelled.

"You okay? You look a bit off," Eoin said.

I swallowed the last bite of charred burger with some difficulty. "Nah, just remembering some things I have to do. Ready to haul that stove down?"

"Sure thing," Eoin agreed.

I kept myself busy. First hooking up the stove in Eoin's lair, then cleaning up the kitchen. I moved on to sweeping debris out of the truck bed, and from there, to cleaning out the rain gutters. When I found myself soaping the squeaky bottom of my sock drawer, I had to face the truth. I just sat there on my bed, the upside-down drawer in my lap, socks and underwear scattered across the quilt, and contemplated it.

I had a monster crush on this woman. It was destined to crash and burn. And I didn't even have the good sense to back away. Just couldn't do it.

I was so fucked.

Chapter Four

Beep. *Beep. Beep.* John Esposito rolled over on the couch and punched the button to silence the alarm. Yes, fuck you very much, it was five to midnight. He got it.

The big guy was about to check in. He'd set the alarm in advance, to be sure he was sufficiently alert. He had to be razor sharp to deal with Haupt.

Truth was, he slept very little when he was on the job. Didn't miss it, either. Stalkings, interrogations, punishments, executions, they stoked him like petroleum fuel. He loved his work. When the gig was over and the fee was safely tucked into his offshore account, he'd sleep for two weeks straight and make up for lost time.

He peered out the window, across the street. A glance at the monitors of the vidcams he'd installed while the Contessa lay dead on her living room floor confirmed that nothing interesting was happening in the empty house. Eight vidcams. Living room, kitchen, bathrooms, basement, and the three upstairs bedrooms.

He stood up and stretched out his shoulders. Any second,

Haupt would call. John knew very little about the man person-ally, only that he paid well and that job failure would be dangerous for John's health. John was fine with that. He held himself to very high professional standards. That was why he charged the big bucks. The element of risk even gave the proceeding an extra zing. A plus, in his book.

The terms of this job were complicated, not a cut-and-dried hit. John preferred to get half up front, but Haupt had only given him a third, plus expenses. The rest of his fee was contin-gent on a successful outcome, but the promised sum was so egregiously large, he'd decided it was worth it. He hadn't factored in what a pain in the ass Haupt was going to be, though. It was worse than dealing with his own mother.

His employer had been unimpressed when John let the Contessa slip away, but was it his fault the old bitch croaked before he could question her? He wasn't even the one who killed her, so how was that a reflection on his professionalism? In his line of work, he'd never bothered to learn CPR. Sneaky old hag. He particularly hated that she'd put herself beyond punishment. He did not like to be thwarted by a woman. Not ever.

His only consolation was the delightful discovery of the Contessa's three fuckable daughters. He couldn't decide which one he liked best. Looked like he'd have to sample them all. They might try to resist him, too, during the course of this job, if he was lucky. And if they did? Ahhh yes. He was oh so ready for them.

He'd video-streamed a segment of last night's drunken henfest in the kitchen to Haupt, but the humorless prick had been unamused. All that had interested the boss last night had been the jeweled pendants.

The three identical letters that John had taken from the Contessa's house made cryptic references to necklaces but had offered no clear explanation. John had studied every piece of jewelry he'd taken from Lucia D'Onofrio's bureau, to no avail. None of it seemed relevant to those fucking letters. He'd had the stuff delivered by courier to Haupt, but the old bastard hadn't made any more sense of the jewelry than he had.

It seemed logical that this new delivery of pendants was significant. That goddamn letter was full of coy, cryptic clues designed to annoy the shit out of a straightforward professional. *"Music will open the door."* What the fuck did that mean? *"It's up to you three to decipher the key together,"* the stupid hag had written. *"Consider beauty, faith, knowledge, and above all, love —the keys to all secrets worth knowing."*

Fucking drivel. Beauty, faith, knowledge, and love? Not his field of expertise. He'd faxed the thing to his employer, who had been unable to make anything of it, either.

But John hadn't exhausted all possibilities yet. Given the proper incentive, the daughters could probably figure out their batty old adoptive mother's letter. And he had all the incentive necessary in the black plastic case he kept under the bed.

The old bitch was fucking with him. From the grave. He flexed his knuckles. He wanted to wrap them around her stringy old neck and squeeze. But her daughters' necks were velvety soft and smooth. He could punish Lucia through them.

He took his phone in hand. His internal stopwatch warned him the time had come. Five seconds to midnight—four ... three ... two ... one ...

Beeep. Right on cue. John opened the call. "Yes?"

"What do you have to report?" came the soft, faintly accented voice. "Something more interesting than weeping, bingeing females?"

John meditated for a second on how many zeros that would be on his final bank draft. "There's a carpenter crew coming tomorrow morning to start renovating the place."

"Renovating? Now?" The usually soft, dead-calm voice on the other end of the line rose to a squeak of outrage. "Did you search again?"

"As requested. I went through the place after the carpenters—"

"Carpenters? You mean they have already begun?"

"They unloaded their supplies," John said. "They start tomorrow."

"Did you get the paperwork on the pendants, at least?"

At least? What was this "at least" shit? As if he'd failed? Asshole. "Of course," John said. "I found the delivery slip with the jeweler's store address. I also found his home address."

"And?" The old guy waited.

"And what? It's past business hours, and the guy was probably eating dinner or fucking his mistress, so I figured I'd wait to—"

"Wait? For the carpenter's crew to rip the house apart and find what you are unable to find? And what then, John? What then?"

John's mouth worked. The dickhead went on before he could reply.

"Assume that the pendants are part of the Contessa's puzzle," Haupt said. "The daughters know nothing. The Contessa is dead, thanks to you—"

"I did not kill her!"

"The only person who could conceivably know more about this situation is the jeweler himself," Haupt said. "And? So? Do I really need to say it, John?"

John blew a breath through flared nostrils. "All right. Tomorrow I'll—"

"Never put off until tomorrow what you can do today."

"You mean right now? But it's past midnight, and I—"

"I know what time it is. Past midnight is an ideal time for an interrogation. It's an ideal time for many things."

John reordered his mind around this new imperative. "You are implying an ultimate solution for the jeweler, I take it?"

The man let out a low growling sound of frustration. "When you were recommended to me, I was told that I would not have to micromanage."

John ground his teeth. "I'll take care of it."

"I do not want that crew in that house until we know more."

A muscle twitched in John's cheek. "I can't stop it from going forward without making a big mess," he said. "Should I arrange an accident for the carpenter?"

"No. No more bodies in that house, not unless it is strictly necessary. A break-in, some vandalism. Delay the work. Search everything again, from the ground up. Not that I hold up much hope, after your failure so far."

"Yes," John said, after a brief pause. "I will search the place. Exhaustively."

"Good. Very well, then. Until tomorrow."

John laid the phone down and dragged his black plastic box out from under the bed. It was full of curiosities that he'd acquired over the years, devices he'd made and adapted himself, even some antique originals with a dark and storied past. He pulled out a few of his old favorite standbys and loaded his kit bag.

The thought of the job ahead was getting him revved up. Knives and picks in hand, the jeweler screaming, begging. But first, the bitch Contessa's house.

He selected the lock drill. Even if the contents of the house were inanimate, smashing them to bits was going to feel good.

It was a tantalizing precursor of softer, juicier things to come.

Chapter Five

Nancy

I took a bracing gulp of coffee, finished typing the latest edits into Peter's CD liner notes in my laptop, and closed the program. Moxie flung herself at my feet and writhed.

I picked up Moxie and buried my face in her long fur. She'd been feeling neglected. And now she had to spend yet another day alone while I went to clear the stuff out of Lucia's kitchen.

I had not gathered up the strength to go back there and clean up the mess in the kitchen, not after my spine-tingling encounter with Liam Knightly, so I had my work cut out for me today.

I hadn't asked my sisters to help, either. Not that they could've, despite all their brave words. Nell was working, as always, teaching classes all morning and waitressing all afternoon, and Vivi was working a craft show upstate. I had a million things of my own I had to cancel.

But the rock-bottom truth was, I preferred to see Liam Knightly alone.

Nothing got past Vivi and Nell's sharp eyes. I didn't want my curious sisters intercepting any smoldering glances or catching stray waves of throbbing sexual heat. They'd draw their conclusions and start to tease. Or worse, start to worry.

First order of business: what to wear? The jeans and T-shirt I'd thrown on this morning after my shower were perfect for cleaning, mopping and packing kitchenware, but they were utterly inadequate for being seen by Liam Knightly.

Moxie sprawled, purring and stretching, on a growing heap of rejects on the futon couch as I yanked item after item out of my closet.

I finally settled on a pair of snug, faded jeans and a tailored, dark blue cotton blouse, primly buttoned up, with just the last button undone, so that the luscious sapphire pendant at my throat showed, ever so slightly. A glint of color, a flash of light. Crisp, businesslike, no-nonsense, but subtly feminine.

I fixed my hair twelve different ways. In a paroxysm of disgust, I fell back on my old emergency standby: slicked back with gel into a wet-looking braid. I spritzed on hairspray to underscore the no-nonsense message of the tough hair. Some cover-up under my eyes, a dash of brown mascara, and a dab of sandalwood oil to infuse the look with an air of sensual mystery. There. That should do it.

I stared into the mirror, wishing I could make the anxious crease between my brows disappear. What was I even trying to accomplish? A come-on, or a back-off?

Aw, hell with it. It was 8:20, and I was wasting the guy's time with my crushed-out primping. I perched my glasses on my nose, stuck my chest out, and gave myself a hard smile in the mirror. Ta-da. I scooped Moxie into my arms and pressed my face into her soft fur. "Time to scram," I told her apologetically. "Sorry, sweetie. I'll make it up to you."

My phone buzzed. I almost ignored it, late as I was, but ingrained professionalism prevailed. Or obsessive paranoia, depending on how you looked at it.

I saw the display. Liam Knightly. Moxie plopped to the ground with a yowl as my arm went limp. I hit "talk." "Hello?"

"Nancy? This is Liam Knightly."

"Ah. Um, hi," I stammered. "Are you already at the house?"

"Yes, and I—"

"Oh, no. We must have crossed wires about the meeting time. I'm so sorry. I'm running a little late because of some—"

"Nancy." He cut her off, his voice grim. "There's a problem."

"A problem?" A creeping sense of icy cold began to spread its tendrils out to my belly and limbs. "What do you mean, a problem?"

"There's been another break-in."

Another break-in? "No," I said, my voice high. "That's not possible."

"I was driving by on my way to breakfast to see if your car was there yet. I wanted to pass a broom through the place before you saw it, since Eoin and I tracked in a lot of mud yesterday. I saw that the door was open, so I thought maybe you drove a different car up. Then I looked inside."

His eloquent pause chilled my blood. I was starting to shake. "And?"

"It's been trashed," he said. "Badly. I'm so sorry to tell you this."

I was crumpling—on my knees, hands braced against the floor like it was trying to rise up and smack me in the face. My phone lay next to Moxie's bowl of kitty crunchies. Fish-shaped pellets were scattered on the little black-and-white tiles.

The floor was cold against my hands. Liam Knightly's urgent voice came through the phone. I let my butt drop to the floor so that I could support myself on one hand and picked up the phone again.

"Here I am," I gasped out. "Sorry. Dropped the phone."

"Jesus! You scared me! I thought you'd fainted. Are you okay?"

"I'm good," I croaked. "I just had, you know. A moment. Did you call the—"

"The police? Yeah. They're on their way. You were my second call."

Unreasonable panic ballooned inside me into something monstrous. I saw Lucia's body on the ground, her wide-open eyes, her livid face. "Don't go in there!" I told him wildly. "Get away from the place! Right now! What if whoever did it is still inside?"

"I'll be okay," he soothed. "I won't go in. I'll leave it for the cops. They wouldn't want me touching things or tracking though the crime scene anyhow."

"It's just a house." The words made no sense, I realized, as they flew out of my mouth—and oh shit, now my face and throat were shaking. "It's just a goddamn *house!*"

"Yes, that is absolutely true," he soothed. "Hey, Nancy? Nancy? Hey! Answer me!"

I tried, but my throat was shaking too hard. I made a word-less sound, just so he'd know I was still conscious.

"Nancy, give me one of your sisters' phone numbers, okay? You shouldn't be alone. I'll call one of them for you. Give me the number."

Oh, God. He thought I was losing my shit. Embarrassment stiffened my spine.

"No," I said thinly. "They're both busy. I'll be out there as soon as I can."

"No! You're upset! You should not drive!"

"I will be *fine*. I'll see you in an hour and ten, barring traffic."

"Hey! Wait! Nancy—"

I hung up on him and lurched over to the kitchen counter. The little espresso pot had a mouthful of powerful coffee left in the bottom. I poured it into a cup, cold though it was, and dosed it with sugar.

My cell began to tinkle. I checked. It was Liam again. No freaking way was I answering him now. Ten rings. A pause. Ten more. Silence. Take that, buddy.

Then, the chime of a text message. I opened it.

At least get a goddamn rideshare please do not drive yourself

Hah. Like I had hundreds of extra bucks to burn. Dream on, buddy.

I tossed on my jacket, legs wobbling. This news had taken all the starch out of me, but a secret warmth unfurled in my chest at the thought that he'd been worried about me. Awww. I cherished the feeling, silly though it was. Bossy though he'd been.

I spent the drive up to Hempton trying to calm myself down. I tried to remind myself that it was just a deserted house. A break-in was upsetting, yes. Expensive, a huge waste of time, a rotten inconvenience. That was all. Nothing, in the grand scheme of things. Lucia was no longer in that house. The very worst that could possibly happen had already happened. This was nothing. Absolutely nothing at all, in comparison.

So why did I feel so scared?

Chapter Six

Liam

I lurked in my truck, watching cops and forensics techs trooping in and out of the D'Onofrio house. Finding the place tossed had been a shock. Weird as hell for lightning to strike the same place twice, and just a week after Lucia's death, too. It made me nervous and queasy, like I was missing something important. A vague, discomforting almost-thought that kept flitting out of sight before I could put my finger on it.

Maybe because I was short on sleep. Around two-thirty a.m, I'd given up on sleeping and headed to my furniture workshop. The slow, detailed work of joining without glue or nails was one of my favorite pastimes. It put me in a mellow, focused, zen kind of place. The next best thing to sleep.

Currently, I was working on a dining room table. For my future family. One long enough to feed a dynasty. Sometimes I imagined what it would feel to see it loaded with food, my family gathered around it. Just a vague, hopeful fantasy in my head.

It usually gave me a connected feeling. I'd figured that working on that table would be just the thing to link me with reality, and my true, bedrock values.

But I'd bombed on that. My fantasy future wife was a bland, formless fog of vague possibilities, whereas Nancy D'Onofrio stood out, brilliantly sharp and clear, every vivid, stylish detail of her. Those cool, slender fingers, twisted through mine.

At a certain point, erotic fantasies had overtaken me. They involved Nancy, and the dining room table. Her, perched on the edge, graceful legs spread wide. Me, on my knees, my tongue deep inside her. Her hands wound into my hair. Writhing and whimpering.

Working on that table would never be the same again.

I'd gotten out of the house before Eoin was up, and the first thing I'd done was to drive by the D'Onofrio house. The bitch of it was, Nancy wasn't even in the damn house. It was enough for me that she'd been in it the day before, and that she'd be in it again today. How childish was that. I was pretty far gone.

Well, I'd paid for my fatuous bullshit. I got to be the dickhead who bore the bad tidings. Because that was what happened when a guy started poking around in the hornet's nest of a woman's messy, complicated life. He got stung.

Even so, I was glad it fell out this way. Better me than her. If she'd been that upset hearing about it on the phone, it would have scared her out of her wits to see the house trashed, all alone, with no warning, after finding her mother dead less than a week ago.

Nancy's battered black Volkswagen appeared, and pulled in behind my truck. My heart rate kicked way up. She'd driven herself up here. Of course. Stubborn female.

She didn't spare me so much as a glance as she got out. The wind fluttered her dark blue blouse, but did not budge a wisp of her smooth hair. Her profile was stark and pure as she stared at the house. Her face was so pale, she looked like she might faint.

I got out of my truck and folded my arms over the heavy thud in my rib cage, as if the woman didn't have more serious things to worry about than my horn-dog crush. She turned at the sound of the car door, and her chin went up.

I considered my options and went for it. Full-on overbearing. "I see you decided to drive yourself after all."

"Of course," was her cool retort. "I can't afford to call a car all the way up here. It would cost me a fortune."

I let my silence criticize that decision, and a flush of anger bloomed on her cheeks. "Did you call your sisters?" I demanded, just to double down on the scold.

"Not that it's any of your business, but no. Not yet. Nell's teaching and never answers her phone anyway, and Vivi's upstate doing a crafts fair. I'll tell them about all of this later. Once I know exactly what happened."

"Huh," I said. "It always seems to be you who has to take care of the messy details."

Her eyes narrowed. "That is not their fault! They're perfectly willing to help me! They're just busy, and you had my number, not theirs!"

Now her head was high, her eyes snapping. Excellent. She looked better now. Nothing like putting a man in his place to perk a woman up.

"Uh, yeah. Of course," I murmured, suitably chastened.

She trotted up the stairs with a spring in her step that she hadn't had before. I caught up with her, saw marks under her eyes that the makeup did not hide. I wanted to offer her my arm, but her hands were white-knuckled. Bracing herself.

I followed her in as she looked around. The place had been brutally tossed. Every piece of furniture was upended, every sofa cushion and pillow slashed, every breakable thing crushed.

The tiles he and Eoin had hauled in were scattered every-where, shattered to pieces. Lengths of lumber were scattered around like huge matchsticks. There were jagged holes in the walls. A photograph of Lucia and her three daughters smiled up from the floor, covered with chunks of broken glass.

Nancy bent down and reached for the pieces. Her hand shook.

"Please don't touch anything, ma'am," said an evidence tech, a frowning middle-aged woman. "It might be better if you waited outside. Until we've finished."

"Oh. Um, let me just take a look," Nancy said. "I'll be quick." She took a step farther into the room and let out a cry of distress when she saw what lay at her feet. To me, it looked like a formless tangle of wire and chunks of broken glass and stone.

"Oh, no." Nancy's voice shook. "The sculpture that Vivi did for Lucia. 'The Three Sisters.' It was one of Lucia's prize possessions." Then she turned and saw the *intaglio* writing table. Her hand flew up over her mouth. "Oh, dear God. No."

The plastic cover she'd bought had been tossed aside, and the plane of the table smashed in. The two pieces lay collapsed in on themselves, splintered edges ragged. The four-by-four used to break it lay among the broken pieces. The jade plant was torn apart on the floor, chunks of dirt and leaves scattered everywhere.

Better judgment clamored at me, but I ignored it and grabbed her hand.

Chapter Seven

Nancy

My fingers curled gratefully around his, and a rush of sustaining energy flooded into my body through his hand. He was so solid. An oak that would never bend or break.

The romantic metaphor almost made me smile. It was lifted right out of the haunting ballad that Enid had just cut for the album, a song I had finished mixing in the studio only a few days ago. Of course, the oak in that particular folk song did break, in the end. The girl was left barefoot in the snow, an illegitimate baby in her arms.

Just a little something to think about.

I stared down at the ruined table, thinking about the vast sweep of history that it had seen. Lucia's family line and this historic table had both come to an abrupt, violent end right here in this room, within a week of each other.

As if the table could not continue to exist without Lucia.

One thought kept coming back to me, circling around and

around in my mind. I opened my mouth and voiced it. "He wasn't satisfied the last time. He's still angry."

Liam slanted me a cautious glance. "You really think it's the same person?" he asked, his voice even. "From what the cop said, it's a very different kind of crime."

I shook my head, reluctant to speak. Anything I said was just going to sound like grief-stricken rambling. I pressed my hand hard against my mouth as I stared at the ruined table, painstakingly crafted by some nameless artisan hundreds of years ago—smashed to splinters by a brain-dead hoodlum. It was as if someone had defaced Lucia's grave. Ugly, vicious, and very personal.

I shuddered, and Liam's hand tightened. "Want to go outside and get some air?"

I snapped myself to attention and shook my head.

"I am so sorry," he said. "It was such a beautiful thing."

I nodded, swallowing hard. "Yes, exactly. A thing. On the one hand, it's a precious heirloom full of history and memory. On the other, it's just an inanimate old thing, carved from ancient wood. I just don't know how to feel about it."

"You don't have to choose," he suggested gently. "Both things can be true at once."

I was moved by the comprehension in his eyes. I looked away quickly, but there was no place to rest my eyes in that entire room that did not hurt to look upon.

"I, uh ..." He stopped himself, looking doubtful.

"What?" I demanded.

"I could try to repair it," he said carefully. "I've done a lot of furniture restoration. It's a thing I really enjoy. My mother was heavy into antiques, and I've been working on wood joining for years. I wouldn't expect payment for the labor. It would be a privilege to work on it. Even so, you might be better off contacting a specialist."

I stared at him for the briefest of moments. "I accept," I said.

"Hold on," he warned. "Not so fast. I couldn't make guarantees. It'll never be the same as before. There's a lot of damage, and it would take a long time. With something like this, I'd go one splinter at a time, in my off hours. You'd better talk it over with your sisters first and see if you—"

"Yes," I said. "They'll agree. I want you to do it. Only you. No one else."

He studied my face, looking worried. "Well, fine, then. I'm willing to try, but I won't hold you to it. Not until you talk to your sisters."

"I'll hold *you* to it." I glared at him, daring him to rescind his offer.

"Uh, okay," he murmured. "My pleasure."

I realized I was clutching his fingers. Heat flooded into my face, and I whipped my hand away. "Sorry." I headed toward the kitchen. His light footfalls followed, broken glass crunching.

The kitchen was just as bad. Cupboard doors had been torn off their hinges, their contents hurled to the floor with a violence that had shattered the floor tiles. The table was upended, the chairs were tossed, every dish was smashed. The garbage we'd forgotten about had been dragged out from under the sink, the plastic bag slashed open, its contents spread out over the floor.

"Guess I won't have to go looking for packing boxes," I said.

That was when I saw it. A crumpled piece of white bond paper, and something written on it, in Lucia's elegant, slanted handwriting. I snatched it up, heart thudding.

"Nancy, hey. You're not supposed to—"

"I know, I know," I said impatiently, shaking coffee grounds off the paper. The page was covered with scribbled handwriting, marked with small edits, some words crossed out, others scribbled in:

> *...will come as a shock to you girls, and no doubt you think me Machiavellian and foolish for creating this elaborate system of checks and balances, but after what happened to my father, after what this thing did to my marriage, I feel I cannot be too careful. Just please know this: I made these arrangements not because I do not trust you, but because I love you, and because you love each other. Love, like any precious thing, should be protected by every means possible. The older I get, the more I understand that it is the only thing worth protecting.*

Then a couple of lines, both of which had been savagely crossed out, as if Lucia had been frustrated, searching for the right words:

> *The necklaces are the key to*
> *You must use the necklaces together to discover the secret of*

It continued with a new paragraph:

> *You are each in your own unique way great lovers of beauty—music, literature, and the visual arts, and so I devised the key to reflect*

And the page ended. I could hear Lucia's soft, accented voice echoing in my head.

"What is that?" Liam picked his way across the rubble.

"A draft of a letter." My voice wavered, then broke. "To us, from Lucia." I held it up.

He scanned it rapidly and met my gaze, his mouth grim.

"Wow," he said. "That's intense. Any clue what she was talking about?"

"None," I said. "But it was just a first draft. Of a letter to the three of us."

"Right." He paused, thoughtfully. "But if this is the draft …"

"Then where the hell is the finished version?" I finished.

We stared at each other. I wanted to grab his arm, to steady myself. The ground beneath my feet had become the thinnest crust of apparent normality, and beneath it churned an abyss of dangerous, shifting possibilities.

"Why didn't we find the finished letter?" I asked. "Why?"

He pondered that. "Could she have mailed it to you? Could it still be on its way?"

"Eight days have gone by," I said. "It takes two, four at most, for a letter to get to the city. This was an extremely important letter. She was putting a lot of thought into it. Writing and rewriting it. This did not get forgotten or lost in the mail. No way."

He finished the thought. "You think it got lost in some more sinister way."

"After what this thing did to my marriage'?" I quoted softly. "What thing? What marriage? What the hell is this thing that she's talking about?"

"Maybe it's what she installed the safe for," Liam suggested.

I glanced up at him, freshly startled. "Safe? What safe?"

His eyes widened. "She didn't tell you about that?"

My blank face answered his question, and he whistled silently. "A few weeks ago, she hired me to install a hidden safe in her upstairs closet. That's how we met in the first place. I'm so sorry I didn't say anything. I assumed you knew about it."

The woman from the forensics team came into the kitchen and frowned at me. "Miss, I asked you not to touch anything," she scolded.

"I found something important." I held out the letter. "The investigating officer needs to see it. Please, be on the lookout for more possible pages of this letter, okay?"

The woman snatched the sheet of paper out of my fingers with her latex-gloved hand and tucked it into a plastic envelope. "I'll bring it to her attention. And since you can't keep your hands to yourself, could you please wait outside until we're finished?"

She sternly herded the two of us out onto the front porch. We looked at each other, eyes still full of awed wonder. Too boggled to be embarrassed by the scolding.

"I want to look at that safe," I said. "Not that I could open it. I don't have the combination. I don't imagine you...?"

He shook his head. "No. Lucia had to choose the combination herself."

I chewed my lip. "I wish I had a copy of that letter. God knows when they'll let me see it. I need to show it to Nell and Vivi."

"One second." Liam went to his truck and pulled a sheet of paper from the dashboard. He plucked a pencil from his shirt and began to scribble against the hood of his truck.

He handed it to me. It was the text of Lucia's letter, transcribed in a bold, angular cursive script. "It's not word for word, but that's the gist of it," he said.

"That's incredible! What, do you have a photographic memory?"

"Not really. In an hour, I wouldn't be able to write more than a rough paraphrase. And it has to really interest me. Otherwise, I don't retain a damn thing."

I broke eye contact and busied myself by folding the paper

into a neat little square. "Well, thanks for being so interested. I, um ... appreciate that."

"Anything having to do with you or Lucia interests me. You don't have to thank me for something involuntary."

"Involuntary?" I let out a self-conscious snort. "Like a sneeze?"

"No. More like breathing."

His quiet response abruptly halted that very bodily function to which he referred. I shoved the folded paper into my pocket. "Um, great. Okay. Thanks."

"The investigating officer's going to want to talk with you," Liam said. "I told her you were on your way over here. But you haven't had breakfast yet, have you?"

I floundered, thrown off course. "I, ah ... what?"

"Breakfast?" His subtle smile flashed. "First meal of the day? Familiar with it?"

"I've had coffee," I offered.

"You've got me beat, then. There's that diner downtown. We could get some food into you before you talk to the detective. Might not be a bad idea."

I started groping for excuses. *Calm down. At mealtimes, normal people get food. They don't read hidden significance into it. Lighten up.*

"Some food would be great," I said faintly.

Chapter Eight

Nancy

I regretted my decision once I was seated across from Liam in the mirrored pink interior of Luigi's Diner. I also regretted that I hadn't left my hair loose or worn contacts instead of glasses. And something a little lower cut.

Not that I had cleavage to speak of, but still.

He just waited patiently across the table from me, sipping his tea. After a couple of minutes of that, my control snapped. "What?" I demanded. "What are you waiting for? What are you looking at?"

He discreetly looked away. "I was looking at you. You look …"

"What?" I demanded. "Unapproachable? Aggressive?"

His mouth twitched. "Not at all."

"What, then?" I demanded.

"Great. You look great, Nancy." His velvety voice was low, caressing.

I wrapped my arms across my chest. "I'm sorry. Long,

significant silences make me twitchy. I appreciate you being nice, but I look like hell, so please stop saying that."

His eyes narrowed. "You look stressed and scared, but that doesn't keep you from looking good. And I'm sorry about the long, significant silences. They're hardwired into me. I'm not much of a chatterbox."

"Oh. That's okay." I stared down into my coffee and fished Liam's copy of Lucia's letter out of my pocket, unfolding it. "And yes, I am scared. Very scared. Mostly, I'm scared that things didn't happen the way the cops think they did. Lucia wrote this letter, but we never received it. Someone took it during the first break-in. And your classic dickhead burglar looking to trade a TV or a diamond ring for a hit of meth? That guy is not going to take this letter. That guy does not give a shit about this letter."

Liam nodded. "Agreed. He absolutely doesn't."

His quiet agreement rattled me even more. I'd been half-hoping that he would talk me down from this terrifying line of reasoning, but now it looked like I had to face it head on.

"So who took it?" I went on. "And what is this 'thing' she's referring to? What's the deal with these pendants she gave us? And if she had this great big hairy family secret, why didn't she tell us before, goddamnit?"

Liam cleared his throat. "Maybe she was—"

"What the hell does she mean by that crack about 'what it did to her father'? And who even knew she was married at all? What kind of mom just sort of forgets to mention that pesky detail to her daughters? Even if they are adopted?"

Liam waited patiently for me to get my ya-yas out. People were starting to peek at the scene I was making. I hunched over my coffee cup, embarrassed. "Sorry," I said. "I'm freaking out on you in public. The breakfast date from hell."

"You're a great breakfast date," he said. "Very entertaining.

It's just one humdinger after another. I can't wait for the car chase."

My snorting giggle sprayed coffee over the table, but when I looked up from sponging coffee off my cuffs, he was looking pleased with himself.

"You know what scares me the most?" I said. "The responsibility. Because I have no proof. Nothing to help the cops. Nothing to convince them things are different from what they've already concluded. Just spooky hints about a menacing secret. Some mysterious, sinister 'thing' that I've never heard of. I don't know what or where it is, just that somebody wants it. And that somebody might have killed my mother. And gotten away with it. And I'm the only one who knows."

There it was. I'd said the unsayable. I let out a shaky breath. Liam just accepted my words, not reacting, not negating, just acknowledging them with a grave nod.

I hid my face with shaking hands. "If somebody killed Lucia, I have to do something about it," I said, my voice low. "I can't just let it go. But what?"

"One step at a time," he said in a soothing voice. "Let's start with the necklaces. She said that they're a key. Do you know what she's referring to?"

I held up the pendant that glittered at my throat. "She has to be referring to these. They came the day before yesterday, hand delivered directly from the jeweler's shop. Evidently, she'd commissioned them for us before ... before it happened. Three pendants, each one decorated with our three birthstones. They're reproductions of Renaissance jewelry, but knowing Lucia, the gold and the gems are definitely real."

He leaned forward, peering at the pendant. I unclasped it and handed it to him. He examined it from every angle and passed it back. "Very pretty. Looks great on you."

"Thank you," I said, reclasping it. "That's what I thought,

too. It's just pretty. A beautiful replica of a fifteenth-century noblewoman's pretty bauble. No mysterious keys to menacing secrets that I can tell. And probably expensive. More than Lucia should have spent, considering that she was renovating the house."

He drummed his fingers thoughtfully on the table. "It might be worthwhile to talk to the jeweler who made them. Find out more."

I nodded. "An excellent idea. I will do that. This very day."

"I'll take you," he suggested. "We can go together."

"Oh, no, don't worry about it. I have my car, and you must have all kinds of things to do, so—"

"Nope. Nothing at all to do. I was going to work on Lucia's house today, and I can't do that now, so I'm just kicking my heels. Don't fight me on this. You'll lose."

Whew. There it was, a naked challenge, right out there in the open. I blinked as I studied his set jaw, his narrowed eyes. Hello, Mr. Alpha Dog.

Here it was: the part in the script where I made it abundantly clear that he was not the boss here, that he was not dealing with a fluttery pushover, and that my decisions were entirely my own, thank you very much. Buh-bye.

The words wouldn't come out. Just a strangled silence and lots of nervous blinking.

The truth was, having some company today would be very nice. Having big, tough, hard-muscled, keen-eyed, hyper-protective company? Even better. Stellar, in fact.

Maybe, just maybe, I could let him have this one. Like a chunk of meat flung to a hungry wolf. But just this once, mind you. Never again.

"Let's talk about something else," I said.

He lifted his teacup, eyes smiling over the rim, figuring he'd scored a point. "Whatever you like," he said magnanimously. "Be my guest."

His expression made me squirm on the cushion. "What do we talk about, then?"

His lips twitched. "You were the one who wanted to change the subject. I was fine with the subject."

"Don't start with me," I warned.

"Not at all. Relax." He reached out, pausing as I flinched, and touched my forehead with the tip of his finger, massaging the anxious crease between my brows as if trying to erase it. Hah. Good luck with that.

"Oh, that's just my face," I said. "That never goes away."

His boldness made me feel naked. I hadn't known there was a good side to feeling naked, but with Liam Knightly, there was. The feeling was both exciting and unsettling.

I stiffened my spine. "So, Liam," I said. "Tell me about yourself. Lucia told you about me, and that puts me at a disadvantage."

His smile faded. I felt a flash of regret for killing the charged moment, but I hardened myself. I had to be tough with this guy. Guarded.

"What do you want to know?" he asked.

"Whatever is relevant. You're not married, engaged, or seriously involved, I assume. Lucia wouldn't have thrown me at your head if you were."

"True enough," he agreed.

"So what's wrong with you?" I threw out the challenge.

He looked mildly curious. "What do you mean, 'wrong with me'?"

I shrugged. "One would think that a guy like you would've been taken by now. You must be, what, thirty-five?"

"Thirty-six," he confirmed.

"Thirty-six," I repeated. "How have you escaped the noose for so long?"

"I don't see it as a noose. I haven't met the right woman yet, and I won't settle."

My phone rang as the waitress arrived with our food. It was the manager of the venue in Indianapolis where Peter was performing in three weeks, calling to postpone the date. I made a note, promised to check the artist's availability, then hung up and gave Liam a tight smile. "Back to this ideal woman. What's she like?"

His eyes narrowed. "How would I know? I haven't met her yet."

"You must have a list of qualities you want. What's on your list?"

Liam eyed me over his cup as he sipped his tea. "Not really a list," he said. "None of these items are dealbreakers, just preferences. My ideal woman is a good cook, I guess. Likes to bake. Wants children. Would consider being a stay-at-home mom, but I'm flex on that. She's relaxed, mellow, likes flowers, gardening. Loves to hike. Likes animals. Dogs, cats, horses."

My heart sank like a stone. Which was dumb. After all, I had no designs on the guy. Why should it matter if I was the opposite of his ideal woman? I loved my cat, but I couldn't tell a pumpkin from a hollyhock. Children? What a concept. I hadn't given up hope of maybe having at least one someday. But cooking? Baking? Hah.

Liam went on. "She puts home and family first. She's content with simplicity."

"I get the vibe," I said. "Earth mother. Cultures her own yogurt. Dips her own candles, makes her own soap, carves her own toothpicks."

His lips twitched. "You're jerking me around."

My cell rang again. It was a presenter of a concert series in Portland, Oregon, who wanted Mandrake's promo packet. I took down his data and promised to send it.

"You know, that thing has an off button," Liam said.

I looked at him blankly. "What's your point?"

He sighed. "Never mind. You haven't touched your sandwich."

I looked down at my turkey club. "I'm not really that hungry," I admitted.

Liam frowned. "Try to get down at least half of it."

"I don't want to argue about my sandwich. I want to know more about this ideal—"

"You're not going to learn anything worth knowing if you come at me with that attitude," he said.

I carefully set down my coffee, startled. "Oh. I didn't mean to offend you."

"Okay," he said. "Didn't mean to snarl. You get a free pass after what happened today. Multiple free passes, actually."

I stared down while Liam finished his omelet. "I'm not sure what just happened," I said after a few minutes. "But it was definitely my fault."

"All I know is, one minute I was talking to you, and the next minute I had an uptight, bitchy stranger wearing a Nancy mask all up in my face. It was jarring."

"Sorry." I blinked back a startling rush of tears.

"Don't be. Come on, Nancy. Indulge me. Eat some of your sandwich. Please."

Oh, please. What did I have to lose by obliging him? I picked it up and took a bite.

We talked, carefully, about neutral topics. I managed to eat almost three quarters of my sandwich. When the bill came, he snatched it from my hand and looked offended when I tried to pay my share. Wow. I'd never met one of those guys, although I'd heard that they existed in the wild.

Liam opened the truck door for me, then climbed in. "Where's the jeweler located?"

The paperwork was now buried in the rubble at Lucia's house, but the name, Baruchin's Fine Jewelers, was burned into my mind, and the search engine on my phone revealed that it was a couple of towns away. The time it took to drive there was spent in conversation that was probably calculated to keep me calm, but it didn't work.

We pulled up in front of the jeweler's storefront, but the metal sliding doors were down. Closed, on a Saturday at noon? Those were prime shopping hours. Everything else around was open and bustling with activity.

My neck prickled as I got out of the truck. A small restaurant, Tony's Diner, was next door. I went inside and slid onto a stool at the counter. Liam followed.

A middle-aged lady with a dark red bouffant came over with a coffeepot. I smiled and held out my cup. "Coffee, please. I have a question. I need to speak to the jeweler next door about a delivery. Are they on vacation, or something?"

Hot coffee slopped out of the pot and onto my thumb. I jerked back with a gasp as the red-bouffant lady's face crumpled.

She set her coffee down, covered her face, and fled into the kitchen.

I glanced at Liam as I sucked on my scalded thumb. "Not a good sign," I said.

"It sure isn't," he agreed grimly.

After a moment, a bent, scowling elderly man with bushy white eyebrows and a paper cook's cap came out of the kitchen, wiping his hands on his apron. He scanned the counter and headed straight for us.

"You folks was askin' Donna about Sol Baruchin?"

"That's right," I said. "I don't know Mr. Baruchin personally. I just needed to ask a professional question—"

"Old Sol's dead," the man said heavily. "He got murdered."

Cold silence seemed to grip the entire room. Everyone was frozen, listening. Not a spoon clinked.

"M-m-murdered?" I echoed, in a tiny whisper.

"When?" Liam asked.

"Last night sometime. Hell of a thing. Him, his wife and his mother-in-law, all three of 'em. Christ, the mother-in-law was bedridden. Musta been ninety, ninety-five years old. Goddamn animals. I got this cop buddy, comes here for breakfast. He tipped me off about it. Frickin' horrible mess. Just horrible."

I covered my mouth with my hands. I couldn't breathe. Cold pooled in my belly and spread in every direction. My vision swam.

"Sol's been having breakfast and lunch in this joint every day for the last thirty-five years," the old man said, his voice dull. "Donna's all broke up. Christ, it's hard enough at my age, with friends dropping like flies from heart attacks and strokes, without some sick bastard murdering 'em. So, anyhows." He shook his head, his wrinkled mouth compressed into a grim line. "Sol's shop ain't gonna be open anytime soon, miss."

I tried to answer him politely. Nothing would come out of my mouth.

Liam smoothly filled the gap for me. "Thanks for telling us what happened," he said. "I'm so sorry for the loss of your friend."

"Yeah. Yeah, thanks." The old man turned and shuffled back toward the kitchen, shoulders bowed.

I stumbled out into the street, desperate for a gulp of air, but it was worse out there, with the murdered Baruchin's shuttered shop right in my face. "Let's get away from here."

"Sure thing." Liam unlocked her door, hoisted her in. "Where to?"

"I don't care. Anywhere."

Chapter Nine

Liam

I took her at her word. Old Tony's bombshell had rattled the hell out of me, too. My mind raced madly with ominous possibilities.

But I was genuinely surprised when I found myself pulling up under the big maple that shaded my own driveway. This was a tricky choice to sell in her current mood. It had started raining as we drove there. Water drummed down on the truck in the silence.

At the diner, she had been grilling me about my ideal woman. Which meant that she was skeptical about our chances, just like I was. That she was thinking about it anyway, just like I was.

Nancy looked around, as if waking from a dream. "Huh? Where are we?"

I braced myself. "This is my house."

Her gaze cut nervously away. "Oh. I didn't even see where

we were going. It's, ah ... pretty." She twisted her hands and stared, wide-eyed, at the water sluicing down the windshield. "That poor guy," she said. "And his wife. And her mother. How awful." She looked back at him, her eyes haunted. "This is not a coincidence. You know that, right?"

I hesitated for a moment, unwilling to scare her any further, but honesty prevailed.

"You might be right," I said. "What happened to Lucia was bad enough on its own. Then the break-in, the letter you found, and now the jeweler. God knows I'm no expert, but it's such a tight cluster of events. Seems improbable that they aren't connected."

We sat there in the cab, watching the rain on the windshield. I reached for her hand. It was as cold as ice. I put my other hand on top, gently rubbing it. Wishing I could lift it to my lips, but that was still a bridge too far.

"Come on in," I urged her. "Let me make you a cup of tea."

She stared down at her hand, clasped in mine, not agreeing, not pulling away.

"I'm the opposite of your ideal woman, you know," she blurted out.

My jaw clenched. "The whole 'ideal woman' thing is made up out of nothing," I said, hoping it was true. "Let's pretend we never talked about it."

She shook her head, ignoring my suggestion. "All that bread-making and flower-growing and candle-dipping and mellowness," she said. "It ain't me, babe. Let that be right up front. Right out in the open."

"The candle-dipping and the toothpick carving is a bit much," I commented.

"Not really," she said. "So where does that leave us?"

I looked up at the bare, dripping tree, the heavy clouds. "At the moment, it leaves us parked outside, in a truck, in the rain."

Her face turned pink. "You want me to come in?"

"Only if you want to," I said. Hah. I wanted her to come in more than I wanted my next lungful of air.

"I hardly know you," she whispered. "I know zero about you."

"We can fix that. Come in for a cup of tea. We'll tell each other stories."

"That's very nice of you. But it's not a good idea to have a first date in one's own private space." Her voice sounded prim.

I felt myself start to grin. "Is that what it would be? Doesn't breakfast count?"

She looked flustered. "I don't know. Second date, then. What would you call it?"

I drummed my fingers on the wheel. "I'd call it a cup of tea."

Nancy wrapped her arms around herself. "Well. Actually, I don't think that breakfast counts. It wasn't premeditated. And a first date—that is, um, any first encounter—should take place on a mutually agreed-upon neutral ground. A public place, like a bar, or a restaurant. And just a drink, not dinner. Just to see how it goes."

"Is that how it's done?" I dared to lift her hand and press a soft kiss against her knuckles. "All right, then. Tea's a drink, right? But I still think breakfast counts."

"No." She sounded breathless. "No way. We're nowhere yet. Breakfast doesn't count. Intention is everything."

"Now that is the God's own truth." It almost felt like I was in a dream, watching myself stroke her cheek. Warm, soft, as exquisitely smooth as I'd imagined. She smelled good. Warm. Sweet. Like honey. Like rain.

She made a low, inarticulate sound as I stroked her again, feeling the sharp angle of her jaw, studying the fine, delicate details. Dazed by her softness.

I leaned forward in tiny increments, until our faces nearly touched. We commenced a slow, careful dance of advance, retreat. Feeling her breath against my cheek, stroking her jaw. Tracing that elegant jut of delicately sculpted cheekbone beneath her skin.

I hung onto my control, sensing her caution and her longing, waiting patiently until caution and longing found their perfect balancing point, and ... ah. *Yes.*

Her eyes shut as my lips brushed hers. So lightly, so carefully. Tasting them. The contact made me gasp. She tasted like light. Incredible, electrifying. Her lips felt so soft and shy beneath mine. Trembling. A shimmering heat swelled inside my chest.

I explored her face with my fingertips, stroking her jaw, her throat. She drew in a sharp breath as my hand slid down her back, settling on the deep curve of her hip. Her nipples jutted against her blouse, and my fingers ached to brush over them, caress them.

I touched the first button, tugged it loose, revealing the hollow of her throat, and a warm cloud of her exotic, woodsy scent rose up. I wanted to gulp it in. To not waste a single precious breath of it.

I pulled her closer, kissing her jaw, her throat. My lips brushed over the gold of the pendant Lucia had given her, warmed by her body. My hand brushed over her breast. Her nipple brushed my palm. The little nub was hard, tight.

I deepened the kiss, my arm tightening around her, tasting her sweet flavor—

Whoa. I felt it, the very second the door slammed shut inside her. One moment she was melting in my arms, her fingernails digging into my shirt. Then suddenly, she went stiff and arched away, rigid and brittle. I was so in tune with her, I could feel the alarm jangling inside her, like her surge of anxiety was my own.

I forced myself to let go. Eased back, hands clenched, giving her the space she needed. I was at it again, pushing and grabbing. It was a piss-poor time for this. I'd scolded myself for being a greedy dickhead already, but apparently, it hadn't taken.

She was a complicated woman, grief stricken, stressed out, and I was being an asshole, forcing the issue. I had to struggle not to pant.

Fists clenched. Slow breathing. *Don't even look at her. Eyes straight ahead.*

Minutes ticked by, measured by drops of water making their way down the windshield. By the ragged breathing I struggled to keep silent. By my pounding heart.

At length, I heard her rustling, the soft sounds of fabric shushing together. Buttoning her blouse, getting herself in order. A cough. Clearing her throat. "Ah . . . um, Liam? That was, ah—"

"Amazing." I stared fixedly at the lean-to, and the pattern of the carefully stacked wood for my fireplace beneath the eaves. "But I pushed you too hard. I'm sorry."

She looked at her lap. "No, I'm the one who's sorry. I sent out, um, mixed signals, I guess. But I didn't mean to lead you on. Look, I need to get back. I need to talk to the cops about that letter, the jeweler, and clue my sisters into all these new developments. You've been great, and I appreciate the company, but I'm—"

"Scared," I said. "Of me. For some reason that I can't imagine."

She sighed. "Not of you." Her voice was low. "You're a good guy. I can feel that. I know it when I see it. It's just ... well. Everything."

"Yeah?" Frustration hardened my voice, despite my best efforts. "Everything's not here in the cab of this truck, Nancy. It's just me in here with you."

She shook her head. "I just...I can't."

"It's just a cup of tea," I reminded her. "Not the end of the world."

She let out a dubious snort. "You know exactly what would happen if I went into your house, Liam."

"Yes, actually, I do. I'd pull up a chair for you, put the kettle on the stove. Rummage around in the pantry for that tin of ginger butter crisps that I know is in there somewhere. I already know that you take milk and sugar. I'd make pleasant conversation. Ask leading questions about your childhood. Say nice things about your eyes, your hair, your earlobes. I'd try my best to be witty and charming."

"My earlobes?" A smile flickered on her face.

I nodded, willing it to be true. That scenario required iron-clad self-control.

"It sounds...very nice," she said demurely. "But...oh, never mind."

Yeah, she didn't have to say it. I saw that alternative scenario, too. The one where my iron-clad control faltered, and I ended up peeling the clothes off her luscious, sinuous body, pinned her against the wall and pounded her until we both exploded.

My heart thudded as the fantasy roared through my head, uncontrollably vivid.

Cool it. The moment was so fragile. She was so sensitive to my every word, my every thought. The air between us was a shimmering force field, alive with possibilities.

I caught her eye flicking to my lap and then darting nervously away. Yeah, there it was. Exhibit A, the boner of the century, aching with each thud of my heart for the soft touch of that cool hand, gripping and squeezing me. Heat burned into my cheekbones.

I gave her a shrug that said, *yeah, and so?* Maybe I couldn't control my body's response to her, but I could by God control my actions. I wanted her to know that, beyond all doubt, but there was no good way to say it without overstating it, sounding stiff and stupid. Anything could blurt out of my open mouth. Better to keep it shut.

"I just need things to be ... under control," she whispered. "I have enough to be scared of right now without piling on, you know?"

I rubbed my hand against my face, feeling around instinctively with my senses for a way through this maze. But I couldn't turn around and go back. That was not an option.

I flung the door of the truck open. The rain on the earth had released a deep, sweet, spicy perfume, just like hers. Raindrops pattered heavily down onto my head, my shoulders. I circled the old truck, and stood outside the passenger-side door, staring into Nancy's big, worried eyes through the rain-spotted glass.

I mimed rolling down the window. She did so, frowning in perplexity.

"What are you doing out there in the pouring rain?"

"Proving a point," I said. "Continuing our conversation. You need control? Fine. Take control. The car door's the limit, and I will not violate it. I swear upon my sacred honor that I will not touch any part of you that's inside that truck door."

She looked away with a nervous, embarrassed laugh. "Liam. Come on. You don't have to play elaborate games like that. You're getting soaked."

"That's my problem, not yours," I told her.

"But it makes me feel guilty!"

Ah, yes. Progress. "Guilt is your problem. I can't help with that. Sorry."

She laughed, and something primitive inside me capered with glee. *Yes.* It was working. She was lightening up. Praise God.

"So?" Her eyes sparkled. "You're just going to stand out there and get drenched, then? That's so silly, Liam. And completely unnecessary."

"It's a crafty attempt to disarm you with my gallant moves," I told her. "Is it working? Are you charmed? Disarmed?"

She wrinkled her nose and leaned out the window a little. "Nope. I think you're out of your freaking mind."

I felt jubilant as I sensed the change in her energy. "You're charmed," I said softly. "You're also outside the established limit. Any part of you outside the plane of the truck's window is fair game, remember? Which means that the tip of your nose and your forehead are currently at risk of getting kissed. This is a courtesy warning."

"Very gentlemanly of you," she said demurely.

"I'm trying," I said, with stark sincerity.

She didn't pull back. In fact, she leaned farther out, her fingers curled over the truck's door.

I jerked my chin toward her hands. "You're outside the limit," I reminded her.

Her lips formed words that didn't quite make it out of her mouth. She swallowed and tried again. "I know," she whispered.

My heart thudded harder. The force of the rain was increasing. The patter beginning to pound, soaking my hair, beading on my face and hers.

Over the limit. Fair game. She'd been warned.

I reached out slowly, as if she were a bird that might take

flight at any sudden movement, and touched the backs of her cool, slender fingers. Wet with rain.

Unexpectedly, her hands turned beneath mine, and excitement jolted through my chest. Palm up, like flowers, blooming beneath my hands. Fingers opening like petals.

I leaned closer. The rain murmured, pattering against the earth in a soft sigh. She glowed like a pearl, a faint blush of pink in her cheeks. Her huge eyes were wide and luminous, a greenish amber-brown, like leaves in the water. Her pupils dilated, deep and endless and inviting. There was a ruddy sprinkle of freckles on her nose. A frivolous detail that made her beauty even more earthy, more kissable.

The drops of water beading her forehead and cheeks were glittering adornments. They trembled on the grain of her dark eyebrows and clung to her thick mahogany hair, making the jut of her sharp cheekbone gleam. I was dazzled. Lost.

She extricated her hand and stroked my face from cheekbone to jaw. The trail of her finger was a path of light, like moonlight on water. Rain dripped into my collar, soaking my shoulders. It defined the dimensions of this liquid otherworld: pearly gray, green, brown, silvery, glittering and cool. Beneath that was Nancy's secret, hidden heat. The blush in her cheeks, the warmth of her lips, all sweet with rain. Her scent, so elusive and maddening, vanishing like a violet's perfume every time I tried to inhale it.

I swayed closer. Our lips touched.

The kiss pierced through me and broke something open. I clutched the edge of the door to steady myself. That shy, cautious, trembling kiss moved me. My eyes were wet.

Luckily, my face was already soaked with rain. *Keep it together, Knightly.*

I closed my eyes, drank in her scent, savored the delicate, silky texture of the inside skin of her lips, the uncertain flick of her shy tongue. I drank it up, slowly, tasting every drop. Like fine liquor. So much the sweeter for being given, not taken.

Nancy had shifted on the seat, rising onto her knees and leaning out toward me, into the rain. I cupped her face, and she clutched my forearms—her hands chilly and cool, but full of frantic energy as she offered herself up to be kissed.

Her slim torso was fully outside the window now, getting soaked in the shower of rain that neither of us seemed to notice. All I could feel was her strong, trembling body. All I could taste was her lips. Then I realized it. Whoa, her whole torso was outside the limit I'd established. She realized it, too. Awareness shimmered in the air between us.

I rested my forehead against hers, curling my fingers into the collar of her shirt. "A whole lot more of you is outside the window now," I stated, just to keep things clear.

She swallowed a few times. "Um. Yes. I am aware of that."

"So you're good if I do...this?" I unbuttoned the top button of her shirt.

She leaned forward, and the sapphire pendant swung free, glittering and swaying. She laughed softly under her breath. "I'm good," she whispered. "I'm more than good."

"Great." My heart raced so fast, I felt giddy. "Then it won't be that much of a stretch to do this." I plucked the second button loose. "And this." I undid the third. "And finally, this." I popped open the last one.

Her shirt was open now, showing a long stripe of bare, pale, shadowy skin beneath. I slid my hands inside, into that damp warmth beneath to rain-dampened cloth, and pushed the shirt open, and off her shoulders. It clung to her upper arms.

Oh God, she was beautiful. Like a naiad rising from the lake, hair slicked back, water-beaded skin, fathomless eyes. And those breasts—small, high and firm—with deep crimson, puckered nipples, tight and stiff at the cold kiss of rain. Flushed, gleaming red lips, moistened by her pink tongue. Yielding to my kiss.

She clutched my shoulders as I kissed my way reverently down her skin. She was trembling, but not with tension. Like a lake ruffled by currents, by the wind. She wound her fingers through my hair as I worshiped those perfect breasts with my hands, my lips, my tongue. Kissing, licking, suckling, coaxing. The tension pulled tight inside me. I was going to shatter...but she broke first.

Her fingers dug in as she cried out. I felt her climax throb through her and echo through me. So intense, I nearly came in my jeans, right then and there.

I pressed my face against her perfect breasts, panting. Sobered by the hugeness of what had just happened. If this was how I felt just kissing and caressing her, parked outside, in the pouring rain, in a driveway, with a car door between us—well, damn.

Getting her naked in my bed might just stop my heart.

I slowly kissed my way back up, straightening up, resting my forehead against hers again. My eyes gazing into hers. Speechless with wonder.

Then I heard the angry buzz of her phone in her purse.

It could have been ringing for ten minutes, for all I knew. I didn't want for either of us to leave our magic bubble, but the sound's insistent buzzing was a grappling hook that Nancy couldn't hope to resist. I felt tension grip her, and then I felt it drag her away from me.

I begged her, in my mind. *Turn it off. Don't go. Stay right here. Stay with me.*

She pulled away, crawling back into the cab of the truck, groping for her purse. "Hello?" She listened to a loud burst of talking on the other side, and her eyes flicked up to me. "Just a sec, Eugene. Um, Liam? This is going to take a few minutes. You might as well get back into the truck, out of the rain."

Yes, the moment was over. *Fuck.* I stood there, fists clenched, fighting unreasonable anger, but she didn't notice. She was focused elsewhere. All business now.

I got into the truck, feeling dismissed. What a chump asshole. Winding myself up into a state. Convincing myself that we were on the verge of something important.

But not more important than a fucking phone call.

Chapter Ten

Nancy

"Thank God you picked up. We've got a disaster on our hands!" Eugene was the fiddler from Mandrake, my Afro-Celt fusion band. I avoided looking at Liam as he got back into the truck. "What's the matter?"

"It's Dennis! He's deserting! The traitor!"

"Calm down. Let's take this step by step."

"He just got a gig with a touring show of *Celtic Dreamsong*! He's blowing us off! A week before the tour! The gigs in Boston, Albany and Atlanta all specified Uilleann pipes in the contract! We can't show up without a piper!" Eugene's voice cracked.

"Calm down," I said again. "This is bad, but we'll fix it."

"How, Nance? Every decent piper we know is booked solid those weeks! I've already made seven phone calls! We're completely screwed!"

"We'll fix it!" I insisted. "I'll be back tonight. When I get home, I'll call you and we'll work something out. Don't panic."

I listened with half an ear to Eugene's carrying-on, my body still quivering.

God. After all my resolutions to be tough. Making out madly with a stranger in his truck. Having a rain-soaked orgasm like none I even knew existed. Getting swept toward God alone knew what—his house, his couch, his rug, his bed. I hadn't been swept away since ... well, never, really.

I'd never known anyone that good. Hell, I'd never known *that good* existed. I was squirming, hot, wet, desperate. And that was after just some sweet talk, some gallant moves, a light kiss, a few buttons undone and my breasts expertly caressed. He'd barely touched me, and I'd gone off like a bomb. How on earth was that even possible?

I jerked my attention back to Eugene before I lost the thread. "All this work for nothing," he moaned. "I can't take it, Nance. It's too much for me. I'm going back to school. I'm going to be an accountant, like Mom wanted."

"You're not going to be an accountant," I soothed with practiced ease. "It's too late for that. You're not fit for any work but being a fiddler now, so get yourself a cup of tea and just calm down."

"Where the hell are you, anyway?" Eugene demanded.

My eyes flicked up to the side of Liam's impassive face. "I'll call you back, Eugene. Later, okay?" I closed the call and dropped the phone back into my purse.

The rain was now driving sideways into my open window. I rolled it up.

"I'll take you back to your car," he said.

The warmth was gone from his voice. I missed it.

It took twenty-odd minutes to get back to Lucia's house, and every minute that passed, his reproachful silence made me shrink further back into myself. As if I'd done something wrong, but I wasn't sure what.

When we arrived, he parked behind my car. So much had happened since I'd been there last, though it had been less than two hours. The whole gamut of human emotions had blazed through me, in waves. I felt hollowed-out.

I stared up at Lucia's shabby old house with the bright yellow crime scene tape festooned across the door, and started rummaging for my car keys.

"Thanks for the ride," I said. "And for keeping me company when we went to Baruchin's." *And for the most mind-blowing orgasm I ever felt. That, too.*

I wanted to say something to him after that moment of incredible intimacy, but his face looked so closed. The words just stopped in my throat.

I flung the door open and slid out of the truck. My legs almost buckled, and I steadied myself on the door before heading to my car. I tried to unlock it, but the key slipped from my stiff fingers, splashing into a puddle on the cracked old sidewalk.

Suddenly, Liam was beside me, fishing the keys out of the water, wiping them on his jeans. He opened the door and helped me into the car. I sat heavily in the driver's seat, glad to be off my feet.

"You need protection," he told me. "Twenty-four seven."

I snorted before I could stop myself. "Do I, now? Well, isn't that a shame. In a perfect world, I might agree with you. But I live alone, Liam. I work, all the time. I have a cat. And most importantly, I can't afford a bodyguard. So there it is."

"You could stay with me," he said. "Bring your cat. I like cats."

I gaped at him, at a total loss. "What?"

He shrugged. "It's a possible solution."

"But I...but what about your work?"

"I cleared my schedule for three weeks for Lucia's house,"

he said. "I'm overdue a vacation. I'd take some time for this. Just say the word."

"But your assistant—"

"I can find Eoin work on someone else's crew in five minutes. Don't worry about Eoin."

That finished all the obvious objections to the outrageous proposal. Now, I had to get down to the actual, awkward truth. "Liam. Get real. We don't have the kind of relationship where I could move in with you. Not even close."

"But you need protection," he repeated. "I feel it. Something bad is happening. You shouldn't be alone."

I shivered. "Well, maybe so, but I just met you yesterday. All we have is … well, hell. I don't even know what we had."

"We had breakfast," he offered.

"Do not make fun of me. This is no joke."

"It wouldn't be much of a leap," he said.

"What leap?" she asked crabbily.

"Us," he said. "From where we are now to the kind of relationship where I could have you to stay with me. There's a gap of …" He held up his thumb and forefinger with barely any space between them. "That much. Depending on what you decide."

Shivery tingles chased themselves across the entire surface of my body. "I can't make a decision like that today. I've known you for what, twenty-four hours?"

"Time is an illusion," he said.

She snorted. "Oh, don't give me that lofty metaphysical crap. Time is not a damned illusion. Not in my world."

"Okay," he agreed. "I won't."

I crossed my arms over my chest. "So what exactly do you have in mind? An exchange of goods and services? I shack up with you, and you protect me, in return for what?"

His eyes hardened. "That was crass, Nancy. I'm not an opportunistic pig."

"Whoa!" His anger gave me something to push against. "I never said you were! And maybe it's just me, but I couldn't help noticing a certain hurricane-force sexual energy coming off you, Liam!"

He wiped rain off his face. "Yes," he admitted. "Sorry. It's been a strange day."

"Tell me about it," I agreed fervently.

He crossed his arms over his chest. Big arms. A lot of chest.

I'd barely touched his body yet. And he was so careful with me, like I was made of glass. Fragile, brittle.

Oh, for God's sake. I was poised to tumble over the edge of disaster already. There was no need to take a running leap for it. "Things are strange now," I said. "It's a bad time for—"

"Strange times call for bold gestures. Brave risks."

I snorted. "I'm actually not that brave, if the truth be told."

"Bullshit. You have titanium for a spine. Like your mother."

The mention of Lucia made my throat seize up, tight and hot.

He let a few moments tick by. "I'm not a cop or an investigator. I'm just a carpenter. I can't promise to help you solve this problem. But I can make damn sure that nobody messes with you while you do it. That, I can absolutely commit to."

My eyes dropped, heat infusing my face.

"Let me help you," he urged. "At least think about it. Please."

Oh, my, yes. Think about it I most definitely would. Every waking second.

"Thanks," I murmured. "I'll bear that in mind."

He crouched until his face was level with mine. "And crash with one of your sisters," he directed. "Do not stay in your apartment alone."

"Liam, you cannot imagine how small our living spaces are—"

"Please, Nancy. Please. For me."

The intensity of his voice moved me. He really cared. He wasn't just throwing his weight around. "Okay," I heard myself say.

"Swear it," he said. "On your mother's grave."

I flinched. "Oh, for God's sake—"

"I said that on purpose, to give you a jolt. For Lucia's sake. She would have wanted you to be safe. I know that for a fact. She worried about you all the time."

I sighed. "Okay, okay. I swear it on my mother's grave. I will stay with my sisters tonight."

"Indefinitely. Until we know what the fuck is going on."

"Wow. You aren't shy about bringing out the big guns, are you?"

"Not in the least."

"Fine." I shut the car door, with energy. Shameless manipulator.

He knocked on my window and I rolled it down.

"Now what?" I said, with bad grace.

"Is an Irish pub in Queens neutral ground?" he asked.

I blinked at him, bewildered. "I don't follow."

"You said a date had to be on neutral ground. I'll be at Malloy's, on Queens Boulevard, tomorrow night. Ever been to a seisiún?"

He waited for her nod, then went on.

"Malloy's is a good one. The Guinness is good, the players are good, the food's good. Irish stew, burgers. The seisiún's from ten until two. I'd like to see you there."

I leaned my arms on the open window and looked out.

"This is ass-backward, you know," I told him. "First you invite me to live with you, and then you ask me out?"

He shrugged. "I try to be original." He sank down, his face level with mine at the open window. "You're over the limit again."

I gave him a jerky nod. "Sure am, buddy. What are you going to do about it?"

A grin flashed across his face. He leaned forward and brushed his lips against mine, and then lingered, tasting me. The burst of delight made my body clench and thrum.

We gazed at each other as he leaned back. "I've never felt anything like this," I said.

"Me neither." He stroked my cheek with his thumb. "It's got me all wound up. You're cold. Get the heat going. You're going to wait in here for the investigating officer?"

"I might as well," I said. "Since the evidence techs don't want me in the house till they've finished doing their thing."

"Okay. Tomorrow night, then. And take care." He smiled at me as he backed away and got into his truck.

After he drove away, I touched the tip of my tongue to my lips with a delicious shiver.

I could still taste him.

Chapter Eleven

Nancy

"Once more," Vivi said. "From the top."

Vivi was stretched out on Nell's sofa, her slender legs propped up on the back, gilded toenails flashing in the candlelight. She peered at her own photocopy of Liam's transcription of Lucia's letter with intense concentration. "So. Something very bad happened in her marriage. Something very bad happened to her father. But was it the same bad thing? And when did she come to America, anyway?"

I racked my brain as I petted the wildly purring cat curled in my lap. "Nineteen sixty-eight, or shortly after, I think. She taught art history at Beardsley for more than forty years before she retired. And that was well over ten years ago."

"And what was the name of the town she came from again?" Vivi asked.

"Castiglione Santangelo," Nell replied. "In Tuscany." She turned the Fabergé picture frame that held the old photograph of Lucia's father over in her hands. "Maybe that's why she

101

changed her name from de Luca to D'Onofrio. Because of this mysterious thing that happened. To her father. With her husband. Or both of them."

"Maybe," I said. "It's just so strange that she never mentioned any of it."

"I asked her once why she changed her name, but she didn't want to talk about it," I said. "She just changed the subject."

"I asked her to go to Italy with me once, for an art and architecture tour, back when I was an undergrad," Nell said, her voice low. "I'd saved up money for it. But she snapped my head off, and I was so taken aback, I never mentioned it again."

"Hmm. Let's run it all down again," Vivi said. "The things we didn't know about Lucia, and sadly, still don't." She ticked them off on her fingers. "Her father. Her marriage. The mysterious object. The terrible event in the past. The unexplained name change. The system of checks and balances designed to protect our sisterly love. Whatever mystery that the necklaces are the key to. Then, to make things even more interesting, we now have the mysteries of the purloined letter, the murdered jeweler, and the pissed-off burglar. That's a lot of mysteries. Makes a girl hungry." She rolled up onto her side and reached for a slice of the pizza in the open box on the coffee table.

"I wish we had access to Lucia's papers," Nell fretted. "I'd like to go through her letters and photographs."

"The burglar trashed Lucia's office," Vivi reminded her.

"He might have missed something," Nell said stubbornly. "He probably didn't stop to read the documents. Some of which are certainly in Italian."

I held out my hand. "Can I see that photo for a second?"

Nell handed it to her. "Of course."

I studied the fierce, hawklike face of the late Conte de Luca, Lucia's father. His intense, blazing dark eyes were so much like Lucia's, they made my chest ache. "I wonder when he died," I mused. "He looks like he was in his fifties in this photo. Maybe there's a date on the back." I fumbled with the back of the delicate gold frame until I managed to carefully loosen the little hook that held it closed, and pried the back loose, shaking the contents into my hand.

We all stared, frozen, at what lay in her hand. Not one photograph, but two—and something else: a small, carefully folded square of yellowed paper.

I gently pushed Moxie out of my lap and scooted over toward the single dim lamp we'd left on. Nell and Vivi scrambled to look over my shoulder. Moxie stalked away, tail high, deeply offended.

"Oh, wow," Vivi breathed softly, as we stared down at the picture. "That's Lucia. Just look at her. What a bombshell."

The young, beautiful Lucia had an elegant pouff of back-combed sixties hair, styled into a curled flip below her ears, and wore a smart little pillbox hat. Her lips were painted into a bold Cupid's bow, and she gazed up into the face of a tall, handsome man who clasped her waist and looked hungry to kiss her. I turned it over. On the back, in faded, brownish ink, was written, *Venezia,Carnevale, 1966.*

"Who is this guy?" Nell murmured. "The missing husband. What's on the paper?"

I unfolded the delicate, yellowing paper. It was lightweight, onion-skin

airmail paper, covered with fine, faded script. I held it to the light. "It's in Italian," I said, passing it promptly to Nell.

Nell fumbled for her glasses and pushed them up her nose. "It's dated April of 1969," she said, and began to translate.

Beloved Lucia,

I do not know why I continue to write while you continue to be silent, but I cannot seem to stop myself, undignified though I must seem, begging on my knees for your return to our life together.

I understand how shocked and horrified you are by what happened to Babbo, but believe me, it was like a knife to my own heart as well. If I could change the terrible events of the past for you, I would, at any cost. But I cannot.

But this is no reason to abandon your home, your family, your nation. You will never heal in a foreign land. You cannot run from this pain, my love. It will follow you wherever you go. Of this, I am sure.

You have always been obstinate. It is a part of your strength, which I love and admire. But true strength must be tempered by softness, reason, compromise.

But why do I waste ink? You are resolved to be cruel and immovable. I try to accept this, but I cannot swallow it. I enclose this photograph, in hopes that it will remind you of happier times.

I continue to work on deciphering your father's map. I have once again completely excavated the palace gardens, this time draining the lake in my search, which you hold to be both stupid and pointless. My efforts were entirely in vain, as I am sure you will be gratified to know.

Forgive my acid tone. I miss you desperately. For the sake of the children we might still have together, please, Lucia, come back to me. Come home.

In faith,
Marco

We all stared at each other after Nell stopped reading, eyes wide with shock.

"Wow," Vivi whispered. "That guy really knew how to lay a guilt trip."

"I bet that's why she never married," Nell said. "She had men chasing her all her life, but she blew them off. She must have still been in love with Marco."

"And they spent their entire lives apart." I stared at the photo. The innocent happiness radiating out of the young couple made my stomach hurt. "All because of some horrible thing that happened to the Conte. Between the years of 1966 and 1968."

"Do you guys think that this horrible thing could possibly be connected to the horrible things happening now?" Vivi's voice was timid.

I folded the letter delicately back into its original creases. "Well, this Marco had a map," I said. "And he was looking for some hidden object. In Lucia's letter, she refers to "this thing," plus what happened to her father and what it did to her marriage. So, yeah. I can't imagine how, but yeah. Somehow, they're all connected."

"And this is not good news," Nell said. "Since we are utterly clueless."

"At least the letter I found in the garbage makes it clear that the 'thing' she's referring to isn't the trio of necklaces that she gave us," I said. "The necklaces are the key, she said. So maybe this secret thing is in that safe that the carpenter installed?"

"Yeah, the safe we have no combination for." Nell held up her pendant. It spun, tiny rubies gleaming in the light of the candles she'd set around her Williamsburg apartment.

"I guess we could count the stones, try the different sequences we come up with as possible combinations to the safe," I mused. "But that doesn't use our love of music, literature, or the visual arts. It seems too obvious. Lucia had a more devious personality than that." I tucked the photograph and the letter carefully back into the picture frame. "She was gearing up to tell us more when she was killed."

"Killed?" Vivi choked on her pizza, coughing. "God, Nance. You really think ... ?"

"The jeweler and his family get murdered the same night the house is trashed, and before I can talk to him about the necklaces? Hell, yes. I do think that."

Nell reclasped her pendant around her neck, her dark eyes worried. "I've never seen you this way, Nance. You'd say you were fine even if you were bleeding to death. I about dropped my teeth when you asked to come over tonight to stay. Not that you aren't more than welcome. I'm scared too, and I'm glad to have you both here."

I fidgeted. "Oh, that's just because I swore a vow," I blurted. "I would've been perfectly fine at home."

"Vow?" Vivi straightened up, eyes wide. "What vow? To whom?"

"To Liam." I picked at the fabric of my jeans, already regretting my incautious words. "The carpenter who was going to do the remodel."

Nell and Vivi exchanged significant looks. "He made you swear not to stay alone?" Nell asked. "This is the carpenter who flash-memorized Lucia's letter? My. He certainly is taking a personal interest, isn't he?"

If they only knew. "I guess you could say that," I hedged.

"Tell us about this carpenter," Nell prompted. "I'm picturing a potbellied guy with a bushy beard, a red nose, and twinkling eyes. Like a young Santa. Jeans slipping down over a big, hairy ass crack. Am I close?"

"Nope," I admitted. "Light-years."

Her sisters exchanged knowing looks. "So?" Vivi asked. "No potbelly? No hairy ass-crack? Do tell."

"His belly's pretty tight," I hedged. "I can't speak for his ass, but shape-wise, it was … well, proportional. In his jeans."

"Proportional, hmm?" Vivi purred. "Height?"

"Maybe six-two," I admitted. "Maybe a little more."

"Six-two," Nell said dreamily. "Nice. Eye color?"

"Very pale green. Dollar bill green."

Nell and Vivi gave each other a high five. "She remembers his eye color! She has fanciful metaphors for it!" Vivi crowed. "It's serious!"

"Oh, shut up," I muttered.

"Let's celebrate." Nell popped open another beer. "At least this guy isn't a musician, right? That's already a big step up."

"Actually, he invited me to a seisiún in Queens tomorrow night, so he's some sort of musician," I said. "Although I have no idea at what level. Or even what instrument."

"Invited you? To a seisiún?" Nell's voice rose to a squeak.

I squirmed. "Not a date. Just a seisiún. A couple of pints in a grotty Irish bar, and Irish tunes until our eyes cross. A date is a much bigger deal than that."

"Yeah, like you're such an expert," Vivi said. "What bar?"

I stared from one to the other. "Don't you dare."

"What bar?" both of my sisters demanded in unison.

"I'm not telling," I said. "So just forget it."

"Fine," Vivi said. "I'll go through other channels. I'll call … let's see … Eugene. We'll tell him you have a hot date tomorrow night, and ask him for a list of the seisiúns tomorrow in Queens. Then Nell and I will make the rounds until we get lucky."

"Vivi," I said. "Don't."

"And then we will roast you so hard, babe. We will have no mercy. None."

My face had gotten hot. "Don't tell Eugene," I said. "He's a terrible gossip. I'll never hear the end of it."

"So give it up," Vivi said, her face relentless. "The seisiún. Let's have it."

I gritted my teeth. "Malloy's," I admitted. "Ten to two. I haven't decided yet whether or not I'm going."

"Oh?" Nell's dark eyes were innocently wide. "Six two, green eyes, perfectly proportional ass? You are *so* going to that seisiún."

"Whether or not, it's my business," I said. "We'll see how you like it when I descend onto one of your dates and try to embarrass you."

Nell's face tightened. "Like that'll happen in this century."

Something in Nell's voice gave us pause. Vivi hoisted herself up onto her elbow.

"Why not?" she asked. "Why shouldn't it happen? You're gorgeous, smart, funny, sweet, creative, amazing. You're a prize. A total pearl. What's not to date?"

Nell shrugged. "I think I'm just one of those women who crushes on unattainable men. You know. Protecting myself by making sure I never have to deal with a real relationship, blah, blah."

"Who?" I demanded. "Who's unattainable? Why is he unattainable?"

"It doesn't matter." Nell looked intensely uncomfortable. "You don't know him, and you won't meet him. Ever. It's just a pointless thing happening inside my own head."

"Is he married?" Vivi demanded.

"No!" Nell snapped. "I mean ... that is to say ... I haven't the faintest idea. He doesn't talk to me. But he doesn't wear any ring, so I guess probably he ... oh, hell. Never mind. It couldn't be more irrelevant. It's just absolutely not, you know ... thing."

But the damage was done, and we had to know more. "Who is he?"

Nell threw up her hands with a frustrated huff. "No one!

Just a random guy who comes into the Sunset Grill for lunch. That's all. I have a monster crush on a guy I serve lunch to. Believe me, it's exactly as stupid and pathetic as it sounds."

"Did you write your number on the check?" Vivi asked. "Do you flirt? Look through your eyelashes? Bring him extra garlic breadsticks?"

Nell rolled her eyes. "If I'd ever established eye contact, that ploy might make sense. But he's never even looked at me. And I mean that literally. He just looks at his laptop. A screen full of code. If he saw me on the street, he wouldn't recognize me."

Vivi clapped a hand over her face. "A techie? God help you."

Nell looked so miserable, I took pity on her and tried to deflect. "How about you, Viv?" I demanded. "Romantic prospects?"

Vivi rolled her eyes. "Nope. I'm making celibacy into a high art."

"Because of Brian?"

Vivi's eyes narrowed. "Maybe. Among other things. There's also the issue of working hard and always being on the road. And besides, the pool of guys who'd be into an oddball like me is pretty small to begin with."

"Brian was six years ago," I said. "He can't derail your life forever."

Vivi's mouth tightened. "Knowing it doesn't really seem to help all that much."

Something in Vivi's voice made me back off. God knows, I wasn't anyone to judge, with my history of romantic train wrecks. I studied my sister's averted face. "I'm sorry," I said. "I didn't mean to be a bitch about it. I just hate him so much. But I love you. Like crazy. And I'm so glad he's out of the picture."

Vivi waved her hand, brushing the subject away. "Forget

Brian. He's a dull, boring little putz. Your six-foot-two carpenter with his tight belly and his proportional ass is way more interesting. I can hardly wait to check him out tomorrow."

"Me, neither," Nell said, with relish.

I let out a puzzled sigh. Somehow, I'd come full circle, and led them both back around to busting my balls again. Ah, the joys of sisterhood.

Moxie started kneading my thigh, claws out. I unsnagged her sharp little nails from my jeans and reached for another beer. "You guys," I muttered. "Please."

Nell nudged my arm. "We don't mean to torture you," she said earnestly. "Well, actually, we kind of do, but it's not malicious, I promise. It's just so nice to have something fun and frivolous to talk about, you know? Be patient. We've been so sad and confused lately. Your proportional-assed carpenter is hard for us to resist."

I squeezed Nell's hand. She was right. It was nice to hear my sisters laughing. To chatter and bicker about men, dating, silly crushes, butthead ex-boyfriends, proportional asses. Silly, nonessential things. Nothing earthshaking.

Not that I would characterize that kiss in the rain as frivolous or lighthearted.

And *earthshaking* was putting it mildly.

Chapter Twelve

Liam

S he wouldn't show up. I was sure of it, but like an idiot, I kept checking my watch every minute or so since I'd walked into Malloy's and took my fiddle, flutes, and whistles out of their bags and cases. I took a swallow of Guinness and wondered why I was torturing myself. The woman's cell phone alone would drive me insane.

I couldn't believe my own idiocy. Offering myself as an unpaid bodyguard? And then getting all up on my high horse when she called me on my bullshit. Oh, sure, I'd keep her real safe, you bet, yesireebob. Nobody would mess with her while she was snug and warm in my bed, pinned to the mattress beneath my heaving body.

But my eyes kept drifting to the bar entrance. I wanted to see her again. Hear her voice. I liked the way her mind worked, the way her brow furrowed when she was thinking. Those big gold-brown eyes. The way she wrinkled her nose when she was disgusted, which appeared to be fairly often. And when I kissed her, oh dear God. The rain that fell on me yesterday should have evaporated into pure steam.

"Yo! Earth to Liam! Come in, Liam!" Mickey the guitar player brayed into my ear. "Do that set of reels you did last week that ends with 'The Tinker's Bride,' okay? I want to try out a new accompaniment."

"Sure." I took another swig of his pint. My watch said 11:07. I had to just get the hell over myself and concentrate on the music. I tuned up my fiddle.

We had just launched into "The Tinker's Bride" when she walked in. I felt her presence even before she pushed through the crowd. A smile spread across my face, and by the time she made it back to the table, it had turned into a big grin. I started speeding up. The other musicians gave me panicked looks, dropping out one by one until only Eoin played with me.

We finished with a flourish, to appreciative hoots and hollers.

She looked softer tonight. Amazingly, her hair was shiny and loose, thick and wavy, hanging long down her back. She was wearing jeans and a snug, low-cut red T-shirt that made her skin glow and showed off the perfect shape of those pert, suckable tits.

Her big eyes were cautious behind her glasses. I put down my fiddle and made my way over to her as the group tore into "The Red-haired Boy." Her eyes widened as I boldly kissed her, as if I had the right. She smelled incredible. Her lips were so soft.

She swayed back. "Whoa," she said with a nervous laugh. "You don't waste time, do you?"

"Fuck no." I slid my arms around her and kissed her again. Doubling down.

It started to happen again, like it had yesterday. The world fell away, the noise of the bar fading, my focus narrowing down to just Nancy and my own pounding heartbeat. I could barely hear the music.

I forced myself to pull away, then glanced over my shoulder to a table-full of smirks, and nudges. Eoin lifted his pint with a smile, his eyes discreetly curious.

Nancy's face was pink. "Did I mess up?" I asked her.

"Ah...not necessarily. I'm not used to guys just grabbing me."

"Did your other boyfriends ask nicely before they kissed you?"

Her eyes narrowed. "That's a loaded question. But no, I don't think they did. To be truthful, I don't think it was ever much of an issue before."

Huh. Maybe this was a can of worms better steered around, rather than dived into. At least until I'd made more progress. "Can I get you a drink?"

"You said the Guinness was good, right?"

"Best this side of the Atlantic." I elbowed my way to the bar and got her a pint.

When I passed it over, she sipped it and sighed with an expert's appreciation.

"I didn't think you'd show," I said.

She licked foam off her lip. "I still don't know if it's a good idea."

"Me neither, but I don't care," I said recklessly. I dragged another chair to the musicians' table and sat her down next to me, boldly taking her hand. Winding my fingers through her cooler ones, to warm them. In the confusion that followed the end of the set, she leaned over to me. "I want to hear you play!" she shouted.

Her warm, sweet breath against my neck was as sweet as a kiss. I picked up my fiddle, Mickey called another set, and we were off and tearing along on a set of jigs.

It was a good group. Guitar, fiddles, bodhrán, accordion, and Eoin, locked in a trance of perfect happiness, his fingers flashing as he played his Uilleann pipes.

Nancy clapped vigorously as we finished the set and leaned over.

"You guys are great!" she said, her eyes alight with pleasure. "You kick ass on that fiddle, Liam! Where'd you learn to play?"

"My stepdad played the fiddle," I replied. "He got me into it when I was a kid. And I picked up the flutes and whistles a few years back, just for fun. I'd rather mess around with them than watch TV."

"You're hot," she said. "Did you ever think of going pro?"

I used the excuse of having to talk over the noise into her ear to kiss the soft skin behind it, and smell her sweet shampoo. "For about ten minutes," I admitted. "Figured that would take all the fun out of it."

"Hmm. I guess you might be right. Who's the piper?"

"Oh, Eoin? He's my cousin. Second cousin, actually. Fresh from County Wicklow. He works for me. Lives in my basement. Good kid."

"He's fabulous," she said.

"Yeah, isn't he? He just lights on fire when he plays those pipes."

That was all there was time to say before we plunged into another set, reels this time, as raucous and wild as the set before.

After the set she leaned over again. "Would your cousin be interested in touring with a hot band that gigs a lot?"

I was taken aback. "Who? You mean, Eoin?"

"I don't want to put you in a bind. You know, poaching from your crew. But we need a piper, and he rocks."

Nancy's eyes glowed. The world was warm and generous tonight, and so was I.

"Ask him," I suggested. "I'm sure he'll be thrilled. He lives to play those pipes."

We played a set of slip jigs as she retreated to the far side of the room to talk into her phone, a big happy smile on her face.

She came back and sat down next to me again looking satisfied. "This is the answer to my prayers," she said. "Matt and Eugene are on their way over, but I'm sure it's a done deal, if he's interested."

"You work fast," I said.

She looked suspicious. "Wait. Are you sure you don't mind me stealing him?"

I shrugged. "Not really. I know he loves playing the pipes more than he loves working on construction crews. It's okay. I'll find someone else to help me."

Her face relaxed. "Oh, good. I love it when things work out perfectly."

"Me, too," I agreed, leaning over to let her thick, silky hair brush against my face.

A stocky redheaded guy with a guitar and a skinny guy carrying a fiddle pushed their way through the crowd about a half hour later. Their eyes fastened on Eoin, lost in the rapture of a set of fast jigs, his eyes closed, arm pumping his bellows. They nodded to Nancy. The redheaded guy's eyes lingered on me. I was still nuzzling her hair.

"That's Matt with the guitar, and Eugene with the fiddle," she said in my ear. "I'll introduce you after the set."

Matt and Eugene pulled out their instruments and dove into the seisiún without delay. Nancy extracted her hand from mine and patted it. "I have to go talk to Eoin," she said. "Be right back."

I watched, fascinated, as she swiveled her way gracefully through the crowd. She waited until the end of the set, then tapped Eoin on the shoulder, and started talking in his ear. Eoin shot me a bewildered look. I gave him a thumbs-up.

Nancy spoke again, and Eoin's freckles disappeared in a deep blush.

Nancy made her way back to me and sat down again, grinning.

"I'll let the boys take it from here. He's shy. Needs some convincing," she said, just as the players tore lustily into "The Abbey Reel."

Not much later, I noticed a man I knew across the bar smiling at me and lifting a pint in salute. It was Charlie Witt, a cop from Latham who'd been partnered with Hank, my stepdad, back when Hank had been on the force. Charlie was a good guy. Past retirement age, but he kept on working.

An impulse struck me, and I leaned in close to Nancy's ear, nuzzling her soft hair, sucking in a greedy chestful of that sweet warm scent that made me want to lick her all over. "There's a guy I want to talk to over there," I said. "Will you come with me?"

Nancy looked puzzled, but she nodded agreeably. We slid out of our chairs, and I clasped her hand and led her through the crowd just as the lads all followed Eoin's lead and struck into another high-speed reel.

Nancy's fingers curled around mine. Her hand was so small. I wanted to kiss it. Drag her out of there. Find someplace private.

I shook Charlie's hand, introduced Nancy, and got a congratulatory thump on the shoulder from the old man as he looked her over. "You got yourself a dish," the older guy said. "Treat her good, huh? Or else I'll steal her for myself."

The next reel had a couple of bodhráns thundering along, so I had to practically yell into Charlie's ear. "I need some advice."

"Anything for Hank's kid," Charlie shot back.

"Remember that elderly Italian American lady in Hempton who died in a burglary attempt about eight, nine days ago? Lucia D'Onofrio?"

Charlie's smile faded. "Yeah, I heard about that. That was a fuckin' shame. They say the house got tossed again. Even worse this time."

"Yeah, it did. And I was the one who reported it yesterday," I told him. "Nancy here is Mrs. D'Onofrio's daughter."

Charlie looked at Nancy again, his round, ruddy face grave. He jerked his chin toward the back of the bar. "Let's go where there's less noise."

We followed Charlie into a quieter room, one with a pool table and a pay phone. Charlie slid into a booth and took a swallow of the pint that he'd brought with him.

"I don't actually know a whole lot about that case," he told us. "It ain't my case, or even my town. I only just heard about it because my partner, Henry, is hangin' out with one of the evidence techs."

"I just wanted your take on it," I said.

I outlined the facts for Charlie with a few interjections from Nancy, clarifying and explaining. Charlie read the transcription of Lucia's letter, peering through his bifocals for several minutes. Then he scowled at Nancy, chewing his lip thoughtfully.

"Your investigating officer knows about this letter, miss? You told him about the connection with the Baruchins?"

"It's a her, actually. Detective Lanaghan. And yes, I told her yesterday," Nancy said. "The letter was bagged up and taken away by the forensics team. They might have even found more of it by now. God, I hope so. It's our only hope of knowing more."

Charlie shook his head. "Bad couple of weeks for senior

citizens around here. The D'Onofrio lady, the clotheshorse. Now the Baruchins."

"The clotheshorse? Who's he?" I asked.

Charlie let out a grunt of disgust. "Nobody knows. Strangest shit I ever heard. Kid finds a body in a vacant lot in Jamaica 'bout a week ago. Some guy in his eighties, neck snapped. No ID, but the guy was dressed head to toe in Italian designer clothes. Like, ten thousand bucks was on the guy's back. Steffi got on the Internet, did some pricing. His shoes alone would have cost two grand. But if he's a rich bigwig, why doesn't somebody report him missing? And if he's a crook, his prints or DNA would turn up some priors, right?" He shrugged. "But no. Nothing. It's like the guy never existed. But somebody popped him. Now somebody pops Baruchin, plus his wife and mother-in-law, and the same night that somebody comes back to the D'Onofrio house and trashes it again? It stinks." He gave Nancy a long, considering look. "You're absolutely sure you don't know what these clowns are looking for, right, miss?"

Nancy's lips tightened. "Not a clue," she said. "Unless it's these necklaces, and Lucia's letter seems to indicate that it's not. The necklaces are the only connection to the Baruchins. Believe me, if I knew more, the first thing I would do would be tell the investigating officer."

"I'm thinking maybe you and your sisters should stop wearin' those necklaces, if somebody might be willing to kill for 'em," Charlie said bluntly.

Nancy's hand shot up and clutched the thing. "They were Lucia's last gifts to us."

"I'm sure she wouldn't have wanted you girls to be in danger," he said.

All the breezy good cheer was gone from Charlie Witt's

face. He was dead serious now. Nancy stared back, polite but stubborn. "Lieutenant Witt, I have a question—"

"Call me Charlie, honey."

Nancy gave him an incandescent smile. "Charlie. In the first break-in, the forensics team found a set of fingerprints on my mother's writing table that did not belong either to her or the three of us. Do you suppose they might try comparing them with Baruchin's prints? Or to this mystery man they found in the vacant lot? Just to see if they might've been in my mother's house?"

Charlie looked doubtful. "I don't see why it would have occurred to anyone, but why not? I'll call Detective Lanaghan tomorrow and talk to her about it. Just don't expect any quick or easy answers, miss."

"Of course not," Nancy murmured. "I'm just trying to cover every possibility."

"Right you are." Charlie turned to Liam with a thoughtful frown. "I wouldn't let her out of my sight, if I were you, kid. Not for a single second."

I nodded. It was a relief to have my own instincts verified. It made me feel less like a slavering hound. I hoped Nancy was paying attention.

"That's what I figured," I said. "But I'm still working on selling that proposal to her. She's not convinced."

"Work harder," Charlie advised, his voice hard. He looked over at Nancy, his eyes sliding over her décolletage. "Not that it would be such a chore to keep your eyes on that, now, mind you."

"That it isn't," I agreed, though the sharp flash in Nancy's eyes indicated that I was definitely going to pay for it.

"Kinda hard to take your eyes off her as it is," Charlie commented.

"Could you two gentlemen please stop talking about me as if I weren't here?" Nancy asked crisply.

Charlie blinked. "Aww, honey. Was I objectifyin' you?"

Nancy snorted, and dangerously, Charlie took it as encouragement. "Had this girlfriend once. Always said I was objectifyin' her when I pissed her off."

"Charlie," I broke in, "put the brakes on, please."

"Never did figure out what the hell she was talkin' about, but she sure had a nice—"

"Charlie! Stop!" I snapped my fingers in front of Charlie's face.

Charlie subsided, eyes twinkling. "Uh, well. Guess I better be heading on home to the wife." His eyes rested thoughtfully on Nancy as he drank his final swallow of beer, and then his eyes cut to my half-empty pint. "I'd switch to coffee, if I was you, kid."

We said our goodbyes and headed back toward the other room after Charlie left. I leaned close, murmuring "Sorry about that. Charlie was trying to lighten the mood."

"I get that," Nancy assured me.

We sat down with the musicians again. I took Charlie's advice and switched to coffee, but even so the night quickly took on a dreamlike quality. The music thundered, and whenever I wasn't playing, Nancy's slender hand rested in mine, fingers entwined.

We didn't talk much, with all the noise, but it didn't matter. Our hands communed.

Some time later, I noticed a disturbance in the group's energy. The driving tempo of the music never faltered, but every male eye at the table — except for Eoin's—was fixed on something right behind me.

I turned to take a look, and the mystery soon resolved itself.

Two strikingly pretty women stood there: one a slender, waiflike girl with big gray eyes and a mop of long, fire-red hair; the other fuller-figured, with long brunette ringlets, flashing dark eyes, luscious curves. Both of them stood by the musicians' table, staring at me intently. I felt like I knew them from somewhere.

Oh. Of course. Lucia's other two daughters. I'd seen the pictures.

I glanced at Nancy and found her rolling her eyes. She gestured for me to lean down so she could speak directly into my ear again. "Those are my nosy, interfering sisters," she called into my ear. "They wanted to check you out. And then roast me."

Her sisters. She had told her sisters about me. Well, hot damn. That was promising.

I wasn't quite ready to talk to them yet, so I went ahead and dove into "The Three Wishes," at Eoin's preferred dangerously fast pace. The rush of energy from being displayed to the sisters made me feel equal to it. I looked at the sisters and gave them a big, friendly "here I am, so check me out" grin.

They gave each other wide-eyed looks, and giggled. Then they took turns whispering into Nancy's ear and giggled some more. Nancy turned brick red.

I freaking loved it.

I was sorry when they left not long after. They ran off before he had a chance to chat with them, maybe make a good impression. Nancy probably glared them away.

Maybe I'd soon get another chance to charm them. Get them onto my side. In a less noisy environment, maybe. Dinner at my place, maybe. I'd push for that. Maybe I was getting ahead of myself, but what the hell. I cooked a good dinner, when I made an effort.

I looked at my watch when the other musicians started packing up, astonished to find that it was well past two in the morning. Eoin was already wangling a ride with Nancy's friends to his next seisiún, hopeless tunehead that he was.

"I should be getting home," Nancy said.

"I'll walk you to your car," I offered.

"Actually, no," she admitted. "I found such a good parking spot for it yesterday that I couldn't bear to move it, so I just took the subway."

I stared at her, appalled. "You're joking, right?"

She looked uncomfortable. "Uh, no. It was perfectly safe. The trains were crowded when I came out. The Seven got me within two blocks of here, and it was full. I always take the subway, whenever I can. It's so much faster, and I—"

"You're not taking it tonight. I'm driving you home."

"Oh, don't worry about it," she scoffed. "I won't take it home. I had every intention of calling a car to get home, given the weird things that have been happening, so—"

"Have you not been listening?" My voice got sharper than I meant it to. "Did you hear what Charlie said? I know you're not stupid, so do you have a death wish?"

Her mouth tightened at my scolding, but there was no way I could have suppressed that. "I do not have a goddamn death wish, Liam. I just try to get through my days as best I can with the resources I have at my disposal, that's all. Plus, I don't like inconveniencing people. And what about Eoin? Didn't he come with you?"

"Eoin's fine. Your friends are taking him to a late-night seisiún someplace in Brooklyn. He'll play tunes all night and wake up God knows where, if he sleeps at all."

She bit her lip. "It's so far out of your way. An Uber would be fine. Really."

It occurred to me that Nancy wasn't used to the people

around her giving a damn whether she got home safely. Not any more than she was used to being kissed.

Well, too bad. She was just going to have to get used to it. I wasn't going to ease into it. I was full-on, one hundred percent.

When it came to keeping her safe, I was dead serious.

Chapter Thirteen

Nancy

I clasped my hands nervously together in Liam's truck. Being alone with him in the dark made all my doubts come rushing back, mixed with a big dose of simmering lust.

So strange, to think how convinced I'd been that I was in love with Freedy, Ron, and Peter, but I'd never felt like this with them. Not ever. This hot buzz. Raw, thrumming, glowing. A live wire with the casing peeled off.

I cast around for something neutral to talk about, but I was too flustered. "What a stroke of luck to find Eoin," I said. "He solves all our problems in one go. Plus, he seems like a total sweetheart. How old is he, anyway?"

"Twenty-one, if I remember correctly."

"God. Just a baby. Looks like he hit it off with Matt and Eugene, too. And he's available for the tour, thank God. Does he have a green card?"

Liam hesitated. "We're working on it," he said guardedly.

"I can help with that," I assured him. "Uilleann pipers are

rare. It's a highly specialized skill. I'll write a raft of urgent letters to the INS about how desperately we need him for this gig or that gig, this recording or that tour. It may take a while, but they'll come through eventually." I caught his smile before he turned away. "Why are you smirking? Do I amuse you, Liam Knightly?"

He pulled up at the Midtown tunnel toll booth, batted away my handful of money, and paid the toll himself. "You're very sweet, Nancy."

My cheeks grew warm. "Thanks for saying that, but I'm actually not doing anything altruistic. Drafting Eoin into Mandrake is good business. In fact, he's saving our asses."

"And the green card?"

"That's in my best interests, too," I retorted.

"Why does it embarrass you when I tell you that you're sweet?"

I thought about it for a minute. "I feel as if you're condescending to me."

"Sweet isn't a bad thing," he said. "You think being sweet equals being vulnerable?"

"Don't tell me how I feel. I'm not in the mood."

"Ah, she's back! The tough broad with the attitude. But you don't fool me. You're tough, but you're sweet. Lucia knew it. She admired it. And I'm not condescending to you at all. On the contrary. I respect you for it."

I was intensely uncomfortable. This exposed feeling was unbearable. The tunnel spat us up into Midtown, thank God, and I busied myself giving him directions.

"Take the FDR Drive south." I held up my hand at his expression. "I swear, I kept my promise. I'm camped out at Nell's, but I had to take my cat, and I didn't have enough arms to carry all her stuff yesterday. I need to get her food, I need toys, I need kitty litter. I'm sorry to inconvenience you, but—"

"Don't apologize again. Please. It bugs me."

That squelched further attempts at conversation. I just muttered "right" and "left" at the appropriate times until I indicated my entryway down in Alphabet City.

Liam took note of the door, drove on past without stopping, and found himself a parking space three blocks down.

That gave me pause. I hadn't expected him to actually find parking near my place. God knows, I never did. I'd expected him to drop me off at the door, and maybe gallantly wait as I fumbled out my keys. But no. Here he was, legally parked. Motor off, with that *what-are-you-going-to-do-about-it* look in his eyes.

Liam Knightly, at my apartment, at three in the morning—wow. It flung open doors in my mind that I wasn't quite ready to walk through.

I sighed. For God's sake, the man had just driven an hour out of his way to take me home in the middle of the night. The least I could do was to offer him coffee for the drive home. I gulped in air. "Do you, uh, want to come up for coffee?"

"Yes," he said.

The word seemed invested with infinite shades of meaning. My knees went rubbery.

"My apartment isn't neutral ground," I said.

His eyes gleamed. "I'll be good."

Would he, now. Loaded words, if there ever were ones.

Liam slung his fiddle and flute and whistle bag cases over his shoulder and took her arm. He looked around at the block of cramped, humble turn-of-the-last-century buildings as if he expected the garbage cans to animate and attack them. They had been built to house the sweatshop workers that had been coming in droves on the boats from Europe to work in the garment district. The apartments were tiny, pinched, light-starved, airless, but you wouldn't know it from the ridiculous rents they charged.

I fished out my house keys. The bulb that lit the stairs was dim and flickering. The place looked tragically shabby at three A.M. I fought the urge to apologize. To say something disparaging about the missing floor tiles or the wall graffiti. To make snide comments about Manhattan real estate prices.

But I would be dignified if it freaking killed me. My high-heeled boots echoed on the stairway, but Liam's footfalls were quiet. I wanted to say something to break the tension, but my brain had ceased all nonessential functioning.

So when the grotesque, faceless ghouls hurtled around the corner of the landing above and leaped at us, I sucked in air. No time to scream.

Chapter Fourteen

Liam

"**F**uck!" I flung her behind me. She hit the wall with a gasp as I flash-assessed the attackers, my body in motion. Nylon stocking masks. Big. Fast. They meant business.

I was spinning before my brain kicked in, my heel connecting to the chin of the closest guy. He reeled back, plowing right into his companion, giving me a second to regroup, and register the knife in the first guy's hand.

I danced back, eyes on the blade, evading my opponent's lunges, but the landing gave me no space to retreat. I had to keep that blade away from Nancy.

My opponent lunged again, jabbing high. I parried with my forearm, glad that I'd worn the heavy leather coat. I rammed the guy's arm against the wall. The knife clattered to the tiles. I spun to jab a knee into the gut of the guy bolting toward Nancy, but the first attacker swept my feet, and I stumbled against the wall and took an elbow slam to the ribs. In my peripheral vision, I saw my own fiddle case slash through the air. *Crack.* A hoarse grunt of pain, limbs flailing, thuds. The second guy was falling down the stairs. Great.

The first guy dove for Nancy. She didn't have time to load another swing with the fiddle case. The asshole barreled into her, knocking her against the wall of the staircase. She slipped, and they toppled in agonizing slow motion together, careening downward, out of my line of vision.

I hurled myself after them so fast my feet probably never touched the stairs. Now they were at the bottom of the stairs, and Nancy dangled under the bastard's meaty arm, her body slack. Stunned.

I barreled into the guy with a shout and looped both arms around his neck. The other attacker was nowhere to be seen. Nancy hit the floor with a muffled grunt. The entryway door yawned open. Light and shadow twirled and spun as the guy took a flying somersaulting leap into the dark off the stoop—and hauled me along with him.

A battering rain of blows as we rolled down—head, shoulders, back, in such quick succession I didn't have time to really feel them. Then, a half second sprawled together on the sidewalk, trembling and panting. Christ, that guy's breath was foul.

The heavy, masked thing twisted against me like some huge, muscular serpent and slammed an elbow into my ear, and the fight exploded freshly.

We grappled, grunted, heaved. I slammed a hand up under my attacker's chin, knocking his teeth together.

The guy was huge, but I whipped his knife hand back with the strength of desperation, ramming it into the rails of the wrought-iron fence that separated the garbage cans from the sidewalk.

And again ... and again.

The knife fell, and I jerked part of my weight out from under the guy so our bodies crossed. He attempted to use his thick legs for traction, spreading them wide, so I reached down, grabbed the guy's balls and squeezed them hard.

He screamed, and I lunged for the knife on the sidewalk, scooping it up. I staggered to my feet in an unsteady crouch, brandishing the blade.

The guy leaped up, wheezing in pain. I couldn't see his eyes, but I could feel the toxic hatred coming off the man in waves. *Yeah. Come at me now, shitbag.*

It would be a fine joke on me if the guy pulled a gun.

The guy hesitated, then turned and ran, boots pounding heavy on the pavement.

I lurched after him, but was brought up short, as if tethered. I wanted so badly to run down my prey. Crush that asshole into a grease spot on the pavement.

Nancy. She hadn't stirred from where the guy dropped her. The entryway door was flung wide open to the night, and it was three in the morning in Alphabet City, and I had no fucking clue in what direction that first guy had gone, or how far.

The attacker had vanished into the dark. It was quiet and still. Both men were gone.

My jaw ached with frustration as I leaped up the steps and sank down next to her inside the doorway, heart pounding.

I brushed the waves of thick, glossy mahogany hair off her face. "Nancy? Are you okay?" My voice was breathless and shaking. "Talk to me, Nancy."

"I'm okay." Her eyes opened, and she dragged herself up onto her hands and knees. "I think I am, anyhow. Are they gone?"

"Yes." I helped her up, scanning for injuries. She looked dazed, disoriented, and as pale as a ghost, but there were no obvious marks on her that I could see.

She let me pull her to her feet, and I seized her. We held

each other for a long moment, swaying and correcting, clinging to each other for balance.

"Wow," she whispered. "That was ... wow."

"Like I said," I murmured into her ear. "One humdinger after another."

Her answering laughter had a choppy, hysterical feel, and I squeezed her closer, stroking her shaking back. She felt so right in my arms. Like she'd always been meant for them. Only two days, I suddenly remembered. We'd known each other for two fucking days. It felt like forever.

"We should call the cops," I said.

Her face contracted. "God. Again."

"Yeah, I know," I said. "But it's not like we have a better plan."

"Let's just get up to my apartment." She sounded exhausted. "I need to sit down. I think my purse and phone must be on the stairs."

We gathered up her stuff and my instruments as we climbed the stairs. A peek inside the fiddle case showed me that the tough fiberglass had done its work well, cracking heads on the outside, protecting the instrument on the inside.

The door didn't look forced, but I took the key from Nancy's stiff, trembling fingers anyway and opened the door myself, hesitating as I peered inside.

"Light's over the stove," Nancy forced out, through chattering teeth. "Yank the string."

She was acting shocky. She by God had the right to, but it still worried me.

I peered inside suspiciously, but there wasn't much to the place. I could take it all in with a single glance.

A long narrow room with a barred, grilled window at one end. A tiny water closet in the back behind the tiny kitchen.

No place for an attacker to hide.

I pulled her inside, grabbed an afghan off the couch, and wrapped it around her. She landed with a *whump* on the couch, legs giving out. I flipped on the light dangling over the minuscule kitchen corner.

"You swing a mean violin," I commented.

That earned me a shaky smile and a swift peek up through those long, dark, curling lashes. "I did what I could," she said. "But you. Whoa. Liam, where did you learn to fight like that?"

I shrugged. "Hank, my stepdad, was a cop and a Marine. He served in Vietnam. He taught me the basics. I did some training on my own, too, later. I like martial arts."

"You were amazing," she said.

"Hardly," I said sourly. "I let the bastard get away. Amazing would've been knocking that dickhead out and tying him up, so that we could hand him over to the police. After we pounded some answers out of him. That would have been useful."

"So you think this is connected to ..." Her voice trailed off as the look on my face answered her question. She shrank into the couch, hands to her mouth. "Liam. My sisters. I have to warn them. Right now. My phone. Where is my fucking phone?"

I helped her find it and handed it over. "Breathe deep," I soothed. "Calm down."

I was grateful to see a teakettle in the small array of kitchen stuff on display. I rummaged for tea bags while she talked to her sisters. She was scolding and haranguing them to go stay with friends, get out of town. Good advice. She should take it herself.

Some digging turned up an off-brand box of stale tea, but I was more concerned with getting sugar and caffeine into her than to worry about flavor.

When she hung up, it was ready, and I held out a sweet,

milky cup to her. "See if you can get some of this down while I call the police."

She sipped it while I called 911. My whole body ached now, and I had no one but myself to blame. This was what happened when a guy poked his nose into a woman's big, hairy problems, and I'd done it voluntarily. I'd insisted on it. I'd bitched and moaned and bullied my way right into this.

When she'd drunk her tea, I took the cup away and sank down in front of her. Her hands were cold, despite clutching the hot cup. So slender. I chafed them tenderly to warm them, and contemplated a potentially life-changing realization.

This woman's life was a fucked-up mess. I was right smack in the middle of it.

And there was no place on earth that I would rather be.

Chapter Fifteen

Nancy

Liam kept my teacup loaded during the whole police routine. He did most of the talking, for which I was grateful. All I had to do was shiver, sip, utter monosyllables.

And that was the least of what I had to be grateful for. If it weren't for him, I would be dead. Or else in the kind of trouble that might make death look good by comparison.

I was afraid to contemplate it, but there was no avoiding the thought. It kept backhanding me whenever I tried to think about something else, or better yet, to not think about anything.

Those guys had not been trying to rob me. Or kill me.

Those guys had been trying to snatch me. To carry me away for some dark purpose that I couldn't fathom. To pry secrets out of me that I didn't have to give them.

That would not have gone well for me.

Shudders of horror kept rippling through me at how close I'd come to an unspeakable fate. But why me? I had twelve hundred and seventy-eight bucks in my checking account, after paying my rent. Most of it spoken for with upcoming bills.

After a while, I found myself drifting loose. I was floating in one bubble—and the two policemen talking to Liam in my apartment were in another. Their voices were tinny, faraway, like a radio chattering in another room.

Liam held the string. He could reel me back in to himself if he wanted to. Otherwise, I'd stay right here in my bubble, thanks very much.

The police finally left. Liam and I had declined to go in for medical observation, in the face of strong disapproval from the female officer, but enough was enough. I desperately wanted a little peace and quiet.

Liam sat down next to me and touched my cheek. "Nancy," he said.

That *"please don't freak out on me"* tone made me brace herself. "Yes?"

"Those guys who attacked us. They were trying to—"

"Kidnap me, yes. I figured out that fun factoid all on my own."

"No need to snap," he replied. "You just need to factor that fun factoid into your future plans."

"Plans?" My voice rose to a squeak. "What plans? You think I'm capable of planning? Someone killed my mother. Then they tried to abduct me. And to murder you while they were at it. I noticed that, too. That knife in his hand. That sucked, Liam."

"Calm down," he soothed.

I let out a shaky sigh. "I'm so sorry. I'm scolding you, but you absolutely don't deserve it. You're a hero. You saved my ass tonight. Don't think I'll forget it."

"Anytime." He fished a cat toy out from under his leg, a

jointed wooden snake. "How can you keep a cat in a place this cramped?"

The disapproval in his voice stung me a little. "It's a hell of a lot better than the life she had on the street! She was half-dead when I found her. I spent fifteen hundred dollars getting her sewn back together, plus getting her spayed, and getting all her shots. And I spend a fortune in kitty litter and tender niblets. I think Moxie knows exactly how lucky she is."

I kept my eyes averted, but the silence that followed was too heavy to bear. When I looked up, Liam had a gleam in his eye. He was trying not to smile.

"What?" I snapped. "You're giving me that look."

"I'm just waiting for you to tell me that getting the cat sewn up, spayed and vaccinated was a hard-assed, self-interested business decision," he said.

I rolled my eyes with a snort. "I liked her," I said loftily. "You're bugging me."

"Get used to it." He picked up Lucia's bronze Cellini satyr that had pride of place on the steamer chest that served as my coffee table, turning it carefully in his hands. "Wow, look at that," he said. "Lucia's, right? You think this thing is safe here?"

"Probably not, considering what just happened. But is anything safe anywhere?"

"Good point." He set the thing carefully down. "Probably not."

"I guess I should put it in a vault," I said wearily. "It got through the Nazi occupation without getting appropriated. The Conte wrapped it in burlap and buried it in the ashes of the kitchen fireplace. It would be ironic if it got stolen now and traded for crack."

"The Conte?" Liam's gaze sharpened. "Lucia's father hid art from the Nazis?"

"Everything he could. I think they got a lot of it, but— Oh, hey! You don't know about the letter, do you?"

"What letter?"

"We found an old letter last night, and a photo, in the Fabergé picture frame at Nell's apartment." I quickly outlined the contents of the letter to him.

Liam listened, his face impassive. When I finished, he turned again to stare at the Cellini bronze. "I'm thinking that there's something else that was hidden from the Nazis, like the Cellini satyr was," he said. "Except that for some reason, it's still hidden—and the old Conte died before he could tell anyone where it is."

I bit my lip, trying to breathe evenly through the anxiety that gripped me. "But then why are they attacking me?" My voice quivered again. "I don't know where this thing is. Or even what it is!"

"They don't know that," he said. "And they'll never believe you if you told them."

Dark spots swam before my eyes. "Great," I said. "So it's the worst of all possible worlds. If this is true, then they'll never stop. And I'll never be able to give them what they want."

"Put your head down." Liam pushed my head between my knees. "Breathe."

I did so. When I dared sit up again, he had a small, thoughtful frown in his eyes.

"Don't think about it anymore," he said. "Please, don't faint."

The thought exploded in my mind. *So give me something else to think about, idiot.* I wanted to yell it, at the top of my voice, but I contented myself with a hysterical crack of laughter.

He looked around my apartment. The cramped room was crammed with floor-to-ceiling shelves, CD racks, books, electronics. A file cabinet, copy machine, and a water cooler crowded around my desk. Liam patted the back of the couch where we sat.

"Does this thing open up into a bed?" he asked.

My hackles rose, sending criticism in formation. "Yes, it does. Anything else? More pronouncements about my apartment, my life, my choices? By all means, Liam. Express yourself."

"So this place is an office. With a couch, for those occasional moments when you want to assume a horizontal position."

Yeah. Like, right now. With you.

I couldn't say that, so I groped for the next best thing, a smart-ass retort. Nothing came to me, but then something did. An unexpected insight formed in my mind as I looked into his clear, keen eyes.

"You're pissing me off on purpose," I said slowly.

"I guess," he said. "A little. Just a couple of snarky zingers, just to get you going. It kicks up your blood pressure. I like to see some color in your face."

I covered my face with my hands. "So I'm being managed."

"Little bit, maybe."

"I must look like death warmed over," I muttered. "Or not even. Death served cold, right out of the fridge."

"No." He reached out, pulled my hands gently off my face. "You're so beautiful, Nancy. You shine. Like a jewel."

I was embarrassed, mortified, and charmed beyond belief. "Sweet of you to say so."

"Sweet has nothing to do with it," he said calmly.

"Ahhh. Now who's defensive when I call him sweet?"

"You don't believe me, do you?" His voice was incredulous.

My face heated. "Well, not exactly. I mean, I, uh, appreciate the compliment, and all. Really. But it's not a matter of believing or not believing. It's just that beauty is such a subjective thing. So it just doesn't mean anything, really."

He looked baffled. "Subjective, my ass. Beautiful is beautiful."

I rushed on, trying to articulate the thought. I'd had it many times, in the course of my disasters with my exes, but I'd never put it into words for someone else. "What I mean is, does it mean anything, when a man says that? Men have told me I was beautiful before. It felt really nice. Then they changed their minds when they met someone they thought was more beautiful. By comparison, I suddenly became less beautiful. That sucks, by the way. When you look into your boyfriend's face and realize that your stock just went down the toilet."

"Nancy," he said gently.

"Who knows what a person sees when he looks at another person?" I went on, my voice tight with emotion. "It changes with his mood, the weather, what he ate that day! How beautiful would I look to you after I'd annoyed you by popping my knuckles, or slurping my soda, or whatever it is that I do that grates on you? Telling me I'm beautiful is meaningless. So just don't do it. You'd have more luck coaxing me into bed if you stayed away from the whole subject."

"You think that's what this is about? Just getting you into bed?"

Damn it, I was doing it again. Babbling nonsense, like an idiot. *I was hoping that was your plan.* I barely managed to swallow the words back.

"Be quiet for just one second." His voice was as soft as drifting smoke. He reached out and carefully lifted a spray of miniature orchids from a vase on the end table by the couch. I'd bought them the week before, in honor of Lucia, who had always loved them. Deep pink, spotted with purple, luminous and mysterious. "Are these beautiful?"

"Yes," I said without hesitation. "Gorgeous. Magical."

"How do you know that they are?"

I bit my lip and hesitated, sensing a trap. "I don't know," I said. "I couldn't say why. I'm not the poetic type. That's Nell's area of expertise, not mine. I just think they are."

He tucked it into the vase and stroked a petal with his fingertip. "That's my point. You don't have to be poetic. Just look at them. Shut up and really look at them. And you feel it. Right here." He put his hand on his chest. "They just are."

I gazed at him, feeling almost hypnotized as his finger stroked the gorgeously purple curve of the orchid petal. I took a deep breath ... and tried it.

I did exactly what he had suggested. I just shut up. The nervous talking, the worries, the fear, the clamorous noise in my head. I just watched Liam touched that flower.

His clear eyes were endlessly patient, gentle. He looked willing to take his time. Willing to wait for me to get it, even if I was slow, or thick. He was in no hurry at all. He reached out, touched my cheek, stroking it as softly as he'd touched the flower petal.

And I got it. Right in my chest, just like he said.

Oh, yes. He was beautiful. The realization pierced through me like a knife.

This was against all my rules, all my better judgment. The power dynamic was whacked, wrong. He was the one who had saved me. He was the one offering protection and comfort. I was the one who was desperately in need of it. He had everything, I had nothing. And for fuck's sake, I couldn't even guarantee him a good time in bed to compensate him for his trouble, not with all my sexual hang-ups. That was a crass assessment of the situation, but I called it how I saw it.

I preferred to have something concrete to offer a man, something that would keep him connected with me after the initial flash of desire flickered and went out, as it inevitably did. Not that the trick had ever worked before, considering my track record.

Liam didn't need me. I had nothing to offer him but myself. When he lost interest in that, I would be destroyed.

Liam sensed the direction my mind was running. I saw it in his eyes.

"What's wrong?" he asked warily.

He sounded exhausted. I didn't blame him. I was nothing but problems, traps, tangled knots, thorny difficulties. My mind raced to come up with a plausible lie. Letting him see how small I felt would embarrass us both.

I shook my head. "Nothing."

He let out a quiet sigh, and leaned back, laying his head against the back of the futon couch. Covering his eyes with his hands, which made me notice his hand.

Crap. His knuckles were torn and raw, encrusted with blood. God, I hadn't even given a thought to his injuries, his trauma, his shock. I'd just zoned out, floated in my vacuous bubble, and leaned on him. As if he were a mighty oak.

But he wasn't an oak. He was a man. He'd fought like a demon for me, and risked his life, and gotten hurt. And I was so self-absorbed, I hadn't even noticed.

I was mortified. I didn't even like to imagine what Lucia would have said. "Liam, your hand! Let me get some disinfectant, and some—"

"It's okay. Forget about it."

"The hell I will! You're bleeding!" I bustled around, muttering and scolding to hide my discomfort, gathering gauze and cotton balls and antibiotic ointment.

He let me fuss, a martyred look on his face. After I finished taping some gauze over his hand, I looked at his scraped, battered face and grabbed a handful of his sweatshirt, tugging it upward. "What about the rest of you? Let me see."

"Just some bruises," he hedged.

"Where?" I persisted, tugging at his shirt. "Show me."

He wrenched the fabric out of my hand. "No." His voice was grim. "If I take off my clothes now, it's not going to be to show you my bruises."

Oh ... my ... goodness. I blinked, swallowed, tried to breathe.

There it was, finally verbalized. "After all this? You still want to, um ..."

"Fuck yes." His tone was low and savage. "I've wanted it since I laid eyes on you. And it keeps getting worse. Plus, combat adrenaline would give me a hard-on like a railroad spike even if there wasn't a beautiful woman in my face, driving me nuts. Which puts me in a bad place, Nancy. The timing's been piss-poor since the moment we met, but it never gets better. It just keeps getting worse and worse."

"It's okay." I patted his shoulder shyly. He was usually so calm. It unnerved me a bit, to see him wound up like this.

"And the worse the timing gets, the more I want it," he went on. "Which makes me feel like a jerk, a user, and an asshole. Promising to protect you—"

"You did protect me," I reminded him. "Spectacularly, I might add."

He waved his hand impatiently. "It wasn't an exchange. You don't owe me sex. You don't owe me anything. And that really fucks me up. Because I can't even remove myself from the situation. I'm scared to leave you alone, but I can't keep my hands off you if I stay. Which puts me between a rock and a hard place."

I put my finger over his mouth. "Wow," I murmured. "I

would've never dreamed you could get worked into such a state, Mr. Liam-let's-contemplate-the-beauty-of-the-flower Knightly."

He snorted, and I shushed him again, enjoying the feel of his lips beneath my finger. "You're not a jerk or a user," I said gently. "You were magnificent. Valiant, selfless, amazing. Thank you. Again."

He looked away. There was a brief, embarrassed pause. "That's generous of you," he said, trying to flex the wounded hand. "But I'm not fishing for compliments."

"I never thought you were," I told him.

I placed my own hand below his and rested them both gently on his thigh. My fingers dug into the thick muscle of his quadriceps, through the dirty, bloodstained denim of his jeans. Beneath the fabric, he was so hot. So strong and solid.

I moved my hand up, slowly but surely, stroking higher toward his groin. His breath caught and stopped as my fingers brushed the thick bulge of his penis beneath the denim.

Here went nothing. "I know what you mean, about the hard place," I whispered, swirling my fingertips over it. Wow. That thick, broad stalk just went on and on. "Or was this what you meant by the rock?"

His face was a mask of tension, neck muscles clenched, tendons standing out. "You don't have to do this."

Aw. Still trying to be the gallant gentleman. What a turn-on. My fingers closed around him, squeezing. A shudder jarred his body. "I can't seem to stop myself," I said.

"Watch out, Nancy," he said. "If you start something now, there's no stopping it."

I stroked him again, tighter, a slow, twisting caress that wrung a keening gasp from his throat. "That's right," I said, my voice low, throaty. "There will be no escape for you."

He reached out, a little awkwardly and clasped his arms

around my shoulders, staring into my eyes as if expecting me to bolt.

He pulled me close, enfolding me in his power, and suddenly we were kissing.

I had no idea who kissed who. The kiss was desperate, achingly sweet. Not a power struggle, not a matter of talent or skill, just a wild, yearning hunger to get as close to each other as humans could be. He held me like he was afraid I'd be torn away.

I tugged his shirt up, and he wrenched it off. I almost purred when I saw him half naked. Oh, yes, please. His skin was pale, and his lean, sinewy muscles were sharply defined in the dim light that dangled over the kitchen stove. He was hot as a furnace. He smelled like soap—and the sharp, salty tang of sweat. From fighting to defend me.

Then he pulled my T-shirt off, and I was just as exposed, blinking through my tousled hair. The chill that hit my skin gave me goosebumps, but I still felt scorched by his eyes, his roving hands. My tight nipples tingled where they brushed his chest.

Shyness gripped me, but it was nothing like that usual cold, sinking feeling I got in these situations, when those iron-plated doors slammed shut, shutting my lover out and trapping my own small, numb self inside. That was how things usually went.

This was so different. I wasn't numb. I was on the verge of shaking into a million pieces. It was almost unbearably intense. I crossed my arms over my chest, eyes squeezed shut. "Can we turn off the light?"

He froze for a few seconds. "Don't hide from me," he said, in a low voice.

"I won't," I assured him. "I just think it would be easier for me."

He started to speak, and I cut him off before he could ruin it. "I don't want to stop, I swear," I said swiftly. "Just the light."

He hesitated, peering at me like he was trying to read me.

"It's because I care about this," I hurried on. "I'll use every trick I can think of not to shut down with you."

Smooth move, Nance. Big turnoff, laying out my sexual problems to a prospective lover before I even got a chance to make him come.

But Liam didn't look put off. "All right," he said. "First, let's put down the bed, though. I don't want to do that in the dark."

Oh. I'd forgotten that detail. I was so turned on, a bed seemed irrelevant.

A few deft tugs and wrenches with Liam's big muscles, and my rickety old futon bed was flat and ready for business. The mattress was already dressed with a sheet beneath the couch cover. Then he went to the stove and yanked the string, and the room was plunged into infinite tones of shadow. Even the blacks and grays took on subtle, delicate meanings—shaded nuances that I could never express in words. And Liam was a fulcrum of deeper gray—an enormous, brooding presence.

Every hair on my body prickled at his proximity. Every sense was heightened. My eyes strained in the dark, my lungs labored for deeper gulps of his scent, my ears were tuned to the pad of his bare feet. I was hungry to touch his skin, to taste his salt.

He unbuckled his belt, kicked off his shoes, and shucked his pants, briefs, and socks. Quick, businesslike movements loaded with pure eroticism.

I admired the angles and contours of his long body in the shadows, the bulk of his thick shoulders. I shoved down my jeans, kicked them off my ankles, and curled up on the futon. Shaky with nerves, but in a good way, strangely. Which was a first, for me.

I saw him moving closer, but my body still jolted with a bright jab of shock when his arms circled me.

I was racked with long, delicious shivers. They throbbed through me in waves, making my breath catch and my fingers dig convulsively into his hot skin, the taut bulge of muscle in his upper arms. His chest pressed against my breasts, his hand stroked down the curve of my back, the swell of my hip, fitting me against him. Skin to skin. So hot. He burned me, and I loved it.

His cock prodded my leg. Thick, stiff, long. I could hardly breathe for the rush of excitement. The wild euphoria, and that keen ache of longing.

And the fear, too. Of how vulnerable this made me. It was there, vibrating like a plucked string. This problem was unique. Before this, sex was never all that central to my thoughts. I could pretty much take it or leave it, and I tended to leave it.

Not with Liam. My hunger for him felt like something clawing inside me. Desperate.

He bent over me, dropping slow, hot, tender kisses at the curve of my neck that made me whimper with excitement. "You're not shutting down," he said.

It was both a statement and a command. And it was true.

"No," I replied, marveling. In spite of the terror we'd just been through, in spite of my tedious list of hang-ups, this was in no danger of derailing.

Always before, the harder a lover tried to get through my walls, the thicker those walls became. It was a reflex. But with Liam, there was no wall. Or maybe there was, but it didn't matter. He was already so far inside it, pushing me deeper into those unknown parts of myself.

It was so new. I had no idea how deep, how endless that inner space was. Alive to feeling. Every sensation, every emotion was a revelation. I felt the wild thrill of leaping into a mysterious, star-bedecked, unknown nowhere, and the glowing tenderness of coming home, all at the same time.

He pulled me down onto the bed and arranged me until I was perched on his thighs, my arms wound around his shoulders, my nose buried in his thick, spiky, sweat-stiffened hair.

His cock pressed against my belly. His thickly muscled arms were tight around me, tense and shaking.

Tenderness for him melted me right down to liquid inside, a hot shimmer around my heart, and lower. I slid my hand down between us and curled my fingers around his cock. Stroking him. Exploring and teasing and inciting him. It made my breath catch with excitement. He was just delicious.

"Slow down," he said. "I don't want to come yet."

I let up my grip. "When, then?"

"You first. Always, it's you first. That's just the rule. The way it needs to be."

I wasn't arguing with that. He slid his hand down over my ass, and slid it between my legs, caressing my exquisitely sensitive places with feather-light fingertips, all while his cock rocked against my clit. He rubbed against me with a, slow pulsing rhythm, his fingers delving inside my pussy—sliding deep into my slick balm.

Feeling me. Petting me. Taking his time. Kissing my cheekbone. My throat.

His teeth dragged against the frantic throb of my heartbeat in there, working me from behind—skillfully thrusting inside while keeping up that slow, sensual pulse with his cock. My pussy felt hot, melting. Sweetly aching. Longing to melt and merge and be filled by him.

Then something opened—an upwelling rush—and all the feelings and sensations converged into a long, pulsing wave of pure rapture.

Chapter Sixteen

Liam

I hung on as the orgasm took her, letting those beautiful rippling vibrations echo through my own body. My breath was ragged with excitement. I kept reminding myself not to let my fingers dig into her perfect skin. I didn't want to leave marks. She was so smooth and soft and strong. A marvel of nature. Every detail so fucking beautiful, it left me breathless and shaking.

And she was naked in my arms. Holy shit.

That orgasm had been a spectacular supernova, right around my fingers. I felt so privileged to be inside the sanctum so I could feel it. I wanted to kneel at her feet, suck her toes, lick her arches, kiss her ankles. I wanted to make my way up, missing nothing, all the way to her beautiful face. I wanted to give thanks for her existence. I wanted to make the whole world bow down when she walked by.

I laid her slowly down on her back, my fingers still inside

her, feeling the tight, clenching flutter of the aftershocks. Her chest shuddered, gasping for breath. Good sign. I folded her legs up wide, wishing the light was on. All I could see were shapes, outlines. None of her colors, her fine, delicate details.

She gazed up at me with big, startled eyes, her hair a swirling mass against the white sheet, gasping and sighing at my every touch as if she were surprised at what was happening to her body. My fingers were in an ecstasy all their own, kissed and clutched in that tight, slick opening. The rich female scent of her drove me wild with lust.

She was lifting herself again, shoving against my thrusting hand, seeking more, deeper, harder. My cock ached with need, and she reached down and gripped me, her cool fingers moving in a tender, twisting caress—and oh *God* …

"Stop," I said, my voice strangled. "I won't be able to wait if you do that again."

Her lips curved in a seductive smile that made my already galloping heart rate kick up further. "Who asked you to wait?"

I panted, my entire existence measured by the throb of my heartbeat in my cock. "Well. I, ah, wanted to make you come at least ten times first."

She shook with silent laughter. "That does sound like fun, but I'm too wound up for anything long and drawn out right now. I really want you. Inside me. Right now. You can lay on the orgasms later, right? There's no pumpkin time for us."

Thank God. I took her at her word and groped in the dark at the corner of the bed where I'd left a condom. I ripped it open by feel, rolling the thing on swiftly, and positioned myself over her, her legs wound around me. I situated myself for maximum control, but she had ideas of her own, wiggling and lifting herself while I nudged my cock tenderly inside her.

She was tight and small, and so wet. Her hot, plush pussy

hugged and clung to me. She arched, grabbing my ass to pull me deeper. Squeezing me.

Damn. Too much. Too soon. I could feel the thundering on the horizon, threatening my control. I should have insisted on the ten orgasms. I should have gone down on her for an hour or so. I would never get this all-important first time with her back again.

But with each slow, cautious stroke of my cock, I slid a little deeper. She relaxed around me, making me slick and wet, her nails digging into my shoulders. I stared hungrily down at her beautiful slim body pinned beneath mine—so fragrant and smooth. Her strong arms, clutching me. Those small, perfect breasts, those tight, dark nipples I hadn't even properly feasted on yet. So much to explore.

A man would need a lifetime for it all.

I rocked forward with a gasp of pure delight. "You good?"

She had to try about three times before she could get words out of her shaking lips. "I, ah...I think I'm going to fall apart."

I went still, arching over her. Holding my breath. "Ah. Is that a good thing, or a bad thing?"

"It's...an unprecedented thing."

That made me cautiously hopeful. "So, that's good, then?"

"You're very large, by the way," she told me.

I stopped breathing again. "Sorry. Am I hurting you?"

"Oh, no, don't apologize. I like it. It's very exciting. Just a little overwhelming, that's all. But I'm down for being over-whelmed. It's working for me. Don't worry." She slid her hands down my back, dug her fingernails into my ass and pulled.

I couldn't say a word. I was trying too hard not to come, second by second, as we rocked and surged together.

We found the perfect rhythm. It was hot, fierce. Heavy, sliding thrusts. Soft, whimpering gasps from her. Her arms twined around my neck, pulling me down.

That kiss ignited a surge of emotion that blew my self-control to hell, and it all went wild. We were clutching, gasping, bucking. She wrapped herself around me with all her strength, lifting, jarred by every thrust. Wild energy thundered through our linked bodies. She held on to me tightly, crying out in pleasure. Riding the crest, triumphant.

My orgasm blasted through me, each pulse propelling me deeper, wider, farther. I was wide open to the stars, the wind, to eternity. To her.

When our hearts slowly eased down into panting stillness, I felt humbled. Nervous to look into her face. The sky beyond the small window had begun to brighten. I could hear the sound of the city slowly waking up around us.

Nancy cupped my face with her hand, pulling. I rolled over onto my side to face her, and we clasped hands, our bodies still joined, slick with sweat. Eyes locked on each other, full of speechless wonder.

This time I was the one who couldn't handle the long, significant silence. I was so afraid I might have hurt her, scared her. I murmured something incoherent and got up to get myself a drink of water. I gulped it thirstily down and got a glass for her, too.

When I brought it back to the bed, she was sitting up, her back regally straight, her hair flung back, legs tucked to the side like a sexy mermaid. I handed her the glass, and she held it up to her bright red cheek for a moment, eyes closed.

I steeled myself and asked, "Are you okay?"

A soft smile curved her lips, but she still didn't speak, and it was driving me crazy.

"What?" I demanded finally. "What the hell is it? What are you thinking?"

Her laughter sounded free and relaxed. "That's funny,

coming from you. I'm just using your trick. And it throws you off balance too."

She saw the bewilderment in my eyes and took pity on me. "I mean the long, smoldering silences," she explained. "I finally get it. Because for the first time, I'm not afraid to just sit with it. Let myself feel what I'm feeling. Right here." She put her hand on her heart. "I don't need to babble, or excuse myself, or justify myself. I feel ... free."

"Okay. Great." I was still lost, but as long as she was happy, we were good.

"I like how it feels," she said. "Perfectly balanced. It's magic."

I was turning red, but the euphoria lifted me a couple inches right up off the floor.

"I don't have a mysterious trick," I admitted. "I appreciate what you said, but it's just my speech patterns. I think you're reading far too much into it."

"No, actually. I really don't think so." She drank the water I'd given her, looking me up and down with a frank approval that made my face heat. It made my dick swell, too.

But not quite yet. Ten more orgasms, and then we'd see how things went. I took the empty glass of water and placed it on the little table next to the futon, then went into her unimaginably small bathroom to get rid of the condom.

When I came back out, I tugged her toward edge of the futon mattress. She sensed my intention and grabbed my hair, as I pushed her shapely thighs open. "Liam—"

"Shhh." Her pussy was beautiful—juicy and glowing, soft in the morning light, adorned with soft ringlets, wet with her lube, sweet, hot.

I kissed my way slowly up her inner thigh, all the way up to the secret tender inside bits and groaned with pleasure when I finally tasted her. Tender, slick folds, juicy and delicious. I could have stayed there forever, slowly teasing her pleasure out of its hiding place. My fingers dug into her smooth thighs, tongue circling gently around the taut nub of her clit ... first a soft gentle pressure, then a flirtatious tongue swirl, slowly around, around ... until she was clutching my hair, making those choked, gasping sounds. I couldn't get enough of that.

And when she was almost there, I slid two fingers inside her, massaging that sweet spot while I sucked her clit into my mouth and gave it a deep pull...

She convulsed, fingers clutching, her pussy fluttering around my fingers. Best moment ever. I realized with a lightning-flash of clarity that I was born for this. To be close to Nancy. To please her, protect her, stand by her.

To love her.

Whoa, ease off. My hormones were running wild. They had left my brain zip-tied to the railroad tracks. I had to slow the fuck down. Two days, I'd known this woman. Two days, and with a murder and an attempted abduction folded in the mix. I needed to take it easy. I needed to breathe, and wait. Be patient.

I lifted my head, wiped my mouth, licked my fingers. Stared up into her eyes. The warning bells jangling in my head were drowned out by the roar of need inside me.

I'd never felt anything like this. I was bewitched. I never wanted the spell to break.

She fished up the other condom from where I'd left it on the corner of the futon, and

I clambered onto the mattress, smoothing it over myself. She seized my shoulders, swinging her thigh up over my lap and straddling me, those beautiful little tight-tipped breasts right at mouth level. I pressed my face to them hungrily, kissing and stroking and suckling those small, puckered nipples while she shivered and gripped me closer. She leaned her head forward, making all her thick, fragrant red-brown hair tumble around my head. I was lost in her scent, her taste, her strong, slender body moving against mine. I suckled those perfect, exquisitely sensitive breasts.

She swayed over me, sliding her pussy lips up and down the length of my cock. The sensual stroke felt like a sweet, teasing lash of a tongue. Undulating up and down, offering her breasts to my mouth. My hands moved hungrily over her, committing every detail to memory. The voluptuous swell of her taut ass cheeks. The sweet little dimple right above them. Her warm, ticklish curtain of hair. The strength and hunger in her embrace, the soft catch in her breath as she moved against my body.

I suckled her, pressing my dick up eagerly against her hot, slick core, petting her clit with it, a slow, slick push and pull. She squirmed and struggled toward her pleasure ... and exploded again, arching and gasping. I held her, braced against me, as pleasure pumped through her.

That was more like it. Maybe it wasn't quite ten orgasms yet, but whatever. I would make my quota. I'd persist through the day, into the night, into tomorrow. Into forever.

I was a man with something to prove.

Color had begun to return to this feast for my eyes. I could see the sheen of sweat on her lip, her forehead. I could see the deep red blush of her lips. The little line between her brows that I had noticed before was almost gone. She looked relaxed. Lush, sensual.

I gripped her hips, and lifted her up off my cock, positioning myself with my fist below her. She steadied herself on my shoulders, swaying, nails digging delicately into my skin like kitten claws as I rolled my cockhead around her slick, drenched opening, and then drove upwards, pulling her down. Letting her take in all of me. Her snug sheath clenched and squeezed eagerly around me.

She made a soft, startled sound. "Oh," she murmured. "I can't move."

"You will," I promised, surging up to thrust deeper inside her hot, slick depths.

Then her cell phone rang.

We froze, staring at each other. *Buzz. Buzz. Buzz.*

"Do you usually get calls at this hour?" I asked.

"A lot of my clients are night owls," she offered. "They've gotten used to me being up at that hour, too."

"At six a.m.? Jesus."

"Sorry, but I just have to see if it's one of my sisters."

I lifted her off me. She slid off the bed and padded over to the table where her phone lay. She stared at it for a moment. The phone kept buzzing.

"Not your sisters," I said.

She shook her head. "No, it's one of my clients." But she didn't decline the call or turn off the phone. She just stood there, frozen and conflicted.

I let out a long, even breath. It would be a dick move to get angry and possessive of her time and attention. Even if all this crazy shit hadn't just happened. I wasn't going to be that guy anymore. Not today. Not ever.

"Answer it," I told her. "Go for it. I know you want to. It'll just torture you if you don't."

She shot me a grateful look and answered the call. The volume was up, and I could hear the guy's voice very clearly.

"Nancy? What the hell? Are you there? Why did it take you so long to pick up?"

"It's six in the morning, Peter." She perched on the edge of the futon. "What do you need?"

"I thought of a great new order for the songs in the liner notes for the vinyl."

"Oh, no," Nancy said. "No way, Peter. You've changed them three times already. Let it go. If Shepard doesn't have those liner notes by nine-thirty, the vinyl won't make it into the catalog at all. You're making it hard for me to make this happen for you."

"But I just realized it now, Nance! It makes way more sense if I put 'The Road to You' at the end. Sometimes these flashes come at the last minute, you know? It's part of the artistic process. Sometimes it requires a deadline."

"Sure, but why is it always me who has to scramble?"

"Don't be crabby, Nance. Enid and I have been busting our asses. We live, eat, sleep, and breathe this album. Believe me."

She let out a sharp sigh. "Yeah. Well, I'll meet you at your place at ..." she peered at the digital clock. "Seven, okay? I don't think I can get there before."

There was a fresh burst of anxious talking on the line, but she cut it off.

"Later, Peter. Really. It's too early. I can't concentrate yet. Tell me about it when I get there."

She closed the call, and looked around, as if waking from a dream. "Whoa. I totally forgot the liner notes for the vinyl, and the appointment with Shepard. My mind was wiped." She shot me an apologetic look. "I'm sorry to cut this short, because this has been the most wonderful night I've ever had. But I've got to get myself moving. I've got a million things to—"

"No," I said. "You cannot do the million things, Nancy."

She froze, eyes narrowing. "Excuse me?"

I couldn't stop the rage from bubbling up, hot and dangerous and caustic. "What would it take to convince you that you can't go flouncing around, la-di-da, and do your fucking errands like nothing even happened tonight?"

"The hell?" she said slowly. "Liam. I do not flounce. And they are not 'fucking errands'. This is my job. It's how I support myself."

"You can't support yourself if you're dead."

She flinched. The words were a blow, as I had meant them to be. "Jesus, Liam. You're overdoing it."

"You're coming up to Latham with me. Where I can protect you."

Her mouth dropped open. She let out an incredulous laugh. "Oh! Am I? Wow. Thanks so much for discussing this decision with me."

"You have no grip on reality," I said.

"On the contrary. It's you who needs to get a grip." Her voice shook. "Don't think that I don't appreciate what you did for me last night. But just because I'm in your debt, don't start thinking that you're the boss. I have a life, and I have to—"

"That's what I'm trying to help you protect! Not your work, Nancy. Not your career. Your *life*. Do you see what I'm trying to say here?"

"Liam, I'll be perfectly safe in the light of day," she assured me. "This city is swarming with millions of people—"

"Two of whom came at us with a knife last night!"

"I promise, I'll be in company the entire day," she said. "And I'll take car services, taxis, rideshares. I have to drop by Peter and Enid's place this morning, and they'll go with me for our appointment in midtown by nine-thirty, and I—"

"I'll take you to your appointments."

Her eyes widened in alarm. "No way. That would be stressful and uncomfortable. I'll be racing from pillar to post, and I can't concentrate if you're watching my every—"

"Deal with me. Or come back to Latham."

That was my father's voice, coming out of my mouth. That overbearing, cringe-inducing, bullying tone. She was responding to it badly, and who could fucking blame her. It was unbearable. I should know.

"To Latham," she repeated, incredulous. "With you. While my livelihood goes to hell. What do I do there, Liam? Spend my days lolling in your bed, legs in the air? It would be fun, but it's not a long-term solution!"

"I never said it was," I snapped.

Aw, shit. Wrong thing to say. The hot color drained from her face. "I see," she said. "Of course. Since this is just a temporary thing. We're fuck buddies, right?"

Shit. "Nancy, that's not what I meant. It's just that you can't—"

"I can do whatever I want, Liam. The meeting this morning is with the biggest production company I've ever done business with. If I flake out on them, they'll never take me seriously again."

I gathered my clothes and pulled them on. "Don't try to justify yourself to me," I said. "You can't convince me that your professional appointments are more important than your safety." I pulled on my shoes. "Get dressed. I'll take you to your client's apartment. But you are not walking out of this place alone."

Her chin went up. "It's not up to you. I can get a car."

Two strides put me in her face, tilting her head back. Words came out that I was powerless to stop. "Don't push me," I snarled. "You will give me this one. You owe me that. Actually, you owe me more than that. But you will do me this courtesy today."

Or else. Her throat bobbed. They both felt the menace in my tone.

I'd never tried to intimidate a woman. Never even dreamed that I would be capable of it. But look at me, throwing my weight around like an asshole. Actually wondering what I'd do if she called my bluff.

My aching dick had some good ideas.

She wrenched her chin away from my hand, turned away and started getting ready.

My bluff had worked. She'd backed down.

And the predatory beast inside me was as disappointed as hell.

Chapter Seventeen

Nancy

"God, Nance. What was the point of you coming down here at all if you're not even going to listen to me?"

I rubbed my eyes until Peter's handsome face swam into focus. "Peter, don't bug me. I haven't slept. I risked death and abduction last night, so spare me the attitude."

"I'm sorry you got mugged, but I highly doubt that anyone was trying to abduct you," Peter said. "I mean, why would they? You're having delusions of grandeur. Do I need to brew you some coffee? Or can you stay conscious long enough for me to run this new song order by you?"

I huffed out a breath and dragged myself to my feet. "Hit me with it," I said grimly. "I'll stand. It'll be easier to stay awake."

"Good idea. So anyhow, my thought was to put 'Glory Road' at the top. Hit 'em with everything we've got, bada-boom. Once we've got their attention, we go with 'The Slippery

Slope.' Then Enid's intro to 'The Far Shore.' And then, we'll put ..."

Despite my best efforts, Peter's voice faded into background noise. I shifted my weight from one foot to the other, thinking of Liam's eyes when he left me outside Peter and Enid's apartment building. It made me want to howl.

But I couldn't just throw my whole life up into the air and leap into his pocket. I'd worked too hard and too long for this.

I pushed the image of Liam's desolate eyes out of my head and studied Peter's face. Those refined, ethereal good looks that had so attracted me back in college.

We'd met our freshman year and formed a band: Peter on lead vocals and guitar, me on acoustic bass, Henry on drums, Chad on keyboards. I'd worked like a maniac finding the band local gigs, planning spring break tours. After a while, I'd begun to fancy myself in love with Peter. He loved me, too. At least, he had assured me he did—even on that unforgettable day when he, Henry, and Chad sat me down and told me they were looking for a new bass player. Someone with a more primal, savage rhythm. A more dangerous vibe.

"We need somebody with a jazzy, rockabilly background, Nance. Someone who can lay down a killer bass line," Peter explained earnestly. "Someone who can really go wild with us."

And I'd just sat there, trying not to cry. Feeling like a fool.

"It's not that we don't love you, Nance. What we're trying to say is, everybody should do what they're best at," Henry coaxed.

"Yeah, and what you're best at is finding gigs," Peter said, in a bracing tone. "You should be the band's business manager. That's where you really shine."

I'd dabbed at the tear-snot with a tissue, and stared at them, eyes blurred.

"For real, we can't do without you, Nance," Henry said

earnestly. "You take care of us, you know? Like how you always make sure that Chad's shirt doesn't clash with his pants before he goes on stage. And the way you find us gigs. That's total magic. That's what we need. Bassists are a dime a dozen. We can find a bassist anywhere."

Peter patted my shoulder. "Come on, Nance. Be a sport."

"Oh, I'm trying," I'd told them, dully.

And it was true. I'd tried to be a sport. Tried very hard.

Then I'd tried again, a couple of years later, when Peter fell in love with Enid. Oddly enough, he'd used almost the same words as when he'd dumped me as a bassist.

"It's not that I don't love you," he'd said, patting my shoulder. "It's just a different kind of love. The love I feel for Enid ... it's like she sets a match to my heart, and I just go up in flames. Match to my heart. Huh. Cool image."

He started humming, then let out an irritated sigh when I burst into tears.

"Oh, God, Nance. Please. Don't," he begged. "It's not like we had this grand passion. Come on. Be a sport."

So I'd choked back my tears and been a sport for Peter and Enid. Then I'd been a sport again when Ron dumped me for Liz. And damned if I hadn't been a sport yet again for Freedy, when he jilted me for Andrea.

I was a real goddamn trouper.

The loss and the humiliation had felt so crushing back then. Strange, how it felt so insignificant now, after losing Lucia. After facing terror and death in a nylon mask, carrying a switchblade. After making love to Liam.

Ron, Freedy, Peter—they all felt like dimly remembered games of hopscotch and dodgeball from grade school. Kid stuff.

Peter was yelling my name. "Nance! Are you having a seizure, or what?"

"I'm fine," I said faintly.

And in that moment, for the first time, I heard the words as I said them. *I'm fine.* I said it all the time, as a reflex. But it was a huge lie right now.

Peter's frown was turning into a pout. "I need feedback, Nance, and I really don't feel like you're there for me. Would you please listen while I play the new order?"

I braced myself for the burst of percussion that opened "Glory Road," but halfway through "The Slippery Slope," I zoned out again, staring blankly at Peter's profile.

It struck me as effeminate. Insubstantial.

Liam's stern, masculine beauty radiated strength, solidity. Peter's had an air of fragility.

My instinct had always been to protect Peter from harsh reality. To bolster his confidence. To manage his career so he could make a living doing what he loved. To make the magic happen for him.

There was nothing fragile about Liam. I would never have to make sure his socks matched. I would never need to find work for him.

Strange, how all these years, I'd been so busy trying to earn what love and attention came my way, it had never even occurred to me how sexy self-sufficiency was in a man.

My revelation brought me no pleasure, however. If anything, it made me more miserable. Liam was so angry and hurt. He probably never wanted to see me again.

The final strains of "The Road to You" were dying away. Peter gazed at me expectantly. "So?" he prompted. "What do you think? Do you get my idea?"

Exhaustion rolled over me. "It's fine, Peter."

His face fell. "Just fine? That's all you can say?"

"I need a nap." I flung myself onto the couch.

Peter's scolding face faded to black. During my nap, a vivid dream came to me. Liam was sitting on a chair, lit by a beam of sunlight, playing a haunting melody on his fiddle. In the unaccountable way of dreams, I knew that the lovely tune was for me.

I woke up smiling, with Enid's big blue eyes right in my face. She was kneeling by the couch, waving a cup of coffee under my nose. I struggled into a sitting position and grabbed the coffee. "Thanks, Enid."

Peter walked in. "Sorry to drag you back to the real world, but it's after eight o'clock, and you'll have to move your butt to get those liner notes reformatted before we head over to meet with Shepard."

A familiar pressure settled on my chest—and I thought about the dream. The sweet melody, still echoing in my head. The painful pressure lightened like magic.

This was not life or death. The liner notes, the meeting—they were insignificant in the grand scheme of things. Close encounters with sex and death did wonders to reorder a woman's priorities. I took a leisurely sip of coffee. "No," I said.

Peter and Enid exchanged alarmed glances. "What do you mean, 'no'?" Peter asked.

"You and Enid can move your butts, not me. The liner notes are no longer my problem."

Peter's face went blank. "The hell they're not! What are you talking about? You said yourself that we have to deliver the layout to Shepard this morning, and if we miss the catalog deadline—"

"You, Peter. Not we. I've revised those notes three times. The thumb drive is in my purse." I fished it out and handed it to him. "Go ahead. Change it on your own computer, if you like. Deliver it to Shepard yourself. I can't make that meeting today."

"Are you nuts?" Peter looked horrified. "Nance, I don't do desktop publishing. I'm an artist, not a secretary."

"You could leave the album order as it is, if you get desperate," I suggested.

"You're not coming with us?" Enid's limpid blue eyes widened with outrage, to the point of bulging, I noticed. "What's gotten into you? What are we supposed to say to Shepard when you don't show?"

"Deal with it. Call and reschedule, if you don't want to go see him without me. Tell him that I'm having personal problems. God knows it's true enough."

"What personal problems could be more important than—"

"Masked kidnappers, Enid." I made my voice hard. "For starters. To say nothing of my mother dying in a home invasion a few days ago."

"We were very sympathetic about Lucia, Nance," Enid said, sounding wounded.

"So you don't even care if the album gets into the catalog, then?"

"Of course I care. But I'm also tired. I'm done pulling rabbits out of hats for you. Peter, get your shoes on. You have to come back with me to my apartment. Right now."

"Now? Why? Don't be ridic—"

"You owe me." My voice was steely. "I work my ass off for you guys, and I almost got killed last night. I'm still shaky. I promised a friend that I would organize to have company for everywhere I go, and I mean to keep that promise. Which means you're up to bat, buddy."

"Your timing is absolutely—"

"I also need some help getting Moxie's pet carrier loaded into the car. I'm going up to Latham for a while. I'm not sure for how long yet."

Enid and Peter exchanged horrified glances.

"Latham?" Peter's voice cracked. "Now? But tonight's the gig at the Bottom Line with Brigid McKeon! Plus the Shepard meeting, the liner notes, and we're going on tour in two weeks, and The FolkWorld Conference is coming up!"

"Latham's not far," I assured him, patting his shoulder. I pulled up my favorite car service on my phone and texted my request for a car. "I'll be in touch. Most of my business is conducted on the phone anyway, so why not do it from Latham?"

Peter accompanied me down to the car I had ordered, with bad grace, but I ignored his fierce sulking. It was turning into a beautiful morning. A brisk wind made the bits of garbage dance and swirl cheerfully over sidewalk grates.

Peter stared stonily out the window as the car service took us back to Avenue B. Peter usually required a lot of attention, but he wasn't getting any from me today. I wouldn't be capable of giving it to him if I wanted to.

Today, I couldn't be bothered. After last night, I felt light, fizzy, floating.

I was going to pack up every part of my life that was portable, collect my cat, drive up to Latham, and throw myself on Liam's mercy.

And a couple of other choice body parts, if I got lucky.

Doubt clutched at me. No way could it work. Not in the long run. A guy like him, with his mellow country lifestyle, his earth mother ideal. A busy, citified madwoman like me. I would drive him nuts. We would crash and burn. Probably sooner rather than later.

Maybe we already had. He'd been so angry at me this morning. And there were the armed abductors, the angry burglars. Add all the other crazy elements, and it looked like having Nancy D'Onofrio for a girlfriend, or hell, even just a casual fuckbuddy, was way too risky.

But at least I no longer felt like I would disappoint him in bed. Oh, no. All my doubts were gone in that regard. I knew exactly what I wanted to do to that big, strong body. I thought about the look in his eyes when he gave me that gorgeous schtick about the beauty of the flower. Sneaky, seductive bastard. He'd just reached right inside my chest, grabbed my heart, and squeezed it. I had felt so seen. So real, and present.

I was going to Latham. And if I got my poor tender crushed-out heart squished into jelly, well. It wouldn't be the first time.

But it would definitely be the worst.

Chapter Eighteen

Liam

Eoin shuffled up the driveway to my house at two in the afternoon, red-eyed and shamefaced, like any guy would who'd guzzled Guinness all night and had faced the new day without sleep or a shower.

I looked up from the chopping block when I saw him. I'd been trying to unload excess adrenaline and misery by chopping wood, so far with no success.

"Well, hell. Look who the cat dragged in," I commented.

Eoin flushed. "I was playing tunes with the lads at this pub in Sheepshead Bay, and I lost track of the time."

I grunted. "Hear you've got a new job."

"Uh, yes. I'm going on tour with this band, Mandrake. Next week."

"Congratulations," I said.

"Don't think I don't appreciate—all you've done for me—"

I held up my hand, and Eoin choked off whatever he was

about to say. "It's okay, Eoin," I said wearily. "You should be making music. You're doing the right thing."

Hope dawned on Eoin's pallid face. "So you're not mad?"

"Nah. Do you want to work on Matigan's crew until you leave, or don't you? If you're too busy, I need to let him know right now."

Eoin straightened his thin shoulders. "I'd be glad to work," he said with dignity. "I start rehearsing Sunday. I can work until then."

"Go get some rest, then," I told him. "You look like hammered shit."

Eoin hesitated.

"So. Ah. Is, ah, something happening between you and Mrs. D'Onofrio's daughter?"

The look on my face made him take off like a shot.

Inviting her to the seisiún had been my first mistake.

Taking her home was the second—though I'd paid for that in full already, by getting my ass pounded by the masked assholes.

But the crowning stupidity? Fucking her.

Now I knew what it felt like. And I could think of nothing else.

I was begging for exactly the trouble I'd spent the first eleven years of my life watching up close. The kind of bitterness that ate away at love until it was all gone.

Was I programmed to repeat this bullshit? Was I fucking doomed?

That thought dragged up memories, like that vacation to Niagara Falls that my mother had planned. A last-ditch effort to unite us as a family. The bags were packed, train tickets in my mother's clutch purse. She'd been waiting, dressed in her eggshell blue pantsuit. But when my father walked in the door,

I took one look at him, and I knew that it wasn't going to happen.

Dad had done it again. You could count on him to let you down the way you could count on the sun to rise.

"It's about time you got here," Mom said, reaching for her coat. "We'll have to hurry to catch the train."

"Something's come up, Fiona."

Mom froze for a moment, then laid her coat down, her face expressionless. "What do you mean, something's come up?"

"There's a problem with a shipment and I have to go look into it."

"Why can't you send Martin, or Brady?"

Dad shook his head. "You want something done right, you got to do it yourself."

"That principle doesn't apply to your family, however," she said, her voice tight.

Dad's mouth became a hard, flat line. "I make sacrifices to keep you in style, Fiona," he said. "And all I ever get from you is whining and nagging."

"Did I ask you to make these sacrifices? No, Frank. I didn't. All I ever wanted was to see you more than once a month." Mom's voice shook. "All I'm asking now is that you call and get someone else to cover whatever the problem is at work. Just keep your word to me, and come with us to Niagara."

My father's fists clenched. "God, Fiona," he ground out. "Why can't I make you understand? It's my responsibility!"

"Fine. Go, then. Your bag's by the door. Don't come back. I've had enough." She walked out of the room. Her back was straight, but her face was crumpled.

Dad looked at me, seated stiff and immobile with dread on the couch. "Sorry, son," he said heavily. "When you've got a family of your own to support, you'll understand."

"Go to hell," I said.

Frank Knightly's face darkened. "Don't speak to me that way. I'm your father. Show some respect."

"You're not my father anymore." I remembered so vividly how clear and cutting my voice had been. "You're a terrible father. You're fired."

Dad just stared at me for a moment. Then he grabbed the suitcase and walked out. That was the last I'd ever seen of him. Twenty-six years. More than two-thirds of my lifetime.

I shook myself back to the present, and attacked the kindling again. *Whack. Whack.* Fuck this. Fuck it all.

A few sweaty minutes of chopping later, the sound of a car made me turn.

My stomach did a somersault as I recognized Nancy's Volkswagen buzzing down the driveway. I clutched the ax handle as she got out of the car, wishing that I'd bathed.

She was elegant in faded jeans that clung enticingly to her hips and a dark, high-necked ribbed sweater that showed off a strip of flat belly. Her hair was wound into a loose braid, backlit by the sun like a halo of fire. She looked gorgeous. And nervous.

"Hey, Liam." She gave me a tentative smile.

I crossed my arms over my chest. My voice was locked in my throat. Her smile faltered.

Then she opened the back door of her car and pulled out a cat carrier. A plaintive meow issued from the plastic crate. I looked into her car windows. The backseat was piled high. A suitcase, a laptop backpack, boxes of files. Was she actually planning to ...

Holy shit. My heart started to gallop. My face got suddenly hot.

"What are you doing here?" I was so wound up, my voice came out hard and unwelcoming. I was more than capable of fucking up this incredible second chance right here and now.

Easy does it, Knightly.

Chapter Nineteen

Nancy

I'd known this was going to be awkward. I couldn't let him psych me out. Not yet, anyway. I stuck out my chin, crossed my arms over my chest, and stared him down.

"I was under the impression that you'd invited me, Liam," I said.

"I did. Then you blew me off."

His tone chilled me. "I did some thinking this morning and realized when I got to Enid and Peter's place that I'd made the wrong choice," I said.

"What changed your mind? Another ambush? Sniper fire? Arson?"

"I made a mistake," I said crisply. "And I regretted it, almost immediately. Can't a person make a mistake?"

He shrugged. "I don't know. People make them whether they're allowed to or not."

"Don't be snide. I'm serious."

He was grimly silent. "That's what I'm afraid of, Nancy," he said. "I think getting serious would be a bad idea for us."

I fought for control of my face. *Be a big girl. Be a sport.* God knows, I'd had plenty of practice. *Forget I ever said anything. Thanks for your help. Sorry for the bother. Sorry for the bruises. Have a nice life. It's been grand.*

It just wouldn't come out. This was worth trying a little harder, damn it. I might end up looking like a pleading, bleating fool, but who cared? Only Liam would ever know.

I cleared my throat with a delicate cough. "So, Liam. Are you all done with the scolding and punishing part yet? Because it's really boring. I'd like to skip it and move right along to the good stuff."

The darkness in his eyes shifted, like clouds in a turbulent sky. "I'm not scolding or punishing you. Just trying to be clear." He waited a moment, eyes narrowed, but he couldn't help himself. "What exactly do you mean by the good stuff?"

Ahhh. Now I had him. I let my eyes drag slowly, appreciatively, over his gorgeous body—the open shirt showing off his ripped belly, cut pecs, that dark, silky treasure trail. "If you have to ask ..." I said throatily.

He started to speak, then stopped himself. "I'm not the kind of person who takes this kind of thing lightly," he said.

"I know," I said. "Neither am I."

His eyes searched my face. "We'll hit a wall eventually," he said.

I ached to touch his face and smooth away that worried look. "You're so sure?"

"I feel very strongly for you," he said. "Even though we've only known each other a few days. But I see that wall, right in our path."

Tears welled up, and I swiped them impatiently away with

my knuckles. "Maybe," I said. "Right now, I don't really give a shit."

A ghost of a smile touched his lips. "No?"

"Let's just go for it. Top speed. We'll hit that wall together."

The wind whipped my hair around my face as we stared into each other's eyes.

"Nancy," he said. "If this is because of those assholes who attacked you—"

"Actually, no," I assured him. "And I'm glad you mentioned that. It's a point I particularly wanted to make. I appreciate your offer to protect me. That's really sweet and generous of you, and it melts my heart. But that isn't what this is about."

"It's not?" He frowned. "Then what is it about?"

I took a deep breath, and went for it. Balls to the wall.

"Nope. This is about unbridled carnal lust, Liam. You rocked my world last night. I want more, like I've never wanted anything, ever. And I don't want to wait. Not one more second."

I held my breath and waited for the verdict.

And waited. And waited. He was doing his silent smoldering thing, and it was agonizing to go this far out on the limb, and just stay there, fighting for balance.

One last, desperate sally before I retreated in ignominy and despair.

"One more thing," I said. "I want to give you a blowjob."

His eyes went blank. "What? You do?"

"Yes. We never got around to that last night, so I'll make it my first priority. I hope you're not too shocked, but the last few days have pretty much burned away all my maidenly shyness. I can't promise any world-class technique, but I think that going down on you right now would be the absolute highlight of my day."

Liam blinked. Swung his ax in a big arc. It landed in the

block with a *thunk* that made me jump. He grabbed my cat carrier and headed toward the house. "Follow me."

I trailed after Liam, up the steps of the wide wraparound porch. So dizzy with the success of my last-ditch ploy, I barely even saw his home. Just a vague impression of fresh-smelling, airy, minimalist rooms, big windows, sparse furnishings.

In the living room, he knelt down and flipped the lever that opened Moxie's carrier. The cat poked her head out, sniffed his hand, and stalked away to investigate this new situation, tail high.

I wanted to break the tension somehow, but the purposeful way that Liam started up the stairs discouraged speech. I hurried after his long strides. He didn't even bother turning to see if I was being pulled along in his wake. He could feel it.

So. It looked like I was going to be making good on my rash offer. My toes were curled up with excitement at the thought. But truth be told, I hadn't pictured going down on him when the weather conditions were this, well ... stormy. Tension and anger in the mix made it a little weird.

He stopped outside one of the upstairs doors. "I'm sweaty," he said. "I need a shower."

"No," I told him. "You absolutely don't."

He gave me a doubtful look, and I waved him in the door. God forbid I lose my nerve, or miss my precious, fleeting window of opportunity. Besides. He looked great gleaming with sweat, hair damp and spiky. Salty, virile.

He opened the door and beckoned me in.

I might have guessed that his bedroom would look like this. The room was stark in its simplicity. An antique brass bed sported a beautiful Irish chain quilt. An earth-toned Navajo rug lay on the wooden floor. Musical instruments from around the world decorated the plain white walls. A straight-backed chair sat next to a narrow, upright antique chest of drawers, decorated with a photograph of an attractive elderly couple, both smiling. An old, turn-of- the-century steamer trunk.

Old-fashioned. Sparse. Neat. A room from another century.

Sunshine blazed through the open window, lighting up the rug. Liam stood in the middle of that patch of sunlight, and turned to face her, in a wide-legged stance.

So, then. No banter, no chitchat, no lead-in. He was still angry, but he wanted his blowjob anyway. Well, fine. It was a weird vibe, but definitely a hot one. And I was getting comfortable with weirdness in these strange days.

Now I just had to behave like a femme fatale. It couldn't be that hard. I'd seen it done in films. But I was excited and flustered. My breath was coming fast, palms damp, knees rubbery. My thighs kept squeezing around a pulse of aching heat, just at the sight of him. At the thought of taking him into my mouth.

A slow, deliberate striptease was the obvious thing, but I was dressed all wrong. I needed more pieces, layers, with delicate straps, complicated lingerie, snaps and ribbons and laces, to draw it out. Not that I owned clothing like that in the first place.

As it was, I could only toss my purse to the floor by the bed, and peel off my sweater with slow, sexy deliberation. I let it fall off my fingertips and walked toward him until the patch of sunlight illuminated my body, too. The air was cool, tightening my nipples to puckered brown nubs.

I twitched my braid over my shoulder, pulled off the elastic, and unraveled it. My wavy hair rose up all around my face, electric and wild. Medusa's locks.

The jeans came next, which revealed the appallingly plain white cotton panties, and there I was. Naked as the day I was born, but for Lucia's sapphire pendant.

He stared at me. His burning eyes said it all. But the thick bulge of his erection backed up the smolder quite nicely.

"Do you, ah, want to sit down?" I asked.

He shook his head. Of course not. That would be too easy.

I sucked in a deep breath and reached for his belt. It took forever to get the thing undone, but he did not help me. His hands were clenched. Big fists held rigidly at his sides. Intense emotion emanated from him. I felt it against my skin, like blazing heat.

I moved to his jeans and shoved them down with his briefs —just far enough to free his cock. It sprang up into my hands, hot and huge and hard, the thick flushed knob at the end dripping with pre-come. Ahhh, yes. No lack of enthusiasm on his part.

I swirled my hands around the slick fluid that gleamed on his big cockhead and gripped him, moving up and down his shaft in a long, tight slide. He jerked, shuddered. His groan sounded as if it had been captured in his throat and wrestled into submission.

My rubbery legs gave way, and I sank down to my knees on the rug. Hungry to make him shudder and gasp, helpless in the grip of intense pleasure.

His cock bobbed in my face. I was kneeling in that patch of brilliant sunshine. The sun was hot, but cool air moved from the open window, and the combination was a subtle caress, like fluttering strokes made with feathers.

I stroked him, gripped him, lashed him with voluptuous strokes of my tongue. His hands slid into my hair, tightening. His whole body was rigid.

I went at him with everything I had, licking and lapping, stroking and swirling with my hands. Flicking my tongue against the sensitive slit of his cockhead, savoring the slick, salty fluid that dripped from it.

I drew him slowly into my mouth, intensely aroused by every part of the experience. My body was flushed and shivering. I relaxed and took him deeper, despite his size, slowly figuring out the sensual choreography. I kept a steady rhythm, drawing him back into my mouth with every slow stroke, tongue teasing along the way. I could taste his climax building. The taut stiffness, the desperate sounds he made.

His hands tightened in my hair, and he pushed my face away. I wiped my mouth, and looked up into his stark, rigid face. "Something wrong?"

"I need to fuck you," he said.

A shiver of delight went through me. I stroked his balls with my fingertips, just to savor the pleasure that racked his big body. "Do you have a condom?"

He shook his head. "I do not. I don't bring women here. Haven't for years."

I pondered that potential disaster for a moment, still squeezing and stroking him, and held up my hand. He took it, hoisting me to my feet.

"Well," I said. "This is the thing. I actually have a contraceptive implant. It dates back from my last relationship, which blew up on me eight months ago. I kept meaning to get it removed, but I'm always so busy, I just put it off. So, ah ... I'm covered. And I've been tested for everything a couple months ago. I'm all clean."

His eyes flashed. "Whoa," he murmured. "I've had clear blood tests, too. So if that's what you want, then hell, yeah. There's nothing I'd love better."

I turned, aiming for a hip-swaying sashay toward the bed, but it was all I could do to stay on my feet, I was so wobbly. I started to circle the bed, but stopped short, gazing at that expanse of quilt. A real femme fatale would not waste such an obvious chance to strike a hot pose for him, so I clambered up onto the bed on my hands and knees, arching my back. Sexy, sinuous, that was the vibe. But I didn't have a chance to let the moment develop, because the effect on him was instantaneous. The bed squeaked and swayed, and there he was—arched over me, his hot body covering my back, his cock swinging and bobbing against my inner thigh.

I tried to turn, but he held me in place, trapped beneath him. My breath came fast and nervous through my open mouth. I'd miscalculated my comfort zone.

Not his fault. I'd presented my ass to him; he could hardly be blamed for taking me up on it. *No.* I was not going to spoil this, for him or for me. I was not chickening out. I wanted this more than I'd ever wanted anything. And I would ... get ... through it.

I braced for it, but there was no invasive shove. Just his enormous warmth poised over me, warming me, waiting. His hot, soft lips caressing my nape, my spine. His hands moved between my legs, stroking my clit. Slow, lazy, circling strokes, petting me expertly until I squirmed against his hand. Delving inside to spread my juice around. Working me, squeezing me, stroking and thrusting ... until I collapsed into waves of shuddering pleasure.

When he finally nudged his cock inside me, I was so primed and desperate, I rocked backward to take him in. He gripped my hips with a low, admonishing murmur, kissed my shoulder blades, licked my spine. My shivering inner flesh clenched around his thick shaft. Every part of me that he touched went slick and tingling, melting with yearning. I squirmed against him, clawing my way closer to that shining prize that beckoned in my mind, crying out as he slid so deep inside ...

I disintegrated into wrenching pulsations of pleasure once again.

When I was fully conscious again, his breath was hot and rhythmic against my back. He set his teeth against my shoulder and licked off the sheen of my sweat.

"Ah, God," he muttered hoarsely. "So good. Do that again. Please."

"Anytime you want," I told him shakily. "I can hardly stop it, when you touch me."

He made a strangled sound, gripped her hips, and thrust harder.

I yielded to the wild, frenetic momentum, clutching the quilt, my face shoved in the pillow. Low cries jerked out of my throat at each slick, driving stroke and swivel of his thick shaft. He was pounding me into a creamy froth, and I didn't shut down or go cold. My body had resculpted itself to cherish every thick, throbbing inch of him.

After his own pleasure finally jolted through him, we lay together in a dream measured by bursts of birdsong and the flickering shadows of clouds from the window. He was heavy, but the pressure felt so good. I loved the deep, wonderful heat of him. So what if my lungs could only expand to ten percent of their capacity? Air, shmair. Who needed air, after sex like that?

But after a moment, he rolled onto his side, still keeping me held tight and close against him. Still inside.

My phone rang, and I felt his body tense. I leaned down, groped for the phone, and checked the display. Peter again. Hah. Later for him. I dropped it back into my purse, letting it ring on unanswered.

I turned back to him, enjoying his startled expression.

A wondering smile dawned on his face. "Wow," he said. "That must've cost you."

"I would turn it off completely if it weren't for my sisters," I told him. "With everything that's going on, I don't want to risk being out of touch with them."

"Give them my landline number," he suggested.

"Landline? How quaint and antique," I murmured. "It really suits your retro analog personality."

His smile widened to a gorgeous grin. "I'll take that as a compliment. But for real. They should have my number. And I want both of theirs."

"Thanks," I said demurely. "We'll organize that. For sure."

He nuzzled the nape of my neck. "Mmm. You smell like something good to eat."

"Vanilla sandalwood essential oil," I told him.

"Yeah? It's wicked good. Drives me crazy."

I arched like a cat. The way he responded to me made me feel like a dangerous, powerful temptress. I liked it. "So, Liam. Are you done being mad at me?"

He looked thoughtful. "I really don't know yet," he said. "I mean, I was pretty upset. Profoundly devastated, in fact. I think we'll have to have a whole lot more sex before I work all the poison out of my system."

I snorted with laughter. "Okay. I'm down for that," I said cheerfully. "Really. Take your own sweet time getting over it."

I feasted my eyes on his naked body. The pattern of dark chest hair arrowing down to his groin, the powerful muscles of his legs and thighs, his heavy arousal, rising proudly out of a thatch of thick black hair. Mmm. Already. Wow.

"Are you hungry?" he asked. "I could fix you something to eat."

"I'm not hungry right now," I said. "Not for food, anyway."

I caressed his thick cock, the stiff, swollen heat of it. He grasped my hand and pulled it to his face, kissing my knuckles before turning it over to kiss my palm and each individual finger. Then he pressed the back of my hand to his cheek.

I reached out for him, drawing him close, and he rolled onto me again, thrusting inside in a seamless slide of such sweet perfection that tears sprang to my eyes.

We clung, rocking, for what could have been hours. I lost all sense of time. The sunlit room was a magical sphere. Suspended dust motes floated lazily above us. The breeze rustled the trees. Wind chimes tinkled and clanked, sweet, hollow sounds

Liam's face filled my mind, overflowed my world. His weight, deliciously sensual between my legs, pressed me down into the bed. I rocked in that slow, lazy pump and swirl. I could have looked into those gorgeous, astonishing eyes forever, but eventually we started moving faster, kissing wildly. Every place his body touched mine was like a kiss, specific, hot, deliberate. I lifted myself, grasping for that shining perfection that beckoned and teased ...

And without warning, it burst upon me. Liam cried out at the same moment.

We soared together, fused.

We took our time drifting back. Liam untangled himself, stroking her back. "Was everything all right for you?"

I laughed. "It was great, and you know it."

He smiled. "I don't want to overdo it. I could do this all night and all the next day."

"You don't say." I laid my head on his broad, solid chest, practically purring as his arms closed possessively around me. "You're amazing," I told him. "I've never been able to ... well. Just amazing."

He lifted his head, eyes sharpening. "Never been able to what?"

I tried to gloss over the moment with a careless laugh. "I don't usually have this good a time in bed, that's all. I tend to shut down. With you, it doesn't happen."

He ran his fingers through my hair. "Why do you shut down?"

"Who cares, since it doesn't happen with you? I'd much rather think about this amazing present moment, and not dwell on my stupid, tedious—"

"Why do you shut down? Did something happen?"

I sighed. Shit. It would seem that Liam would not be guided around this particular crack in the pavement.

"I've got a theory," I offered reluctantly.

"Let's hear it."

I gathered my composure, hoping very hard that talking about my hang-ups would not invoke them back into the bed with me and Liam. "Well. I told you about being in foster care, remember?"

"Yeah, you mentioned that."

"It was the last home I was in before Lucia. I was thirteen. A nice family in Larchmont. I felt lucky. It was better than a lot of places I'd been. Until their son came back from his freshman year at college. Big guy. Body odor problem."

Liam's face contracted. "Oh, Christ."

"Oh, don't get scared," I said quickly. "He never actually … well. Lucky for me, there were always lots of people around, and I shared a room with two other girls. But he took every chance he got to pin me in dark corners and rub his erection against me. That was usually all he had time for."

Liam's hands were clenched. "What a piece of shit."

"He was working up to it, though," I went on. "It was only a matter of time. And he was his mother's firstborn darling. She was never going to believe me over him. Which was really sad. She was a nice lady. Deluded, but nice. I liked her."

I stared up at the ceiling, twiddling with the quilt, lost in unpleasant memories.

Liam nuzzled her with his lips. "And? So?"

I let out a sigh. "So I told my social worker," I said. "She confronted the mother. The mother took his side. Called me a nasty, lying slut. I got a new placement. With Lucia." I stroked his hair. "So you see? My luck turned. It was meant to be. But I still carry some of that around. I never go for guys who are significantly bigger than me, for instance. I hate being pushed around, or feeling squished. I freeze right up." I hoisted myself onto my elbow, and petted his massive chest. "You're a big exception," I added, in a wondering voice. "Very big."

His penis was long and hard, standing up against his belly. He shot me an uncomfortable look. "I know it's inappropriate, after what you just told me. Being close to you just does it to me. I can't help it. Or hide it, either. Since I'm naked."

"It's okay," I murmured. "I know you're one of the good guys."

He gathered me into his arms and I melted into the hug. My arms
trembled with the strain of holding him so tightly, but I wanted it to last forever.

When we finally relaxed, he brushed the hair off my face and cupped my cheek.

"I want to find that guy and kill him," he said.

I was taken aback by that blunt pronouncement. "Ah, I don't recommend that, Liam," I said nervously. "I have enough problems as it is."

He traced my eyebrow with his finger. "It's strange," he said. "I'm not a violent person. I've never gone looking for a fight in my life. But I would kill anyone who hurts you."

I opened and closed my mouth a few times, utterly nonplussed. "I'm not quite sure what to do with that information."

"It's not for you to do anything with," he said. "It's just the truth, for me. Maybe I shouldn't have shared that. Sorry. Didn't mean to make it weird for you."

"It's okay," I assured him. "Just a little, um. Intense."

"Yeah, I guess it is." He pulled away and got up, scooping up his jeans, and I sat up, realizing that our idyll was over. Liam was all business now.

He pulled his jeans up over that stunning ass, and then pulled open his closet, rummaging under a pile of thick wool blankets on a high shelf. After a moment, he pulled down a heavy black fiberglass case and laid it down on the bed.

"What's that?" I asked.

Liam unsnapped the case. "My stepfather's old service revolver."

I flinched. "Oh, my God. What are you going to do with that thing?"

He lifted an eyebrow at my tone. "Keep it close. Just in case."

"You really think that's necessary? Do you know how to use it?"

Liam laughed under his breath as he pulled out a box of bullets, opened the cylinder, and loaded it. "Yes and yes. I could have used this in your stairwell last night. Of course I know how to use it. God, what a question." He tucked it into the back of his jeans and shrugged on his shirt over it.

I shivered at the thought of the deadly thing, cold against the warm skin of his back. "Do you have a license to carry concealed?" I asked.

"I can get one," he said. "I've never needed one before, so I never bothered."

"Well. Until you get one, maybe you'd just better—"

"Think it through, Nancy," he said. "If the cops catch me carrying concealed, they'll give me a really hard time. If the bad guys catch me without it, they'll kill me, and take you. Which of those two scenarios scares you more?"

My belly contracted into a hard knot. I hugged my knees to my chest.

Liam sat down beside me and put his arm around my shoulders. "It's just a precaution," he said. "I'm sorry it upsets you. But I'll feel better carrying it."

I leaned into his hug. We clung to each other. The patch of sun on the floor had moved all the way across the room to the wall by the time he lifted his head.

"You hungry?" he asked.

"That's the second time you've asked," I commented. "I'm thinking you're definitely hungry. Am I right?"

"Starving," he said promptly. "Haven't eaten since before the seisiún last night."

Hmmm. I hadn't eaten since that sandwich at the diner, which was the morning before that, but he would almost certainly have something critical to say about it.

"You poor thing," I said. "Wasting away. Why didn't you say something?"

"Didn't seem important until now," he said. "Lucky for us, I fixed the neighbor lady's porch steps a month ago, and she gave me a lifetime supply of frozen pot roast stew. She's an artist when it comes to pot roast. Get dressed."

"Why? It feels good to be naked. Are you expecting company?"

"Eoin's around here somewhere," he warned. "I'm sure he has the good sense to keep his distance, but there are no curtains on the kitchen window."

That convinced me to clothe myself. We freshened up in his bathroom, pulled on our clothes and went down to feast in Liam's big kitchen on rich, savory beef stew, sourdough toast, crisp apples, and wedges of cheese.

I ate with appetite. Having a man stare at me like that made me giddy. I practiced my femme fatale act, licking fruit juice off my fingers, and was gratified when he dragged me right back up to the bedroom for another passionate collision in his bed.

I could get used to this. Hell, maybe I could even get good at it.

Chapter Twenty

Nancy

The day passed in a lazy blur of caresses, embraces, meals —and then caresses and embraces all over again. The revolver sat on the bedside table, a small, dark sentinel, grimly reminding me of the fear and violence that lurked outside this magic bubble.

But it didn't intrude. Liam's place felt safe. Home free.

The sun was low and the window pink with sunset clouds when I opened my eyes and found him twirling a lock of my hair and staring into my face.

"What's on your mind?" I asked.

"Lucia," he said. "I was thinking of her showing me your picture. I feel honored."

I blinked at him. "By what?"

"That Lucia thought I was good enough for you."

I rolled my eyes. "Please," I said. "I loved that woman tremendously, but I'm still furious with her for setting me up like that."

He propped his head up on one hand. "What's so mortifying about it? She wanted you to be happy, right? What's the harm?"

I shifted uncomfortably. "Lucia never quite grasped one of the basic laws of the animal kingdom."

"And what law might that be?"

I let out a sigh. "Men only want what they can't have," I told him. "They chase things that run. Babbling about my availability is like the kiss of death."

Liam pondered that, looking disapproving. "I'm no animal."

"I never said you were," I snapped. "You're taking this way too personally."

"I don't know any other way to take things. But you don't have to run away to make me take notice. I was interested from the first photo Lucia showed me."

"She showed you more than one?"

"Two photo albums," he admitted. "Your high school graduation photo was cute. Hell of a hairdo you had back then. I personally like it better long."

I groaned. "Don't tell me you didn't wonder why a reasonably attractive young woman would need her mother to find her a date."

He smoothed a lock of hair out of my eyes. "Strike out 'reasonably attractive' and insert 'drop-dead gorgeous.' And yeah. Of course I wondered."

I blew a lock of hair out of my mouth. "So, to get back to what I was saying—"

"Stunning," he added.

"Liam, we've been through the beauty-of-the-flower lecture. It was lovely, and I got it, okay? Do you want to hear the rest of this or don't you?"

He leaned back and folded his arms behind his head. "Go for it."

"Well, to start with, Lucia hated all of my fiancés," I told him.

That got his attention. "All your fiancés? How many did you have?"

I huddled into the quilt. "She didn't tell you about my train wrecks?"

Liam shook his head.

"I give her credit for masterful restraint, then," I said. "I was engaged three times. All three of them dumped me. Not exactly at the altar, but uncomfortably close. Two happened to be my clients. Which was probably not a great idea from the get-go, but hey. Mistakes were made."

He looked incredulous. "So what happened with these idiots?"

I plucked the quilt, embarrassed. "They fell in love with someone else."

He winced. "Ouch."

"Yeah, it sucked. At least by the time Freedy dumped me, I knew better than to get the wedding dress made in advance. I've only got two wedding gowns in storage, not three. One takes comfort in the little things." I kept my eyes down, so I wouldn't have to see pity in his eyes.

"They did you a favor," he said. "They did me one, too."

"How do you figure?"

"If you were married to one of those boneheads, you wouldn't be here with me right now," he said.

A silent giggle shook me. "It really is just as well. Lucia nagged and nagged about how they took advantage of me, but I never really saw what she meant until this morning. After last night, those guys with the knife, then being with you...it finally came together for me. Lucia was right all along."

"This morning?" He looked confused. "You're still in contact with these assholes?"

"Of course, but they're not assholes. Just temperamental artistic types. Two of them are my clients, as I said. Or three, I suppose I should say, counting Enid. I manage her, too, since she and Peter are a duo now."

His jaw dropped. "These dickheads dumped you for other women, and you still work sixteen hours a day managing their careers?"

"Don't you start," I said huffily. "I will admit that I have problems setting limits, putting my foot down, defending my own interests, yada yada. Those character defects have been exhaustively pointed out to me by Lucia and my sisters. I have gotten all the sermons and lectures in full, multiple times. Trust me. But these people are genuinely my friends, and they're very talented musicians, too. We've put it behind us."

"That guy who called this morning—was he one of your exes?"

I hesitated. "Uh, well, yes," I admitted. "That was Peter, my first fiancé. He's married to Enid now. She's another singer whom I manage. I was the one who introduced them, ironically enough. He's an incredibly talented—"

"Manipulator. Self-serving, self-indulgent user."

My chin went up as tension thrummed through me. "You don't know him."

"I don't want to. Actions speak louder than words. I know what I need to know."

I breathed down the tension. "That's pretty fucking inappropriate, Liam," I said. "You don't hear me making judgments about how you've lived your life all wrong."

"I just call it how I see it. I didn't mean to sound judgmental."

"No? And I don't mean 'Liam, you arrogant, know-it-all bastard' in a *rude* way."

He rolled on top of me, leaning down to nuzzle my throat.

"I'm sorry," he said. "You're right. You got my protective instincts all fired up. Emotions are running really hot, and stuff just comes out of my mouth. Sorry."

"Um." I stared at the ceiling, biting my lip. "Right."

"I didn't mean to be a dick. I can be way too opinionated."

"I'm starting to notice that," I murmured.

My face was inches from his bright, pale green eyes. So freaking beautiful. Then he started kissing his way across my collarbone … and then down to my breasts. Licking, suckling, stroking. Then my belly.

That slick bastard. I was embarrassed to feel my anger and tension fizzling away under the blunt force of his masculine allure. I had to at least try to push back.

"Liam," I said. "You can't win an argument by seducing me."

"This isn't me arguing." He pushed my legs wide. "This is me apologizing."

I let out a soft cry as he put his mouth to me. "Smart-ass," I whispered.

His laughter vibrated against my clit, and then he started in with his tongue, melting me down into a helpless, writhing frenzy.

Chapter Twenty-One

Liam

The haunting sound of the Uilleann pipes woke me up. Nancy's light weight on my shoulder gave me a jolt of startled joy.

I turned to look at the clock. 2:17 A.M. Eoin. That sneaky, sentimental little bastard.

Nancy murmured softly and raised her head. Moonlight flooded through the window, illuminating her big, shadowy eyes. She brushed her hair out of her face.

"That's gorgeous," she said. "'The Soldier's Vow.' One of my favorites."

"Yeah, Eoin goes for the real heartbreakers," I muttered.

She cuddled up next to me. "It's so romantic."

"Yeah. It's also two in the morning."

She punched me in the shoulder. "Oh, give in! There's moonlight, there's music, it's romantic. Surrender, already!"

"I already have. See?" I pulled her hand down and showed her the effect she had on my body.

She laughed. "Uilleann pipes are a real turn-on for you?"

"I like them fine, but you're the turn-on, Nancy."

"Aww. That's sweet. Don't you ever get tired?"

"Not yet," I admitted. "What about you? Are you sore?"

"I'm fine. I'm great. But I'd rather just talk for a while."

"Okay." I rolled onto my side, facing her, stroking the curve of her side, the beautiful swell of her hip. "What about?"

"Not quite sure yet," she said. "Let's take it take it one minute at a time. Let's listen to the tune. We'll see what comes to us."

We just stared at each other in the moonlight as I ran my fingers back up her body, and through her silky hair. Eoin ended "The Soldier's Vow" and launched into "The Women of Ireland."

"God, that kid is good," she murmured as the plaintive tune filled the air. "So he rents your basement?"

"Not exactly. He just bunks there. It's a space for him to crash."

"You give him a job and a place to stay, for free? That's awfully nice of you."

"Not really," I said. "People helped me when I was young. I figure that this is the best way to pay them back. Besides, he's family. My mom's cousin's boy."

"People helped you how?" Her slender hand trailed over my shoulders, exploring my body with her fingertips. The tender caress seemed to zing straight to my dick, making it pulse and throb. I let out a slow, controlling breath, resolving to keep it together. I'd told her just a couple of hours ago that I wasn't an animal. Now I had to live up to those rash words.

I wrangled my attention back to her question by brute force of will. "When I was Eoin's age, I did a lot of traveling. I worked my way across America on cattle ranches. I crewed on a yacht in the Pacific. I worked on sheep stations in Australia for a while. I had a great time, learned a lot, met a bunch of great people who gave me a meal, a job, or a place to sleep. It was a good education."

"Wow. That's adventurous. How did your parents take it?"

"They worried. My stepfather wanted me to be a cop, like him. He thought I'd be good at it, and maybe he was right. I considered it for a while. But that job wears you down on a soul level. There's so much cruelty and ugliness, and as a cop, you have to witness it firsthand. I didn't want to. Hank was disappointed, but he understood."

"Hank," she murmured. "He was your stepfather?"

"Yeah. He was a good man. He was the one who taught me music. Carpentry, too. It was what he did to relax." I traced the curve of her cheekbone with my finger as Eoin's pipes began to sob out yet another haunting tune.

"You never thought about going to college?"

"Sure, I thought about it. But I wanted to travel. And I wasn't interested in any careers that require a certificate, so why go to all that expense? Anything you want to learn, you can just go to the library and study up for the cost of a library card. You just have to care enough to actually do it. That's the hard part. Self-starting."

She slid her hand up my chest, winding her fingers through my chest hair. "I never thought of it that way, but you're probably right. What's the story on your real dad?"

I stiffened. "Haven't laid eyes on him in twenty-six years."

Her eyes sharpened. "Oh. You don't even know where he is?"

"Maybe there was an address with the flowers he sent to Mom's funeral. I didn't look."

Nancy sat up, chilled. "Sorry," she said. "Did I hit a nerve?"

"It's okay," I said.

She caressed my shoulder. "Do you, um...want to talk about it?"

"No," I said flatly.

Silence followed. She looked worried.

I felt like shit for using that tone with her, but my guts were clenched up in irrational tension. Hers had been a completely innocent, reasonable question, and yet somehow, every word seemed to propel us closer to that brick wall that lay in wait for us.

Emergency detour. I grabbed her arm, yanking her down. She cried out.

I froze. "Did I hurt you?"

"No, you just surprised me. I thought—"

I cut her off with a kiss, using all my skill to drag her back into the burning present moment, which was where we needed to stay. I rolled on top of her, sliding inside in one heavy lunge. No future, no past. Just the melody that throbbed outside the window, full of pained longing. Just the moonlight spilling in. Just Nancy's strong, slender body moving beneath mine. Holding me, clasping me.

I didn't want to think about that wall we were racing toward. Or the look on my father's face right before he walked away forever. Or Lucia's freshly dug grave, or the masked attackers in the stairwell, or the destroyed heirloom table, or the gun by his bed.

Violence lurked around every blind corner. Uncertainty, danger, risk. Pain and loss lurked in the shadows, just waiting for their opportunity to rend and smash and destroy.

And this beautiful, delicate thing between us. So fragile. Beset on every side.

She gripped me, arching and crying out as her climax shivered through her.

Yes. The satisfaction that exploded in me felt almost like anger.

I buried my face against her hair and hung on as my own pleasure detonated deep inside me, mind and body, launching me out into sweet, blessed oblivion.

I was going to cheat Fate for as long as I could.

Fuck them all.

Chapter Twenty-Two

Nancy

The sky was pink outside Liam's window when I woke. The bed beside me was empty. I flopped back onto the pillow and studied the room. A photo of a younger Liam was hung on the wall across the room. He had a big carefree grin, and his arm around the shoulder of a handsome older woman with a smile like his.

I took a shower in Liam's big bathroom. Muscles I didn't know I had were pleasurably sore. When I came down the stairs, bacon was sizzling on a skillet, a teakettle was whistling, and Liam was spooning pancake batter onto a griddle. It smelled delicious.

Liam looked over his shoulder. "What tea would you like? I've got Darjeeling, or this great Nepali stuff."

"No coffee?" I stared at him in blank dismay. I hadn't thought to bring my own.

"Not in this house," he said.

"You are kidding me. This will not do." I plugged my phone

into a countertop outlet to recharge. "There's got to be an espresso bar somewhere in Latham."

"I wouldn't know," he said. "Do you like your bacon crisp or chewy?"

"Right in the middle of the range, please. Could I use your landline? I want to give my sisters your home number."

"Be my guest." He scribbled a number on a scrap of paper and slid it across the bar to me with a smile. "There you go."

I forked wet food into a bowl for Moxie as Vivi's phone rang and rang. She finally picked up, though her voice was sleepy. "Yeah?"

"Get a pen, Viv. I have to give you a phone number."

"Omigod. Is it the number of that big, tall green-eyed drink of water? Hey, Nell! Wake up! Nancy got laid!"

"Get the pen, Viv," I repeated through my teeth.

Vivi hummed as she copied down the number I dictated. "Okay, it's on Nell's fridge, plus it's written on my hand. So? Details, honey, details! Is he, well, as vigorous as he looks when you guys ... well, you know?"

"I will not be drawn into any discussion," I said primly.

"I should think not, since he must be right there with you. Am I right?"

"Bingo. Making pancakes as we speak. And bacon."

"Whoo-hoo! Sounds tasty. So go upstairs, or outside, or whatever, and I'll call you back on your mobile phone. You've got to tell us everything!"

"I can't use my phone right now. It's charging right. That's why I'm calling with the landline."

There was a dramatic silence from the other end of the line.

"Your phone isn't charged?" Vivi repeated. "Hold on. Who is this? And what have you done with my sister?"

"Oh, stop. You're being ridiculous."

"Tell us all about it tonight. And I mean every juicy detail. When are you getting back? Let's hit that great little Indian place down the street from Nell's and then huddle down all together at her apartment for safety. With a few bottles of wine."

I hemmed and hawed. "I don't exactly know when I'll be coming back. I brought Moxie up here, see, and he's asked me to stay—"

"You brought up Moxie? Nell!" Vivi howled "Get this! Nancy's shacked up!"

"Stop it, Vivi," I begged. "Don't jinx this for me."

"Okay, you big scaredy-cat. But we worry, so call us whenever you get the chance, between sweaty bouts of bed-play. And say hello from the two of us!"

Vivi hung up, and I clutched the receiver with a hand that shook.

Liam's hand touched my shoulder, making me jump. He took the phone and hung it up. "My sisters say hello," I offered.

"Great. I say hello right back. Why do you look so worried?"

"Because they're having this big, happy freak-out about me being up here with you, and it's making me nervous."

Liam's mouth tightened. "Ah." He was silent for a moment. "So you think that they'll be crushed when they find out that it's no big deal."

My throat started to burn. "I didn't say that," I said. "You're the one who said we were going to hit that wall."

"So I did," he said.

I laid my hand upon his chest, feeling the strong, steady throb of his heart. "It's a very big deal, to me," I said.

He covered my hand with his own. "Yeah? How big?"

"Huge."

We came together into a tight embrace, and I pressed my

shaking face to his chest. Silently agreeing to let the dangerous moment pass.

An alarming smell a couple minutes later made them look up.

"Oh my God. The pancakes." Liam lunged for the griddle.

There were plenty of pancakes, so we feasted on pancakes and bacon. I ate twice as much as I usually did, and loved every bite. We cleaned up the kitchen, then looked at each other, embarrassed.

"So, ah, what now?" I asked.

His lips twitched. "You tell me, Nancy."

The gleam in his eye was hard to resist, but the reality of my work life was breathing down my neck. "I really do need to get some work done," I told him. "Is there a place I could set up shop where I wouldn't be in your way?"

"I'll set up an office for you. I'd give you the spare room, but if you want a phone line, it'll have to be in the living room. I'll get the stuff from your car."

When he'd hauled in and set up all of my office equipment at the desk, he gave me a brief, hard kiss. "I'll try to stay out of your way," he said. "The temptation will be strong, though. Don't be creeped out if I look in on you, just to make sure I'm not daydreaming. That this is actually happening."

I tried not to smile. "Don't freak if I turn my smartphone on, okay? I need to check my messages."

"Be my guest," he said magnanimously. "It should be close to charged by now. I'll be in my workshop if you need me."

My voice mail was loaded with petulant messages from Peter and Enid. Peter was her first call.

"Well! It's about damn time!" Peter scolded. "I've been trying to get in touch with you for twelve hours!"

"Horrors," I said mildly. "What's up?"

"No need to be snotty." Peter sounded hurt. "Enid and I

did the opening act at the Bottom Line last night for Brigid McKeon and the Beltane Beldames, remember?"

"Of course. I sweated for months to get you that gig."

"Oh. I figured you'd forgotten, since you didn't bother to come. Well, get this. Brigid liked Enid's voice so much, she wants her to go on tour with the Beldames!"

"Wow," I said. "That's really great. Did you tell her to call me?"

"Of course I did, but you've been unreachable, so I expect you've missed her call. So? It's not like Enid can say no at this point in her career to Brigid McKeon."

"True. She shouldn't," I said.

"But she can't throw away her solo career to be a Beldame, either. Enid belongs in front of the band, not singing backup."

I lost the thread when I glimpsed Liam in the doorway, listening. I waved at him.

"Relax, Peter," I soothed him. "I'll talk to Brigid's manager and get the dates, and see if I can switch Enid's concert schedule, or maybe agree to just one tour, and use it as a selling point for her own tour." I squeaked, startled, as Liam materialized behind me. He started to kiss my neck, and I batted his head away.

"You're up there with some guy, right? The graphics are overdue for my album, it's a week until FolkWorld, it's a critical moment in mine and Enid's careers, and all you can think of is your hormones? We're talking serious money, here!"

"Speaking of money, I advanced you the registration fees for the FolkWorld Conference, remember?"

"Yeah, but we still haven't gotten paid for those five gigs upstate!"

I wiggled as his hand slid down my belly and into the waistband of my jeans. "But my credit cards are maxed."

"I can't believe you're nagging me like this when we've got

this huge decision to make," Peter bitched. "I don't want to talk to you again until you're ready to act professional." He hung up on her.

I let the phone drop. "Damn. Now he's pissed."

"Good." Liam's hand delved deeper. "I heard the name Peter," he murmured. "It got me going. I just couldn't help myself. Let him stew in his own juices."

"Easy for you to say!"

"What have you got to lose?" he demanded. "The cheap bastard doesn't even pay you what he owes you, right?"

"Butt out of things that don't concern you, Liam. I appreciate your help, but do not interrupt my business calls with inappropriate sexual advances."

"Inappropriate? I'll show you inappropriate."

"Not today, you won't." She stuck out her chin. "I have stuff to do. Off with you."

He backed away, hands up in surrender. "Later, then."

I was riveted by the hot erotic promise in his eyes. "Um. Yeah. Later."

The day raced by. I spent most of it on the phone rearranging concert dates and dealing with Brigid McKeon's agency. Liam was unobtrusive, but I was intensely aware of him, sneaking hungry glances at the grace and power of his every movement. More than once he caught me peeking. His grin made my heart float up.

Daylight faded. I mocked up the new Mandrake promo brochure that had Eoin's name on it, entered some new email addresses onto the newsletter sub list, and exited out of my computer. I hesitated for a moment—and then turned off my smartphone too.

It was the professional kiss of death, but right now, I didn't give a shit. I went to the door that led to his workshop, which was dominated by a large and beautiful dining room table. He'd left the door open.

He was bending over a workbench, sanding some piece too small for me to identify. He looked up, though I was barefoot, and made no sound.

He put the piece down. "You done for the night?"

I nodded. "I just shut down the computer."

He held out his arms. "So you're all mine."

"Yeah." She wrapped her arms around him and breathed in the fresh smell of wind, rain, and fresh-cut wood that clung to him. "I even turned off the phone."

Silent laughter vibrated his big frame. "Wow. That's huge."

"It is," I agreed. "Shall we think about dinner?"

"In a bit. First, there's something I wanted to try. I've been thinking about it ever since I met you. It's been keeping me up at night."

I kissed the triangle of skin at the vee of his shirt. "What's that?"

Suddenly, my jeans were tugged down around my hips and knees. He'd sneakily unbuttoned them. My panties soon followed.

I stepped out of them, giggling, and he seized me, hoisting me up onto the edge of the table he was making. The surface was cool and smooth against my bare ass.

I gasped and wiggled as he gently pushed me onto my back, easing my thighs apart. "Hey! What exactly do you have in mind?"

He leaned to kiss my belly and kissed his way lower. "Let me show you."

Chapter Twenty-Three

Liam

"Another slice of lamb?" I offered. "There's more potatoes, too."

Nell and Vivi, Nancy's two sisters, shot each other a discreetly delighted glance and held out their plates without hesitation.

"Don't mind if I do," Nell said. "Yum."

"Oh, hell yeah," Vivi said. "You're a great cook, Liam." She shot Nancy a teasing glance. "Lucky girl."

Nancy held out her plate, too, for another serving of the meltingly tender leg of lamb I'd roasted according to Mom's recipe, which called for a ton of sweet roasted red onions. That recipe was a sure thing, and the baby potatoes had turned out well, too—sauteed in olive oil, garlic, and a mix of fresh herbs from my garden. I'd done a big platter of roasted asparagus, lightly golden and crispy on the outside, meltingly tender inside. A big frilly salad and some freshly baked bread rounded it all out. The meal had earned me points, particularly since I'd gotten it all onto the table in record time, after that long, hard day dealing with the mess of Lucia's house.

Nancy and I had gotten the word that the crime scene investigators were done, and the crime tape had been taken down. It was time to go and face it head-on, but I'd insisted that Nancy call her sisters to share in the physical and emotional burden of dealing with Lucia's trashed house. Nancy was too quick to shield her sisters and take it all on herself, but that just wasn't fair. Or efficient, for that matter.

I'd invited them to dinner, just to make sure they came up to keep Nancy company. It was time to meet them and pass whatever mysterious sisterly tests needed to be passed to gain their blessing and approval.

So far, it seemed to be working. I refilled everyone's glasses with red wine.

Nell took a sip. "It's wonderful, to have a fabulous meal after a day like today," she commented. "I can't believe how relaxed and mellow I feel."

"Amen. I'm all topped up. We'll be full until next week." Vivi smeared butter on a piece of bread to accompany her final scraps of lamb. "How on earth did you pull this dinner off? You were working at the house with us all day long. Then we come back here, and hey presto—you pull a meal like this right out of thin air?"

I shrugged. "I just prepped it. It was all ready to go. The meat was marinating, the potatoes were already parboiled, the salad was ready. It was just a matter of putting the roast in the oven."

The sisters exchanged looks. "Mmm," Nell said archly, eyeing me. "All that and mental organization, too."

Now I was just being fucked with, but with good humor, so whatever. I smiled and lifted my glass to the D'Onofio girls,, resting squarely on my laurels.

Nell and Vivi D'Onofrio had exceeded my expectations. They hadn't skived off from the work. They'd shown up bright and early at Lucia's house for the painful walk-through to assess damage. They worked as hard as he or Nancy had, cleaning, sorting, sweeping, and assessing what was irreparably damaged and what was worth salvaging.

These two women didn't shirk hard work. They were both fiercely pursuing their passions and ambitions in unconventional ways, like Nancy did. They were bright, tough, engaged, interesting. I saw Lucia's influence in them, the way I'd seen it in Nancy. They were a cut above the average. Several cuts, actually.

"I called Giselle, my art restoration friend, before dinner," Vivi said. "She's already getting her A team organized to restore the slashed canvases."

"Good," Liam said. "I don't know much about art, but even I could tell that the stuff on Lucia's walls was next-level. I hope your friend can restore them."

"If anyone can, Giselle and her crew can," Vivi said.

I glanced at Nancy. "Maybe Giselle knows someone who should look at the carved table. Someone other than me. Like I told you, I don't have art restoration experience. Certainly not with an antique that valuable."

"No. I want you to do it. You promised, and I'm holding you to it." Nancy's voice was forceful. She looked at her sisters. "I want him to do it. He has a feel for that table. He vibes with it. And he's incredible at joining work."

"Is he, now." Vivi tried not to smile.

"Yeah," Nancy went on. "You should see the table he's been working on in his workshop. It's a work of art." But as she mentioned the table, her face flushed a rosy pink. Both of her sisters giggled helplessly under their breath.

"Fine," Nell said, eyes sparkling. "I trust your judgment

completely when it comes to your good friend's expertise in, er...joining."

Damn. That was my cue to get the hell out of the room for a while, to let them get their ya-yas out with no witnesses. I stood up. "You all ready for some dessert? I got lemon profiteroles from Fanelli's Italian Bakery. They're the real deal."

Nell moaned with delight under her breath. "Omigod, I'm stuffed. But I can't say no to lemon profiteroles."

"Same," Vivi said promptly. "Lay it on me. I'll suffer if I must."

Nancy was grinning. "Of course. Bring it on. Want help bringing it out?"

"Nah." I backed away swiftly, toward the kitchen. "You stay here. I got it."

I tried not to listen from the kitchen, but couldn't help hearing the smothered giggles, bursts of whispered talk, more giggles. Then Nancy's sharper protests, met with still more laughter from her sisters.

I was glad to hear them laugh, even if it was at my expense. Their day had been a long, exhausting series of unpleasant shocks and painful losses. They had been forced to throw away treasured furniture, sweep up the shards of Lucia's fine china and shattered crystal. They'd salvaged what they could, and we'd all been on the alert for another letter. So far, no such luck.

I scooped the goopy profiterole onto one of Mom's cut crystal serving dishes. It occurred to me that none of Mom's nice china or crystal had been used since she died. My own stuff was very plain. Mom's stuff hadn't even made it out of the box in storage until today. It didn't fit with my austere, monastic bachelor life.

I'd hung onto the stuff, though, figuring it might come in

handy when I got married. I'd thought, vaguely, that my future wife might appreciate things like that.

But I didn't even want to meet that future wife. There was no place for her in my head. All the space, all the air, was taken up by Nancy.

I came out carrying the serving dish piled with goopy pale yellow pastries swimming in lemon cream in one hand and a handful of small crystal bowls from the same dessert set in the other. I dished up the sweet using Mom's nice silver dessert serving spoon, laying on heavy lashings of the cream.

All the while, Vivi and Nell shot each other speaking glances and kicked each other under the table. Those two were having the time of their lives.

"Nancy looks great, since she's been hanging out with you, Liam," Vivi said. "So relaxed. Great color. Lips as red as cherries."

"Oh, stop. I think I've gained about eight pounds," Nancy grumbled.

"I think she looks perfect." I passed Nancy a dish of pastry.

Nell accepted her bowl. "Liam," she said. "Thanks for helping us with Lucia's house. But we have to pay you for your time and energy. Really."

I shook my head. "Lucia was my friend. It's my privilege to help."

"Well," Nell said. "Isn't that refreshing to hear. What a change of pace."

"Nell." Nancy's voice had a warning tone. "Don't start."

"I'm not," Nell said, rolling her eyes. "Just let me be pleased and happy for you, okay? Is that allowed?"

Nancy sniffed. "Far be it from me to impede anyone's pleasure or happiness."

Tension in the air made me search for a change of subject. I scooped up a bite of profiterole. "So. Since you three have cleared away all of Lucia's household stuff, me and my crew can start salvaging the building supplies," I said. "Maybe two-thirds of it is still usable, if we can find some matching tiles."

"Good," Vivi said. "I can't stay to help right now, though. I need to head out to Ohio in the next couple days for another couple of back-to-back craft fairs."

I gave her a narrow look. "Isn't that dangerous? Traveling alone?"

Vivi lifted her hands. "I can't afford to stop working. And I doubt this guy is going to track me along the forgotten highways and byways of America."

I turned to Nell. "Doesn't that leave you all alone in Williamsburg?"

Nell shook a finger in negation while she savored a mouthful of her dessert. "Not at all. I'm being good, I promise. While Vivi's gone, I'll stay at my thesis advisor's apartment. She knows what's happening, and she has a doorman building on the Upper West Side with good security. I'll be safe there."

I nodded. "Okay, good. Even so, I get the sense that you two aren't taking the danger seriously. I think you should both disappear for a while. Lay low."

Vivi and Nell exchanged somber glances. "We can't afford to stop our lives like that," Nell said. "Nor can either of us afford to hide out anywhere."

"You could come here," I offered rashly. "I have two spare bedrooms. I'd be happy to have you. Until this thing is definitively handled, anyhow."

All three women stared at me, openmouthed.

Vivi recovered first. "Uh...wow, Liam. That is incredibly nice of you."

"But you can't take me up on it, right?" I glanced at Nancy. "Gee. Where have I heard this song before?"

Nell made an airy gesture with her hand. "We're just like

that. Those D'Onofrio girls. Stubborn as goats. But really, thank you so much. It's good to know that we have a place to run to if things get weird."

"You do," I reiterated. "Anytime. It would be fine."

"Thank you, Liam." Nancy's voice caught. Her eyes were shining. It made my heart thud heavily with some emotion I did not dare examine.

Vivi dabbed her napkin to her nose. "Well," she said soggily. "I see why Lucia hand-picked him for you."

"Yeah," Nell said. "She always did have perfect taste."

My face had gone beet read. "Uh. Yeah. Whatever. You ladies want coffee?"

"Not for me," Nell said. "Vivi should have a cup, I think, since she's the driver. We should be on our way."

We walked them out. Nell and Vivi hugged their sister, whispering into her ear until she snorted. Then they took turns giving me tight hugs with a hard thump on the back for good measure. They got into Vivi's Volkswagen van and took off.

When the lights of the vehicle had disappeared, Nancy looked up at me. "Damn, Liam," she said. "You really pulled out all the stops. That meal? My God."

I shrugged, sliding an arm around her waist. "It was a pleasure. I liked them."

"I think they could tell." She turned to face me, pressing her face to my chest. "Thanks for being so sweet. But inviting them to live with you here? Wow. A heads-up would have been nice."

"Sorry." I nuzzled her hair. "It just came to me. There's room. And I want them to be safe. I want you all to be safe. I want to fix this goddamn thing for you."

"Thank you for wanting that," she said. "But if they had said yes, it would have seriously cramped our sexual style. You know that, right?"

I snorted with laughter. "Ah. Guess so. Just as well they blew me off, then."

Nancy's smile faded. "Lucia should have been at this dinner tonight," she said. "Telling us her stories. Holding forth. Ordering us around."

"That would have been great," I said. "I can see her, looking proudly around the table at her crowning jewels. Three beautiful daughters that she hand-picked herself."

Nancy's laugh was soggy. "Right. From the thrift stores and pawn shops."

"It doesn't matter where she found you. Like Nell said. She had perfect taste. She knew a treasure when she saw it. Never forget that."

"I miss her so much," she whispered.

I held her close, and we swayed on the porch to the song of the crickets and the wind. Painfully aware of how dangerous it was to care this much about precious, delicate, breakable human beings. So easily hurt, so easily destroyed.

It was terrifying, but together, we were strong enough to let ourselves feel it.

Chapter Twenty-Four

Nancy

My time at Liam's place was wonderful and disorienting. A seesaw of emotional extremes. My days were spent in the makeshift office in Liam's living room, trying to work. Focus was hard to find. I vacillated between wiggling my toes with manic joy, laughing out loud for no reason, worrying about my sisters, and stressing about the stairwell thugs.

And missing Lucia so sharply I could taste it. Grief had left a hard, permanent lump in my throat that only Liam's embrace could ease.

I had gotten over my embarrassment at being fixed up by Lucia. At this point, it comforted me that she had picked him out. A benediction from beyond.

He'd won my sisters over completely. They were blatantly rooting for him now, but somehow, that ratcheted the pressure up even higher.

Feasting on abundant home-cooked food was having its

inevitable effect. My jeans were tighter, to my chagrin. Liam certainly didn't seem to care. I bought an espresso pot in Latham, a bean grinder, and a sizable stash of coffee beans, and with that small but crucial detail handled, I was in a state of total bliss. I hadn't realized how badly I needed to slow down. We stayed close to home for security's sake, other than trips to Lucia's house. Eventually it would be time to venture out again. But for now, Liam's safe, beautiful house was just what I had desperately needed.

No. Liam was what I needed. The house was just an expression of him.

In the evenings, we would wrap ourselves in a blanket and sit together on his porch swing, listening to birds, crickets, frogs, wind chimes. Sometimes talking about anything and everything. Sometimes sitting in a companionable silence. Sometimes kissing madly. A fearful little voice in my head kept whispering cynically, *get it while you can.* I did my best not to pay attention.

Liam was still carrying the gun around, but over a week had passed with no attacks on me, so the immediacy of the threat had eased. I was as ready as I would ever be to broach the subject they had been avoiding until now.

Which was to say...what came next.

It had been wonderful, staying up here. Relaxing, healing, delicious. Just what the doctor ordered. But I couldn't stay up here cloistered in his bed forever. In any case, Liam had other jobs scheduled. The real world beckoned to both of us.

My best-case scenario, which was also my wildest romantic fantasy, was to integrate my two realities. Make him part of my actual life. I liked the person I was with him. That woman was so much happier, more relaxed, more joyful. And so very pleasured.

I'd make the adjustments. I'd be flexible. I'd make it work. He was so worth it.

I made the leap one evening while we were making soda bread in his kitchen, a tasty stew bubbling on the stove. I told him I needed to drive back to New York.

His expression did not change. "What for?"

"To leave Moxie with Freedy's wife, Andrea, when I go to the FolkWorld Conference next week," I explained.

He looked alarmed. "A conference?"

"It's important," I said. "For me and for all my artists. Freedy and Peter and Enid and Mandrake are all performing. Eoin will be playing, too. And I won't be alone for one second. I promise you. I'll be surrounded by everyone I know, in fact."

He let out a skeptical grunt. "Is Freedy another of your exes?"

"Yes, but it's very amicable," I assured him. "Particularly now. I'm so over it, I can't even tell you. Freedy has a showcase Friday night at FolkWorld, but Andrea has to work, so she's staying in the city. She promised to look after Moxie for me."

"Why not just leave her here with me?"

I studied his unreadable profile and gathered my nerve for the big play. "Thank you for offering. That brings me to another thing I wanted to ask you."

"Ask away." He mixed milk into the batter with a wooden spoon, waiting.

I took a deep breath and blurted it out. "Want to come with me?"

He froze, his hands buried in dough. "To your conference?"

I hastened on. "Yes. It's in Boston, at the Amory Lodge. I could get you a listener's pass. You'd stay in my room. And seeing as how it's a weekend, and you have a job scheduled for next week, I figured, maybe you could drive up Saturday."

"Hmph." He looked unconvinced.

"This is the thing," I went on. "I've been experiencing your life since I've been here, staying in your house, eating your food, sharing your bed, and it's wonderful. I love it. But I have my own life, and it's calling me. I'd like you to come to get to know my world the way I've gotten to know yours. The conference will be crazy, and I'll be networking with agents and presenters, and we probably won't sleep much, but you'll hear some great music and meet some interesting people. And Eoin would be ecstatic to have a friend in the audience. Mandrake's showcase will be his first performance. It kicks off their spring tour."

He gathered the dough into a loose ball. "What night is Eoin's thing?"

"Saturday night. At eleven-thirty, if you can believe it."

He laid the dough on the floury countertop, still not meeting my eyes. "I was thinking of taking a few more days off," he admitted.

"You were?" I said hopefully.

"But I was thinking along the lines of running away with you. Someplace where I won't have to share you with hundreds of people. I know a guy on the coast who charters sailboats. I thought, four or five days, no worries, no looking over our shoulders. No cell coverage."

I snorted. "You do like to push your luck, don't you?"

"Oh yeah," he said. "All the way to the very end."

I watched his floury fingers patting dough into the loaf shape. "It does sound wonderful," I said. "But I was hoping—" I stopped, still unsure of myself.

"What were you hoping?" He laid the dough onto a floured baking sheet. He flicked his gaze up, frowning impatiently when I didn't answer. "Tell me."

"I want this to be real, Liam," I said. "Right now it's just a fairy tale, totally removed from my real life. I have to pinch myself to make sure you exist."

He slipped his arms around my waist, careful not to touch me with his floury hands. "Let me prove to you that I exist, sweetheart."

I swatted him. "Stop trying to distract me, damn it. I want my friends to meet you. I want you to hear my artists. I want this to be real."

He pondered that. "How long is this conference?"

"Four days. Thursday through Sunday."

He tapped his fingers on the counter. "I propose a compromise."

"Yeah? Lay it on me."

"How about I come to the conference Saturday night, see Eoin's showcase, and experience your life Sunday. Then Monday we go sailing for a few days. Deal?"

My heart soared. "Deal. That sounds amazing."

"Great," he said. "I'll call the guy and make the reservation. Now, let me put this in the oven and wash my hands so I can touch you properly." He scrubbed and rinsed his hands and pulled me into a tight embrace. I felt the emotional intensity in his hard, urgent grip, and gave it right back to him. Clinging like a vine.

"I'm glad we're doing this," I said. "It makes me feel like there's hope for us."

He was so quiet for so long, apprehension gripped me. "Sorry," I said, through gritted teeth. "Forget I said that, if it makes you uncomfortable."

"It's all right," he said. "I'm hoping for that, too."

Huh. Didn't seem like he was hoping too hard, judging from his tone, but a girl could try. I buried my face against his sweater and hung on with all my strength.

As if strength had anything to do with hanging on to a man's love.

Chapter Twenty-Five

John adjusted the angle of the flexible head of the video camera he was threading between the slats of the heating vent, checking the monitor to be sure it would cover the whole miserable little apartment.

He was in a foul mood, and had been ever since that bruising encounter with the asshole carpenter who'd taken it upon himself to be Nancy D'Onofrio's champion. Knightly had been an unpleasant surprise, causing John to lose even more face with his employer—something he could ill afford to do. For that, Knightly would die screaming. After this shitbag job was behind him, he would take care of that little item. The carpenter's gruesome death would be a personal side project. There were occasional things he did purely for love of the craft, not for the money.

But first, the money. And the helpless, luscious, fuckable D'Onofrio girls.

He'd taken care of the worthless turd he'd hired for local backup, but that did nothing to satisfy the bloodlust raging inside him, which made it uncomfortably hard to concentrate.

That had been just a matter of taking out the garbage before it began to stink. Pure practicality. No element of recreation, so it blew off no steam.

He looked around Nancy D'Onofrio's wretched apartment and quickly concluded that she hadn't located the sketches, or she'd be living much better than this. He'd searched her sister Antonella's apartment in Brooklyn the day before. It was lined with books rather than CDs, but had more or less the same pathetic square footage. He'd searched every nook and cranny, studied every scrap of correspondence, and rigged watching and listening devices.

Vivien, of course, was currently unhoused, crashing with her sister. He'd been through her ramshackle van, but had found nothing of interest.

The carpenter's house was the next step, but patience was key to not getting caught or killed. Hard though that was to justify to a demanding boss.

They were always home, and the carpenter never left her alone. No doubt the dirty pig was fucking her for most of the day. John didn't blame the guy. God knows, he was looking forward to his turn. He thought about that a lot as he sat in the woods, staring through binoculars at the carpenter's house.

His search of the D'Onofrio daughters' living spaces had turned up nothing useful. The time had come to make another attempt upon the D'Onofrio daughters themselves. At first, he'd leaned toward the younger ones, who were more careless and distracted, but his instincts prodded him in the direction of the oldest daughter. If one of them knew something, she would probably know the most. Besides, having her snatched from his jaws had sharpened his appetite for her to a knife's edge. He was constantly imagining it. Her, beneath him, begging and struggling and writhing.

Knightly couldn't afford to hover over her forever. Eventually, he would falter. And John would be ready.

His phone chirped, and he cursed. He'd hacked Nancy's phone so that he could monitor her voicemail, and the app alerted him any time a new message was left for her. He now knew far too much about the personal and professional problems of the musicians she represented. They had bored him to the point of wondering if he should obliterate the whole entitled, whining pack of them, just to make them shut up. But that was just his frustration talking. He had to stay under the radar. He selected the most recent message and played it back.

"Hey, Nancy," a woman said. "This is Andrea. I've been calling your cell, but it's not on, which seems odd. Anyhow, I hope you're checking messages. I'm just calling to tell you that I'm really sorry, but you're going to have to find some other cat-sitter for Moxie. I decided to take a personal-leave day and drive up to Boston Thursday night so I can see Freedy's showcase. I know I promised you kitty coverage, but Freedy and I get so little time together as it is, you know? Hope you don't have problems finding another solution. See you at the conference. Bye!"

Boston? Conference? John went back to Nancy's cluttered desk and shuffled with his plastic-gloved hands through the paperwork scattered over it, looking for something that had flickered at the edge of his attention. Ah, yes. There it was.

A conference program for The FolkWorld Conference. Thursday through Sunday. The Amory Lodge Hotel in Boston. It would be crowded, but she would be distracted, and open to meeting new people, schmoozing, networking. Interesting.

Nancy D'Onofrio was about to have the networking experience of a lifetime.

Chapter Twenty-Six

Nancy

I leaned over the counter in the Amory Lodge lobby. "Are there any messages for me?"

The desk clerk rolled her eyes. "Not in the past fifteen minutes."

Damn. Liam had told me he would arrive around eight. It was a quarter to nine, and Peter and Enid's showcase was scheduled for nine-thirty.

I looked up to find Enid bearing down on me in full performance regalia: a velvet miniskirt, cleavage bulging out of her black leather vest, her hair a mass of luxurious blow-dried curls. "Peter forgot to pack my new mic!" she wailed. "I just spent a thousand bucks on that thing!"

"You bought a thousand-dollar mic before paying me back for the registration fees?" I said wryly. "Seriously?"

"I couldn't sing 'The Far Shore' with that piece of crap! It sounds like I'm singing in a public bathroom!"

I sighed. "This hotel is crawling with musicians who have

good mics. Think of someone who owes you a favor." My eyes flicked to Enid's cleavage. "Shouldn't be that hard," I muttered, and then felt immediately ashamed of myself.

"Hey," came Liam's deep voice from behind me.

I whirled around. There he was, large as life, in a crisp white shirt, jeans, and a long, elegant black coat. Incredibly handsome.

Enid simpered. "Aren't you going to introduce me, Nance?"

I suppressed an impulse to smack that sugary smile right off her face. "Enid, this is Liam Knightly, a friend of mine. Liam, Enid Morrow, one of my clients."

"Delighted," Enid cooed, holding out her hand.

He shook it politely. "You must be Peter's wife."

Enid smiled brilliantly. "Nancy must have told you all about us!"

"Of course." He turned back to me. "Sorry I'm late. I hit traffic." He gave me a hard, possessive kiss right in Enid's face.

An uncontrollable grin spread over my face. "I'm just glad you're here."

My whole body was smiling. Every cell, every atom, every photon of me was happy to see him. He was the handsomest man in the room. By a factor of ten.

"You're just in time to hear our showcase," Enid announced.

"Wouldn't miss it."

"Find Eugene and ask if you can use a Mandrake mic," I suggested. "I think I saw him in the restaurant about ten minutes ago."

A pout marred Enid's heart-shaped face. "Can you take care of it? I have to touch up my makeup and make sure Peter's dressed properly."

"Okay," I said. "I'll do it."

Enid scampered toward the elevators, casting a dimpled smile back at Liam.

I grabbed his hand and towed him toward the restaurant. "Sorry to rush you, but I've got to catch Eugene and chase down that mic."

Liam's fingers curled possessively around mine. "He left you for her?" he said, in an incredulous tone.

I tried to wipe the satisfied grin off my face, with no success. So Enid's sex-kitten appeal didn't affect him. Well, great. My mood soared.

"Pick up the pace," I urged. "I've only got ten minutes to save the world."

He swung me around into a corner alcove full of vending machines. "If you've got ten, you can spare one of them to kiss me. That leaves nine to save the world. For you, that's a generous margin."

He kissed me until I was soft, hazy, and glowing. "Wait. What was I supposed to be doing?" I asked, dazed.

He leaned his forehead against mine and kissed my nose. "The mic. From Eugene. For Enid," he said dutifully.

"Oh, God." I took off running.

He tagged after me companionably as I ran my errands, and finally we were seated in the back of the hall, my hand tucked in Liam's. Peter and Enid were great, and the band that backed them played with energy and precision. When the plaintive strains of "The Road to You" died away, the applause was long and loud.

I nudged Liam as I clapped. "What do you think?"

His face was noncommittal. "Better than I expected."

I tugged on his hand. "Let's congratulate them. Come on."

Enid spotted Liam's tall form first, and she bounced toward them, beaming, her eyes expectantly on Liam. "Hey! Did you like the show?"

"Yes, I enjoyed it very much," he said politely.

Enid took him by the arm, pulling him toward where Peter sat, fingering his guitar. I trailed uncomfortably behind. "Hey, Petey! Meet Liam, Nancy's new friend," Enid said.

Peter's head whipped around. His eyes narrowed. "Ah. So you're the guy who spirited away our manager the most important week of the year?"

Liam gently extricated his arm from Enid's grip. "And you're the guy who left her at the altar and mooches money off her."

Peter's mouth dropped open. He glanced at Nancy, his face looking utterly betrayed. "Who does this asshole think he is?" he hissed.

I pushed closer, horrified. "Peter, I'm sorry. He—"

"Don't tell me. Don't want to know." He grabbed Enid's arm. "Come on, baby. Let's network." Enid shot a bewildered glance over her shoulder as he dragged her away.

I stared after them, aghast. "Liam! What the hell have you done?"

The expression in Liam's eyes was absolutely unapologetic.

I walked away from him, quickly, but Liam kept pace. No matter how fast I went, his stride lengthened to match it.

I kept my back to him in the elevator. I was horrified. I'd known he was opinionated, but this was wantonly destructive. Damaging for me.

Once out of the elevator, he stalked beside me with catlike grace to my room door, waiting as I fumbled for the key. I unlocked it and stumbled inside. The door *ka-thunked* shut behind us.

Liam flipped on the light by the door. "Okay," he said. "Let me have it."

"I cannot believe what you just said!" I exploded. "I told you those things in confidence! I had no idea when I invited you here that you would do your best to sabotage my professional life!"

He frowned. "I didn't mean to sabotage you. I just told it like it was. And about time, too."

"About time for what? To ruin my career? Are you trying deliberately to do that?"

"No," he said. "For a reality check. Peter and Enid are vampires. They suck you dry. And you don't react. You don't draw the line."

"But timing! Why say that right after an important gig, in the earshot of other agents and managers and concert-series presenters? It's a terrible time to—"

"There's never a good time, Nancy."

I plowed on. "Grace, delicacy, and minding your own goddamn business. These are crucial earmarks of maturity."

"So call me immature." The label clearly did not bother him.

I crossed my arms over my chest. "Liam, if I didn't know better, I'd think you were jealous."

He grunted low in his throat. "I'll tell you who's jealous. Peter. He's jealous of me. Afraid of losing you. Or at least, losing control of you."

I gaped at him, bewildered. "No way! Peter's got Enid now, which means he definitely has his hands full! And besides—"

"I got his number the minute I laid eyes on him. 'You're the guy who spirited away our manager,'" he mimicked in a voice so much like Peter's, I almost betrayed myself by smiling, but I caught myself just in time. "Peter and I are old friends. We have a lot of history. It's normal that there's ambivalence—"

"Ambivalence?" His voice was heavy with sarcasm. "For the first time, he doesn't get to have his cake and eat it, too. He took advantage of you when you were together. Then he met Enid, and he wanted her, too, so he figured out a sneaky way to keep you both. It's the perfect setup. You, to do all the scutwork and the secretarial stuff, to get him the gigs, and make sure he gets paid. Enid to suck his dick and fluff his ego. Nobody will give you the respect you deserve for free, Nancy. You've got to demand it. You've got to put your foot down."

I opened her mouth in automatic denial, then closed it.

A dull pain in my belly told her that it was the truth. An ugly, dangerous, ill-timed truth.

"Maybe you're right," I said. "But it was wrong to say it out there. Putting me on the spot. It embarrassed everyone. And reflected very badly on me."

Liam shrugged. Right or wrong, he did not care.

An aching silence spread out between us. I wanted to howl in frustration. "So what do you expect me to do about it?"

"Get rid of them," he said. "Fire their asses."

I snorted. "It's not that simple. They're my clients, Liam, not my employees. And they're also my—"

"Friends, right." His voice was heavily laced with irony.

"Yes! They are! Friendship is complicated. It's never perfect!"

"They suck you dry, and they don't even thank you. They're spoiled children. They don't deserve you. Get rid of them."

"Liam, you can't just fire your friends. You have to find solutions, compromises."

"No, you don't."

I gazed into his grim, unreadable face. "You're not very good at compromise, are you, Liam?" I asked slowly.

His silence answered for him.

I clenched my hands. "I can't deal with this conversation right now. I'm busy. So either keep your mouth zipped around my colleagues, or leave. Understood?"

Liam started to speak, stopped himself. He nodded.

I braced myself. "What does that mean? Does that mean you're staying?"

"I'll stay," he said.

I let out my breath in a sigh of relief. So this wasn't the wall. Not quite. We'd gotten a reprieve. I pulled my key card out of my pocket and handed it to him. "Here. Get another one made at the front desk and get yourself settled. Mandrake plays in about an hour. Same hall as Peter and Enid's showcase. See you there." I opened the door and turned to him. "Liam?"

"Yes?" His voice was wary.

I searched for words to express the yearning in my chest. The hope. How I was so glad to see him, how much I missed him, wanted him. Maybe even loved him.

"Nothing," I whispered as I slipped through the door.

Chapter Twenty-Seven

Liam

I strode down the corridor, my mouth sour with self-disgust.

Being rude to her ex had been bad enough, but spouting preachy crap to Nancy was even worse. Telling her how to conduct her business. Like I had the right.

Damn. I mouthed the word as I stabbed the elevator button. A blue-haired old lady gave me a nervous look and a wide berth. Good instincts. I was an animal tonight. Totally lacking in social skills.

If I could get through the conference without any fuckups or fistfights, I would be rewarded by four days of solitude with Nancy. The elevator pinged. Almost time for the Mandrake showcase. I headed toward the hall.

"Hey, Liam!"

I turned to see Eoin leaning against the wall, freckles standing out in sharp relief in his pale face. I clasped his hand, which was ice cold. "Nancy told me you would be playing. I've been looking forward to it. How's it going?"

Eoin shrugged. "I don't know. We've only rehearsed three times."

I slapped him on the back. "You'll be great. You're amazing. Don't worry."

Eugene and a tall, skinny black guy came charging down the hall, looking excited and self-important. "Come on, man, let's do it!" Eugene said to Eoin as they surrounded him and bore him swiftly away.

"Break a leg!" I called. Eoin shot a final desperate glance over his shoulder. I gave the kid a thumbs-up.

I went into the crowded hall. No chairs left. Nancy was on the other side of the room, talking to Matt, the big redhead that I'd met at the seisiún at Malloy's.

She turned, saw me, and gave me a tentative smile.

I smiled back. Her smile became brilliant. God, she was fine, dressed up in one of her sleek, fitted black outfits, hair pulled into a braided bun, earrings dangling to her jaw. She made every other woman in the room look commonplace. That airhead Enid looked insipid in comparison.

The lights dimmed. Mandrake came onstage to tremendous applause. The lanky black guy laid down a complex, primal rhythm, and Eoin promptly launched into a fiery Irish reel, followed by Matt and Eugene on the guitar and fiddle, and finally a scrawny blond girl who played an endless variety of wind instruments.

They were excellent. I applauded after each piece till my hands stung. The pulsing energy of the music soothed something raw and savage inside me. I was fiercely glad that Eoin had fallen in with this group. They would keep him happy and busy until he found his feet in this country.

After the set finished, I pushed my way through the crush and gave Eoin a quick, hard embrace.

"Great job," I said. "You kicked ass. No surprise."

Eoin grinned. "Thanks," was all he had time to say before he was surrounded by chattering, congratulating people.

Something poked me in the back, and I looked around to find Nancy smiling at me. "Weren't they fine?"

"Excellent." I swept her into my arms. "I'm sorry I was a dick," I whispered.

I offered up a prayer of gratitude as her body softened, went pliant in my arms. I'd gotten through the crisis. This wasn't the wall. There was still time, still grace.

My arms tightened hungrily around her. "Do you have more to do tonight?"

She looked up at me seductively through her eyelashes. "Theoretically, I could network for hours. But I don't have any actual appointments until tomorrow."

I saw Peter scowling at me from across the room. I grinned, baring all my teeth, and nipped Nancy's ear possessively. "How long has it been since you've eaten?"

She looked clouded. "Um ..."

I rolled my eyes. "For God's sake, Nancy."

"Don't scold. Let's get something. Want to ask Eoin and the others if they—"

"No. I want to be alone with you. I missed you." I leaned over, sucked in a whiff of her perfume. "You smell good."

She lifted up onto her tiptoes and kissed my lips. "I missed you, too."

Dinner options were scarce at that hour, but we found an all-night pizza place that delivered. It arrived in our room shortly afterward, and I watched with approval as she enthusiastically devoured several slices of pizza.

"Wow." Nancy licked her fingers. "Yum. Didn't know how hungry I was."

"No wonder people take advantage of you," I chided. "You never eat. It takes energy to put your foot down."

She gave me a narrow, warning look. "Uh-oh," she said. "Don't you dare go off the rails again, Liam. Unless you want to ruin this for us."

I held up my hands. "I don't," I said. "Sorry. So the conference is going well?"

"Excellently." She was fishing for a clean napkin, so I found some under the pizza box and handed them to her. "I've given out tons of promo packets. We'll get bookings. The showcases all went well. I had them all recorded. Eoin will have a high-quality demo, if he wants to gig outside of Mandrake. I'm sure he'll be getting offers right and left."

"That's great," I said.

She took a sip of her soda, eyeing me over the cup. "I've been thinking about our conversation," she offered. "In some ways, you're right. But in others—"

"Let's let it go," I offered swiftly. "I was out of line."

She studied me with those wide, leaf-colored eyes. "Somewhat out of line," she conceded. She took her cell out of her purse, made a show of turning it off. She got up. "Have to wash off pizza grease," she murmured, disappearing into the bathroom.

As soon as the door closed, in the spirit of overkill, I pinched the phone jack of the room phone out of its socket. This was a delicate moment, and I didn't want anyone to interrupt it, from any direction.

I peeled off my shirt to save time and followed her into the bathroom where she was patting her face dry with a towel. Her eyes locked with mine in the mirror, full of longing.

I reached around, trapping her against my body. I plucked off her glasses, pulled her hairpins out, unraveled the coiled braided hair, and smoothed the crimped waves over her shoulders. She was just so damn beautiful.

I wrenched my belt loose, tore off the rest of my clothes.

Nancy gave me that secret sorceress smile that drove me wild and glanced down at my huge erection.

She patted it. "Ever ready," she murmured.

"For you, always," I said. "I live to serve."

I tugged the snug black sweater out of her jeans and peeled it off over her head. Her bra was silvery green, a sheer, lacy thing.

"Wow," I said. "Look at that. Fancy underwear."

Her eyes glowed. "I was hoping I might get lucky."

I unhooked the bra and tossed it away, ran my hands over her velvety softness, feeling the muscles moving sinuously beneath it, staring at the translucent perfection of her high, luscious breasts. "I'm the lucky one," I said. "God. You're so beautiful."

She smiled at me, her eyes catching mine in the mirror, and we both laughed.

"See? I'm making progress, aren't I?" she teased. "I no longer flip out and get all uptight and scared when you say that."

"I want you to know it in your bones," he said.

Her gaze slid away, and she blushed. She liked to hear me say it, but she didn't believe it, not completely. I could see it in her eyes. It made my chest ache. I couldn't get past that invisible barrier inside her. Her caution ran so deep, it was beyond my reach.

I slid my hand down over her belly to the downy tuft of hair between her legs and eased my finger between her tender folds, stroking against that tight, furled slit. "I wish you could see what I see when I look at you," I told her.

Nancy twisted in my arms and looked up at him. Her gaze had suddenly become very focused. "We'll keep at it, then. Things take time. Right?"

We were gripped by tension. "Right," he said hoarsely.

I sank to my knees and buried my face against the hot fuzz of ringlets crowning her pussy. I pried her legs wider—just wide enough to slide my tongue along her pussy seam, teasing and fluttering her clit, thrusting to taste her hot, rich flavor.

I kept at it until she shivered, arched, and cried out, shuddering with her release.

I picked her up and carried her into the other room. Flung her onto the bed. Touching her, kissing her, spreading her out and loving her again with my lips and tongue, again and again. Making her sigh and sob and clutch at me, begging.

When I finally rolled on top of her, she wrapped her strong, shapely thighs around me, taking me in completely. I felt licked by flames of pure pleasure, each stroke an agony of delight, each thrust more perfect than the one before. I clutched her, lost to it, moving with her desperately. My heartbeat clamoring in my ears.

Things took time. Hell yes, they did. All the time she liked. The more time the better.

Forever would suit me fine.

Chapter Twenty-Eight

Nancy

Someone was pounding on my door, and had been pounding for a while. I struggled out of a dream that had a great deal of pounding in it. Liam stirred as I slid out of bed.

I found my nightshirt and slipped it on as I went for the door.

I pulled it open and beheld Peter and Enid, who looked electrified.

"Good God, Nancy! You're not dressed!" Enid peeked into the room, eyes widening as they landed on Liam sitting on the bed, dressed only in his jeans. "Remember yesterday at the Exhibition Hall when you were talking to the promoter for the Jericho Arts Center in D.C.? Where Bonnie Blair is opening next week?"

"Uh, yes, of course. I gave him a packet. He seemed interested in an opening act sometime," I said, rubbing my eyes.

"That's just it! Sammy Phillips with the Phelps Bay Blues

Band was opening for Bonnie, but he wrecked his car yester-day, and—"

"Oh, no!" Dismay shocked me to full consciousness. "Sammy had an accident?"

"Don't worry, Sammy'll be fine," Peter said impatiently. "But he broke his collarbone. Enid and I were having a drink at the bar, and the promoter came up and asked if we're free Wednesday. I told him, are we ever!"

I was wide awake now. "Opening for Bonnie Blair? At the Jericho? *This* Wednesday?"

Enid and Peter nodded, identical grins splitting their faces. "Is that spectacular, or what?" Peter crowed.

"That's incredible! I've got to get on the phone to the presenter. To all the venues in D.C., Maryland, and Virginia. And get pictures to the press."

"But that's not all," Enid said. "There's more. Get this, Nance. There just happened to be this exec from MGM Studios in Hollywood staying at the hotel, and he heard our showcase! He loved it!"

"Hollywood?" I rubbed my stinging eyes. "Excuse me?"

"His name is Maitland Sills, and he's going to put his production department in touch with us," Enid burbled. "He says 'The Far Shore' is perfect for the closing credits of a big-budget feature film they're producing! Talk to him pronto, because he's leaving for Logan Airport in an hour. He's got a meeting this afternoon in L.A."

"Holy crap," I said slowly. "Why didn't you call me?"

Enid and Peter exchanged glances. "Your phone was turned off," they said in unison.

"I would've introduced you to Sills right after the showcase, but you vanished," Peter sounded long-suffering. His eyes flicked over my shoulder, to Liam.

"Why not call the room?" I demanded. "You knew my room number!"

"We tried," Enid said, her voice aggrieved. "It was disconnected."

My head whipped around to check. Sure enough, the jack of the room phone had been disconnected. I stared at it, horrified. Liam met my gaze and gave me an unapologetic shrug.

Tension gathered in my neck. My throat tightened.

"See what I'm saying?" Peter sounded triumphant. "Focus, Nance. No distractions. You'll come to the Jericho gig, right?"

"I definitely should," I said.

"It's finally happening, Nance!" Enid said excitedly. "We're going to totally slay!"

Liam moved around in the room behind me, and I suddenly remembered our sailboat plans. "Oh. Wait. I, um, did have plans for the next few days," I said.

Liam's muscular back was to me as he rifled through his overnight bag.

"Postpone 'em," Peter said, waving a dismissive hand. "This is the chance of a lifetime. Nothing trumps this."

"Yeah," I said, glancing anxiously around.

Peter followed my gaze. His face hardened. "He's not coming with us."

"Don't worry." Liam's voice was remote. "Wouldn't dream of it."

Peter made an impatient sound. "Good. So? Enid will go down and stall Maitland Sills while you get yourself together. But hurry! See you in a few."

I shut the door and turned to face Liam.

His face looked as hard as a mask. "So we can forget our plans, I take it."

I pressed my fist against my mouth. Shit, shit, *shit*. "I'm sorry, Liam, but everything has to stop for this gig. I'll be on the phone nonstop for days to publicize—"

"I understand perfectly."

Hope stirred briefly. "You do?"

"Of course. I should never have put down a deposit. It was stupid. There's always going to be something more important for you. Always."

Hope shriveled and died. I stared at his averted face as he fished under the bed for his shoes. "Liam, I would love to go on this trip! Let's do it when I get back!"

"That's the thing," he said. "We won't. Something else will come up. And something else after that. I know that tune by heart."

"We're not listening to the same tune," I said. "Besides, we couldn't keep up this eternal vigilance routine much longer anyhow. I understand the feelings behind it, but we both have to make money, and this is the biggest—"

He held up his hand. "Stop. You're just making it worse."

My knees weakened with dread. "We've ... we've hit that wall, haven't we?"

Liam dragged a shirt over his head and tucked it into his jeans with swift, economical motions. "We are roadkill," he said.

I laid my hand on his chest. "Liam. It can't be over just because of this. This is stupid. This is just bad timing. That's all!"

He stepped back, and my hand dropped, with nothing to hold on to. My jaw trembled. "I was starting to think we had a chance," I said.

"So come sailing with me." His voice was hard and cold. "You can't, can you? Of course not. You'll never prioritize that. You've made your choice. Own it."

"Liam, I've been working for this moment for my whole adult life!"

"So good luck with it." He took the revolver from the back of his jeans, opened the cylinder and shook the bullets out into his hand. He tossed the empty gun into his bag and looked up at me, his eyes flinty cold. "Better start making those phone calls. No time to lose. And don't you have a producer downstairs to schmooze with?"

"Wow," I whispered. "You are the most rigid, uncompromising person I have ever known."

"Remember what I said last night, about putting my foot down? This is what that looks like. I never said it was pleasant."

"And you don't care what gets crushed under your boot?"

He shrugged on his coat. "This conversation is over."

I grabbed his arm. "You can't just cut me off, Liam!"

He wrenched away, a muscle in his jaw pulsing. "I'll do what has to be done." He walked out, and the door thunked shut behind him.

I sank down onto the bed, shaking. Wrapped in the deafening silence.

Chapter Twenty-Nine

John scanned the shifting crowds. His face itched from the fake goatee, and he sweated heavily in the overheated hall as he listened with half an ear to the self-serving prattle of the blond slut singer.

He'd begun to fantasize about shutting her up definitively. After she'd delivered the services she was so blatantly advertising with the rolling eyes and the heaving tits. At least she wouldn't be chattering while she did that. He'd keep that shiny pink mouth way too busy to talk.

Where the fuck was Nancy, anyway? He did not want to converse with these idiot musicians any longer than was necessary. He was good at improvising a smooth, convincing rap, but his ruse as a Hollywood movie producer was a thin one. Anyone asking the right questions would cop to it in no time.

Fortunately, Enid Morrow was too stupid and self-absorbed to ask the right questions. And Nancy herself would never get the chance to ask them. He fingered the transparent gel capsule in his pocket. A designer drug, exactly calibrated for her size and weight. But where the fuck was she?

He had to get on with it. Instinct was pricking and prodding, saying *now, now, now*. Even with people around, if he started the job at the right moment and pushed on through, hard and swift and decisive, they would probably be too absorbed in their own shit to figure out what was happening. All they'd notice would be a confusing kerfuffle, a brief swell in the noise level, and *voilá*. Back to normal. Nothing to see here.

"... sorry that she's so late this morning. It's totally unlike her," the slut singer burbled.

He smiled, staring at her tits. She obligingly arched her lumbar spine to facilitate his view. "I just hope I have a chance to discuss it with her before I go," he said. "I wanted to present this idea to my team in L.A. this afternoon. Get the ball rolling."

"Of course," Enid cooed. "It's, like, fate! That you happened to be at the hotel by pure chance, and heard us play!"

"Yes, it is." He scanned the room with his peripheral vision beyond the halo of blond ringlets in the foreground.

There! Looking pale and tousled and waiflike, her hair streaming loose. Last night's makeup smudged around her huge eyes. She must not have even taken a shower. Probably had Knightly's nasty spunk still inside her body. Dirty bitch.

His heart rate quickened, his mouth watered, his dick stiffened. His instincts, his senses sharpening. God, he loved this part. She was his succulent little rabbit, and he was the hawk, poised to dive and rend.

Enid craned her neck. The effort popped her bosom further out. "There she is! I'll introduce you, Maitland—can I call you Maitland?"

"Of course," he said. She hooked her arm around his elbow and towed him through the room. Aw. How sweet. His new little best friend.

"Hey! Nancy! This is Maitland! He's the producer I was telling you about from MGM Studios!" Enid sang out.

Nancy looked over at her, her face oddly blank. "Huh? Oh. Enid, hi. Have you seen Liam?"

Enid's jaw dropped. "Um, not lately, Nancy," she said, in a warning tone. "Focus, please. Did you hear me? Maitland Sills? The guy from MGM Studios? Hollywood? Hello? Earth to Nancy?"

But Nancy kept rising onto her tiptoes, her gaze sweeping the room. "Hollywood," she said faintly. "That's nice. Could you folks excuse me for a sec?"

"Nancy!" Enid hissed. "Don't be an idiot!"

"I'll just be a moment. I have to check something in the hall." She slipped like an eel through the crowd and disappeared.

The predator inside him howled and gnashed its teeth.

Enid caught the vibe and shot him a nervous look. "Um, alrighty, then. I'm sure she'll be right back. Say, how about if you just meet with me and Peter? We can speak for ourselves when it comes to big career decisions, if Nancy's not available. Just come with me." She began to tug on his arm.

Nancy had disappeared. The moment might be lost. The slut singer babbled, with a smile he wanted to knock right off her doll-like face. She tugged harder.

His patience came to an abrupt end. He yanked his arm away, and she teetered backward on her spike heels. "What the hell?" she squawked.

He stared into her eyes. "Get the fuck out of my way, you dumb slut." He put a vicious punch of venom behind each softly uttered word.

Enid shrank away, eyes huge, stammering.

He forgot her utterly the second he turned his back on her

and hurried after his prey, blood pumping fast and hot and hungry.

Chapter Thirty

Liam

I avoided Peter Morrow's hostile gaze as I strode through the lobby. I couldn't be bothered to glare back. I was caught in the guts of some big machine, and it would keep grinding whether I was smashed to a pulp in its gears or not.

I didn't want to leave her alone, not with those masked assholes gunning for her. I didn't want to leave her at all. But her safety was no longer my problem.

It never really had been. She wasn't my wife, my fiancée, even my girlfriend. She never would be, because real, lasting relationships weren't based on fleeting perfect moments. Orgasms, long winding conversations, pancakes. Goofy, giggling fights over the relative merits of coffee or tea.

Relationships were based on solid things. Respect. Shared interests. Compatible life goals. Bone-deep trust. Being there for each other. Being on the same page.

Damn. That thought felt so tired and used up as it ran

through my mind. Like I'd thought it a thousand times before and had done it to death. It was limp. Dog-eared.

"Liam!" Eoin bounded across the room toward me like a jackrabbit on crack, his eyes lit up like flashlights in his skinny face. He had partied all night long, but he was still revved as ever. "Hey, what's up?" He looked at my bag, puzzled. "I thought you were staying till tomorrow!"

"Can't," I said, though my mouth felt dusty and dry. "Gotta go."

"Oh. Well, I'm glad I saw you now, then. A favor before you go, eh? I've been telling Eugene about that set of reels you wrote. I remember 'The Dusty Shoon,' and 'Traveler's Joy,' but not the B and C parts of 'The Old Man's Beard.'"

My stomach curdled in dismay. "I have to go. Another time."

"Oh, man, please?" Eoin entreated. "It'll only take five minutes. Eugene can record it. I had this great arrangement worked out, and the lads love it!"

My jaw ached from clenching so hard. "I don't have my fiddle."

"Eugene will lend you his!" Eoin's eyes pleaded. "Five minutes?"

Christ on a crutch. Five minutes of stomach-churning agony. But I didn't want to burden Eoin by telling him that the world had just ended for me. That would be awkward and unfair. This was Eoin's big day, and he should celebrate.

I let myself be towed into a conference room, and obligingly tucked Eugene's fiddle under my chin. Composed myself as I launched into "The Old Man's Beard."

The kid was having a great time. Let him fly, as far as the air currents would take him. A guy crashed down to earth soon enough.

Chapter Thirty-One

Liam wasn't in the lobby. Nor in the parking lot. Nor in the showcase halls, or the alcoves, or the vending machine corners, or the lounge, or the gift shop, or the restaurant. He was gone.

Sadness settled over me, like a smothering blanket. I'd come to depend on him for feeling good. The world looked wretched—empty, flat, boring—without him. I was so angry. I wanted to break windows, smash furniture. What the hell was that stunt he'd pulled, pulling the phone out of the wall without telling me? At a professional networking event? That was manipulative. Controlling boyfriend territory. A huge, scary red flag. A deal-breaker, right there, all on its own merits, but it was piled on top of a bunch of other deal-breakers. A whole mountain of them.

I couldn't have caved to his demands. It took two to make a compromise. If I blew off an opportunity like this out of fear of losing him, I would never respect myself again. And in the end, he wouldn't respect me for it, either.

And that reflection did not help me one little bit.

"Ms. D'Onofrio? Are you all right?"

I dashed away my tears and looked over my shoulder. "Huh? What?"

"Can I help? Can I get you something?"

I blinked back the tears, tried to focus. Oh, yeah. Okay. This was Enid's Hollywood studio exec. Big, beefy guy. Muscle going to fat. He had a sleek black goatee on his broad face, gleaming black hair. His eyes were full of concern.

I vaguely remembered this guy was significant, for some reason. Oh, wait. I was supposed to be kissing his ass. I was so completely not in the right head space for that.

"No," I whispered. "Thanks, I'm fine." I dug around in my pocket for a tissue. It was coming back to me now. Studio exec. Time crunch. Plane, leaving for L.A.

"I'm sorry," I said. "We were supposed to have a meeting, right?"

"Yes, but it's all right. I can see you're not well," the guy said.

My spine stiffened with embarrassment. "No, I'm fine. You've got a plane to catch, right? Let's just go to the bar and have a cup of coffee."

But Sills led her past the bar and into the restaurant. He walked briskly past the few free booths and sat down in the strangest spot—a table, not a booth, and way in the back. It was out of sight to all but a few of the booths, but annoyingly close to the kitchen door, which continually swung open as tray-laden waitresses bumped and bashed their way through with their hips and elbows to carry out breakfast orders.

The waitress brought us a carafe of coffee. Maitland Sills poured and pushed the cup across the table. "You look tired," he said.

I took a deep, grateful gulp of coffee. "It's been quite a night," I said.

I knew in just a couple of seconds that something was wrong. A numb, crawling feeling spread from the tips of my toes and fingers, creeping swiftly inward toward my core. I heard my heart beating loud and fast in my ears. I couldn't move. I fought to breathe as my vision dimmed. What the hell? Was this a panic attack?

Then I looked into the eyes of the MGM studio exec, and my insides contracted. A flash of understanding that came too late. Those dark eyes, fixed and cold and avid. Snake-like. That mouth, so fleshy and wet. He licked his lips.

My eyes fluttered, and in those brief eyelid flickers, I saw like tiny film clips the monstrous thing he was beneath his human mask. Something twisted and foul.

His breath smelled like death.

He leaned forward, his low voice like a snake's hiss. "Do you wonder what your mother's last words were when she was gasping on the floor, Nancy?" he crooned. "Do you want me to tell you?"

I tried to open my mouth, scream for help. Nothing worked.

A waitress burst through the kitchen door and bustled right past us without looking at us. I couldn't speak or raise my hand to get her attention. The open door to the kitchen let in a swell of noise. The volume diminished again as it swung shut.

He reached across the table, seized the pendant Lucia had given me. The burn of the chain around my throat kept me conscious. *Snap.* It broke. He pocketed it.

He got up, came around the table, and reached for me.

Chapter Thirty-Two

"Let us by!" John bawled. "Move over! She's going to be sick!"

He shoved his way through the snarl of employees in the restaurant kitchen. Nancy stumbled alongside him, nearly unconscious. He'd plastered her own hand over her mouth to muffle any sounds she might make, clamping his own hand on top of it. Her hair dangled down to hide her face. He dragged her past a waitress carrying a loaded tray, jostling her hard enough to make her stumble.

Plates of eggs Benedict flew, splattered. Shouts of protest and yammering scolding screams. He hustled on, bellowing, "She's going to be sick!" whenever anyone tried to interact with him, and burst out the kitchen entrance. He loped past the dumpsters toward the corner and the hotel parking lot.

He dragged her into the shrubbery, doubled over, and let her drop to the ground, right next to a big fiberglass instrument case that he'd planted there at four a.m. the previous morning. It was a case for an upright bass. Big enough to carry a slender, curled-up woman.

He made barfing, choking noises, for the benefit of any employees who might have poked their heads out of the kitchen. Probably unnecessary after the mess he'd made. They'd be too busy cleaning up and replacing orders to pay attention to him.

He snapped open the case in feverish haste and followed his choreography. Rip off goatee and wig. Shove them into the case. Shake out his shaggy dark hair. Strip off the jacket. Replace it with a fringed yellow leather coat and aviator sunglasses.

He scooped up the D'Onofrio woman, dumped her slight, limp weight into the wide part of the case, folded and tucked her limbs until she fit. Curled up like a chick in an egg. Soft and helpless. Prey.

He did up the clasps, peeked out of the bushes, and yanked the rolling case onto the asphalt. Walking oh so nonchalantly toward his car. He glanced at his watch. From restaurant table to parking lot, barely over three minutes. Pretty good. He forced himself to stop grinning. It wouldn't do to get sloppy, self-satisfied, or overexcited.

Time enough for excitement later. When it was time to indulge.

Chapter Thirty-Three

Liam

A big-name showcase was about to begin, and I'd gotten stuck in the crowd on my way out. I shoved my way through the crush, having finally extricated myself from Mandrake's clutches. Something inside me was pulled tight, and it kept getting steadily worse. When that part of me finally snapped, I did not know what was going to happen. I just knew that I didn't want it to happen in public.

A high-pitched commotion was taking place. I tried to wiggle around it, but the press of bodies filing into the hall was too thick. It was the singer who was married to the butthead. Enid. She was having a snit fit. I didn't want to know the details, but someone was wheeling a fucking piano into the hall, and it blocked my way.

"... cannot believe that guy! That asshole! Can you believe what he said to me?" She caught my eye and promptly directed her outrage toward me before I could slink away. "He shoved me!" she shrieked. "And called me a slut! How dare he?"

"Calm down, baby. Don't freak. There are concert presenters everywhere," the butthead pretty boy muttered desperately. "You don't want to look unhinged, okay?"

"Calm down? Screw you, Petey! I was, like, attacked in public, and all you can say is just calm down?" She turned her bulging-eyed gaze to me. "He shoved me!" she repeated shrilly. "I almost fell! Right on my ass!"

"Who shoved you?" I asked her, out of sheer reflexive politeness.

"The producer asshole! But you know what I think? I bet he wasn't a producer at all. I mean, he didn't look like one. He didn't have that Hollywood gloss, you know? Plus, he was big and beefy, and he had bad breath. Like, nobody's beefy with bad breath in Hollywood, right? And why would he want to talk to Nancy, and not to me? I mean, like, I'm the talent, right? She's just—" Enid struggled for a word sufficiently dismissive— "administrative help!"

The hairs on my neck prickled. Ice cold talons sank into my gut.

No. Big beefy guy. Bad breath. Wanted Nancy. Oh no, no, no, no, no.

I grabbed Enid's arm. "Did he go with her? Where did he go?"

She goggled at me, and I gave her arm an impatient little shake.

"Do you mind?" she sniffed, wrenching away from my grip. "He went after her, toward the restaurant. She's welcome to him. Rude, violent, sick son of a bitch!"

"What does he look like?" I demanded.

"Hey!" the butthead blustered. "Don't touch my wife!"

"Fuck off." I didn't even turn to look at him. "What does he look like, Enid? Hair color, eyes? Talk to me, goddammit!"

Enid had started to look scared. "Um, longish black hair,

slicked back?" Her voice had gone small and uncertain. "A goatee, and, um, a black leather jacket."

I lost the rest, already shoving my way through the crowd amidst shouts and grunts of protest. Fear propelled me toward the restaurant at a pounding run.

I'd lose too much time if I stopped to get out the gun and load it. I had to run after her without it. I jogged through the restaurant, checking tables. No Nancy.

Think, meathead. *Think.* The door to the kitchen burst open. A harried-looking waitress came bursting out. Behind her, there was some sort of commotion in the kitchen. People were yelling.

Good enough for me. I pushed through the swinging door. A woman caught sight of me and ran forward, holding up her hands to bar my way.

"Hey! No customers in here!" she yelled. "Get back! Right now!"

"What happened?" I demanded.

"It was so gross!" a girl confided. "This lady was sick to her stomach, and the guy gets the bright idea to drag her through the kitchen? Like, that's so unhygienic! She could have had some disgusting virus, right? The Board of Health could shut us down for—hey! Where are you going? Hey!"

I barreled through the press of people in the kitchen, ignoring shouts of protest. I slipped, arms flailing, in a long, harrowing slalom down the straightaway between two rows of range tops, sliding in a skid of yellowish sauce, barely keeping my feet.

I lurched out the door, reeling. This was a loading bay. Garbage dumpsters. Nothing moving here. I took off, heart thudding, for the parking lot.

I scanned the lot. Saw a harried mother pushing a stroller. A young couple. A retirement-age man and his blue-haired wife getting out of a sedan, arguing. Their raised voices floated over. A big guy with shaggy hair in a yellow fringed coat was rolling a string bass behind him. There was no black-haired goateed guy, no black leather jacket.

No Nancy. Goddamnit. *Think.*

I looked around the parking lot again. The man and his wife passed by, still haranguing each other. Their babble did not penetrate my mind. I stared at the parking lot and everyone in it, feeling with my senses. Trying to still my mind.

Doubts assailed me. Maybe Nancy was in the hall, safe and sound, conducting her business. And I was out here chasing phantoms created by my own overheated brain.

Then again ... maybe not. *Big, beefy guy. Bad breath.*

I gave the yellow-coated man a second look. He slowed to a stop and looked around over his shoulder at me. Sun glinted off his mirrored sunglasses. He looked at me for a second, and then turned away, but when he started to move again, he was moving slightly faster. His big instrument case rattled and bumped behind him.

The case. The fucking *case.* Oh sweet suffering Christ.

I took off running. The guy was opening the hatchback of a longish sedan with its back seats folded down. He heaved the instrument into the vehicle, and slammed the hatchback down. He saw me racing toward him, and dove for the driver's seat.

The motor roared. Brake lights came on. I was screaming. The car started to pull out, but it had to stop and correct. I flung himself at the back of the vehicle and yanked the latch of the hatchback.

It opened. The asshole had been in too much of a hurry to lock it. I flung myself inside, right next to the instrument case, which lay like a deformed coffin in a hearse. The guy screamed back incoherently over his shoulder.

I scrabbled for something to grab on to as the guy backed up with a violent burst of speed and then braked abruptly.

I slid out the back, dragging the case with me. It toppled and rolled on the asphalt.

Bam, the asshole shot at me. I jerked to the side. *Zing,* another bullet ricocheted off the asphalt, dangerously close to the instrument case.

A car window exploded. Glass rattled, tinkled. The upright bass case was lying right behind the vehicle's tires.

I guessed the filthy fuck's intentions on the fly and lunged to heave the case out of harm's way, right before the car roared into reverse to run it over.

We landed between parked cars in the opposite row. I flung myself onto the case, in case the bastard stopped to take another shot at us.

Shouts, screams. People had heard the gun. The SUV peeled away, tires screeching. It tore out of the parking lot, ran a light at the corner, and was gone.

I slid off the case onto my ass, shaking violently. My face was wet. My nose streamed with blood. I turned the case gently right side up and unlatched it with trembling hands. My pounding heart felt like it was lodged in my throat.

Nancy was curled inside the padded interior, hair over her face. I felt her throat, and felt a strong, steady pulse. Oh thank God. Thank God.

I scooped her out into my arms and cradled her. Brushed the hair off her forehead, murmuring her name. Alive. Not shot, not broken, not taken.

I was crying now, like a little kid. I couldn't seem to stop. I just sat there on the ground, while the commotion buzzed around me. Rocking her. Holding her. She was unconscious, after all. She couldn't object to it right now. She would never know.

The ambulance came, and they pried her from my grip and loaded her up onto a gurney. They dragged me along to get checked out as well, and I only consented to that because I couldn't leave Nancy until I was sure that she was surrounded by armed people who understood exactly how much danger she was in.

The next few hours were a blur. I called her sisters. I let the doctors look me over. Everything hurt. I was all bruised up, with a broken nose and cracked ribs, they told me.

Minutes crawled by, which turned to hours. Nancy was still unconscious, which scared the shit out of me.

I told the cops who came to talk to me everything I knew about the kidnapper, including his last attack on Nancy in her stairwell. I told them our conviction that his attacks were connected to Lucia D'Onofrio's death, proof or no proof. They looked skeptical, but I was used to that.

Nell and Vivi finally arrived, and Nancy was still unconscious. I felt almost as if I should make some sort of announcement to them. Explain why I couldn't stay, that I no longer fit into their sister's life. But they just hovered over Nancy, ashen-faced and red-eyed. It was definitely not the moment.

I wanted to leave, but I couldn't, until I was sure she would be okay.

Her eyelids started to flutter. Nell and Vivi started to talk to her excitedly.

That was my cue. I beat hell out of there. I called a rideshare to get me back to my truck, parked in the lot behind the Amory Lodge. I was fiercely glad I'd stopped the asshole from hurting her. I only wished I'd managed to kill the fucker. But this episode only made it clearer to me that I was ass-over-head in love with this woman. No one else would do for me, not ever. It was Nancy D'Onofrio, or it was nobody, and this was not good news, because what had just happened, however dramatic, didn't change who we were—the same incompatible people we'd been before that asshole snatched her.

If we kept trying to make an unworkable thing work, we would just hit the same hard, bone-breaking wall again and again.

Until it battered us into bloody pieces.

Chapter Thirty-Four

Nancy

I was so busy, I didn't have time to be miserable. Not when my phone never stopped ringing, my inbox was overflowing, and our social media accounts were exploding with viral videos featuring Peter and Enid. The "it" couple in folk music.

They had been launched into the big time at last. The Bonnie Blair opening gig at the Jericho had done the trick. We were besieged with offers. Even a couple record companies that had previously disdained us were making eager overtures. I boosted our fees and fielded offers right and left. They were an 'overnight sensation.' Hah. All the years of sweaty effort that I had plowed into their careers was invisible to the naked eye. Wasn't that always the way.

But Peter and Enid were ecstatic. I was surrounded by people who needed me. A vital hub of frantic activity. What else had I ever wanted in life? It was finally coming together. My clients would have brilliant careers. All was well in my professional life. That was something. It really was.

I was drinking more coffee than usual, which was saying a lot. My stomach had shriveled into a steel ball about the size of a walnut. Nothing would go into it.

Even Peter noticed, a few days after the Bonnie Blair gig, in their hotel room.

"God, Nance, you're as white as a sheet," he said, frowning.

Enid hastened to get her two cents in. "And you've got dark marks under your eyes. And your pants are hanging right off your butt."

"Gee, thanks," I said, glancing at the mirror. They were right. I looked like hell. I had a brief, bittersweet fantasy of what Liam would say. How he would scold me for not eating, and then make me a big, fragrant stack of pancakes.

The fantasy made my stomach cramp painfully.

"Seriously, Nance," Enid said. "Are you getting the flu?"

"God, no," Peter muttered. "Don't get sick, Nance. You could give it to me or Enid, and we're way too busy for the flu." He strummed an angry sounding chord. "You're not starving yourself or anything dumb like that, are you? You're no use to us if you collapse, you know."

A stab of anger straightened my spine and gave me a zing of energy. "Yeah? Well, God forbid I should fail to be useful to you."

Peter strummed another harsh chord, squinting at my sharp tone. "What the hell is that supposed to mean?"

"That's all you care about," I said. "That's all you've ever cared about."

Peter looked bewildered. "Huh?"

"I could be lying in the road, bleeding out, and all you'd say would be, "How inconvenient, Nance. You're no use to me lying there bleeding." I was almost carried away in a music case a few days ago, to be tortured, probably murdered. That would have been really fucking inconvenient for you, Peter. Did you ever think of that?"

He looked horrified. "What's come over you? Calm down already!"

"I work myself to the bone for you two," I went on. "I went to unheard-of lengths to ensure your success. And all I ever get from you is whining and bitching."

"Nance, that's not true," Enid broke in. "We do appreciate—"

"And you!" I rounded on her. "I introduced you to my fiancé, and you stole him!"

"Nancy!" Peter looked outraged.

"And I forgave you. I put it behind me. And I truly do believe it was for the best, but at the time, neither one of you gave a damn about how I felt."

Peter and Enid exchanged panicked glances in the silence.

"So, uh ... what does all this mean?" Peter asked.

My anger deserted me as quickly as it had come, and only the flat, unlovely truth was left in its wake. "I can't go on like this," I said. "I'm done. With you two."

Enid's eyes went huge with alarm. "Like, done being our manager? Right now? Nance, no way! You've got to be kidding!"

I shook my head. "No. My credit cards are maxed out after advancing your conference registration fees. To say nothing of all the mailings and the demo recordings I produced at my own expense. I'm burned out. Tapped out. Fed up. I'm cutting you both loose, but you're in a good place now. I left you much better than I found you. You'll have no problem finding good management."

"But now is not the time for us to be looking for manage-ment!" Peter bellowed. "We have to strike while the iron is hot! We need you out there fighting for us, like you always have!"

"Sorry," I said. "I'm all out of fight. At least for you two. The cupboard is bare."

Enid's big blue eyes narrowed speculatively. "Wait," she said. "Is this a love thing, Nance? Is it because of the dreamboat?"

"Dreamboat? Who? Are you talking about that rude, arrogant jerk who came to the conference?" Peter was aghast. "But he's just a—"

"Not another word," I snarled.

"Cool it, Petey, baby," Enid said sharply.

Peter flushed, and struck a loud, vicious chord.

I got up, looking from one to the other of them, realizing with a weird sense of lightness that I really was done here. There was no need to say another word.

"I'm heading out," I said. "I wish you well. Good luck with everything."

"Wait! Hold on, Nance," Enid said urgently. She leaned down, whispering fiercely into Peter's ear. He dug his wallet out of his jeans pocket with clear reluctance, looking shamefaced. He pulled out a wad of money, counted it, and passed it to me. "It's not all that we owe you, but I'll get the rest of it to you when we get back to the city."

I stared down at the cash, startled. "Thanks."

"Nance," Enid said. "We'll make this right. We're sorry. I'm definitely sorry. And Petey is, too, even though he doesn't act like it. You know how he is."

I snorted. "Yeah, I certainly do."

"Please reconsider," Enid coaxed. "We don't want to look for other management. You're amazing. The way you care. How you 'get' us. We didn't appreciate that enough. You spoiled us. Not that I put the blame on you, but..."

"But you just did," I said wryly. "I'm not feeling it, Enid. Sorry."

"Just think about it," Enid urged. "Keep an open mind. We'll be good. Good as gold. No more whining. No more tantrums. No more debts."

She looked like she meant it. Gratifying, but I just nodded and left, heading to my own room to grab my own bag. I going home, to figure my shit out. I had bigger problems at the moment. Peter and Enid feeling abandoned just did not make the cut. They needed to grow the fuck up.

And incidentally, so did I.

Chapter Thirty-Five

Liam

There was nothing else I could have done, I repeated as I sanded the table. I was so sick of the images looping endlessly through my brain. Nancy, curled up in that music case, looking so pale and fragile. All the bad outcomes, so narrowly escaped.

It made me want to throw myself in front of her door to keep her safe. But that was not something I had a right to do, unless I was her lover.

Or her husband.

The rhythmic motions of sanding were not chilling me. Working on the table made my misery worse, not better. No matter how hard I tried, I kept seeing that shiny auburn hair spread out in a fan on the smooth, polished wood, those hazel eyes, the long, elegant nose, the wide, luscious mouth. The sounds she made when she came.

I'd never imagined proposing marriage to her, even when things were going well. Idle memories chased themselves through my brain. Inconsequential, silly things, like making sure she ate breakfast. Teasing that anxious little crease away from her brow. Making her smile. Making her laugh.

I sanded away, unable to stop the flood of memories. It had been so easy to talk to her. She'd understood things, even when I couldn't put them into words. I remembered those sweet, companionable silences as we listened to the creak of the porch swing and the song of the wind chimes, the crickets. The wind in the trees as clouds scudded across the evening sky. The moon, shining down on us. Pure magic.

But that wasn't compatibility. That was just hormones, limerence, a cheap trick my mind was playing on me. There were some things in life that a man should not compromise on. Nancy and I were incompatible. She'd demonstrated that time and time again. And blowing off our vacation without a second thought was the last straw. Just like when Dad ...

A chill shuddered through me.

Just like when Dad had done it to me and Mom.

I lay the sandpaper down, my hands suddenly numb. Strange, that I hadn't made that connection sooner. It was obvious, after all. Not a huge revelation. In a lot of ways, the situations were very similar.

Similar, maybe. But not identical.

I ached to talk to Mom. I could see her so clearly in my mind. Her short, iron-gray hair, her clear gray eyes. Smiling as if we always shared some secret joke.

I sank down onto one of my carved benches and closed my eyes. God knows, Mom had never been all that great at compromise herself. I remembered with bemused affection how we'd butted heads. Both of us, hopelessly stubborn.

She had tried to compromise with Dad, but he did not make the same reciprocal effort. At last, she'd been forced to put her foot down, and keep it down.

And as for Dad, forget it. Once he made up his mind, you couldn't budge him with an earthmover. When it came to compromise, I was genetically challenged.

I brushed sawdust on my clothes, wandered out onto the porch and sat down on the steps, deliberately avoiding the porch swing and its memories. I started to let memories of that early part of my life bubble up, uncannily vivid. Those early years with Dad.

It had taken my mother years to get over him. I'd been surprised when she'd finally decided to marry again. But Hank, her second husband, had been an older man. A peach of a guy, mellow, and agreeable.

I had loved Hank, too. I'd learned the trade of carpentry from him, as well as the music, which was a hell of a lot more than I'd gotten from my own dad. Their nine-year marriage had been a good one. I had mourned him like a father when he died.

But there had never been that crackling energy between her and Hank that I remembered between her and Dad. I'd been too young to know what it was, but I'd put a name to it now. That heat. That zing that put a brilliant edge onto things. Made them seem precious and fine.

If I found some nice woman to share my life with, someone who fit my list, it would probably be like it had been with my mother and Hank. Perfectly good. Solid as a rock. Absolutely nothing to complain about.

I rested my aching forehead against my hands. This line of thought made my head hurt. My mom would have liked Nancy. She would've appreciated her spirit and sass. She would have liked that she was Irish stock. Memories of my mother crowded my head. I remembered the funeral parlor, that dull ache in my guts. Like the plug had been pulled from the world.

I remembered staring at that bouquet of tiger lilies that my father had sent.

Tiger lilies. Her favorite. That son of a bitch.

I'd been almost grateful for the anger the flowers provoked. It had given me a break from the ache. I was so furious at my old man. Cowardly bastard. Afraid of his former wife even after she was dead. But he remembered her favorite flowers.

I propped my chin on my hands and stared at the trees. They were bending, swaying gracefully in the wind. Flexible, yielding, singing their sweet, shushing song of rustling leaves ... and a thought popped into my head.

Did I still have the card that came with the bouquet? I remembered stuffing the tiger lilies into the wastebasket set out for the used tissues of the bereaved. Slamming down the lid while people stared and murmured.

But someone had gathered up the sympathy cards for me. I vaguely remembered someone handing me a bag of them.

Maybe I still had them somewhere.

I got up and headed toward the storage shed out back. I had kept boxes of Mom's stuff that I hadn't gotten around to going through. My body hummed with restless urgency.

The stack of boxes was not that large. I hadn't kept much. Just photo albums, letters, clippings. A few of my mother's personal things. I rummaged through them and found the bag of sympathy cards in the second to last box.

There was a tremor in my hand. I observed it as if it belonged to someone else.

Dad's card was there. I hadn't thrown it away.

The envelope bore the company logo. Knightly, Mitchum & McComber, Inc. The card had clouds and a seagull printed on the front, with Deepest Sympathies in a flowery font. Embossed gold lettering.

I opened it. In my father's square, graceless block print, it read, *Liam, I'm thinking of you. Love, Dad.*

Things crumpled and popped beneath my weight as I sank down onto the floor of the shed and stared at those printed words for a long time.

It was full dark by the time I pulled myself up to my feet, stiff, and chilled. I took the card with me to the house, wondering what just happened. This feeling was not unpleasant, just strange. Like a big stick had stirred me up inside, not gently.

I flipped on the kitchen light and stared at the address, which was in San Francisco. So my dad had moved out west. I put on the teakettle and turned on the flame, thinking about the phone number printed beneath the address.

It was three hours earlier in San Francisco. Pacific Standard Time. Still working hours, if he was still working. I did some quick mental arithmetic. Dad would be sixty-nine. No way would he be retired. That tough-as-nails bastard would hang on to control to the bitter end.

The teakettle began to whistle. I made myself a cup of tea with one hand, holding the envelope by the corner with two fingers of my other hand, as if it were a potentially dangerous object. Explosive, or radioactive.

I sipped my tea and pondered the message Dad had written six years ago. The one I'd been too angry and proud, even after nineteen years of silence, even after Mom's death, to read.

A question took form in my mind. I could keep my foot down, and bargain all the color out of my life. In exchange for what? Pride? Righteous anger?

Anger and pride were looking like very cold company right now.

I put down my tea and grabbed the phone. I had to move fast, or I would psych myself out. I dialed the number.

A woman's voice answered. "Knightly, Mitchum & McComber. Can I help you?"

"Frank Knightly, please."

"May I ask what it's regarding?"

"Tell him it's his son."

The woman was silent for a moment, astonished. "Ah ... excuse me?"

"I'm his son," I repeated.

"Oh. I didn't realize that ... um. Sorry. Please hold."

I listened to a Muzak version of "Rocky Mountain High," and then the opening strains of "Tie A Yellow Ribbon" were cut off abruptly.

"Who the hell is this?" said a gruff, suspicious voice.

Intense emotion shivered through me at the familiar voice. "Dad. It's me. Liam."

Dad made an audible swallowing sound. "Liam, eh?"

"Yeah. It's really me."

We waited for a moment, awkward and silent. I suddenly regretted my impulse. It had been stupid to embarrass my dad after all these years. Better to let sleeping dogs lie. I was racking my brains for some slick way to get the hell off the phone and release the both of us from this agony when my father spoke again.

"It's, ah, good to hear your voice. It's deeper than I remember."

I stifled a snort. "Ah, yeah. That happens."

"I've thought about you a lot, these twenty-some years."

"Twenty-five," I corrected.

Dad harrumphed. "Oh. Twenty-five, is it?"

"Yeah," I said. "On June twenty-third."

"Ah." My father cleared his throat. "Long time."

"It is," I agreed.

There was another agonizing pause, and Dad spoke again,

haltingly. "I'm sorry I didn't call when your mother died. Don't know why I didn't. I guess I thought you'd slam the phone down on me."

"I wouldn't have," I said, wondering if it were true.

Frank Knightly sighed. "I guess you wouldn't have. Well, what's done is done."

"That's true." I took a deep breath, and went for it. "Dad. I just wanted to tell you that I'm sorry about what I said before you left."

There was a long silence. "Don't give it a thought, son." My father's voice was gentler than I had ever heard it. "God knows, I deserved every word."

"Maybe you did, but I'm sorry anyhow."

Dad cleared his throat. "I'm sorry, too. About all of it. So, ah ... what made you decide to call?"

A strange impulse propelled the words out of my mouth. "I'm, uh, thinking about getting married," I heard myself say.

"Is that so." Dad's voice was wondering. "Hard to imagine that you're old enough for that sort of thing."

"I'm thirty-six," I reminded him.

"My word," my father said.

I cleared my throat. "Anyway, I just wanted to know ... that is, if it works out, if I should send you an invitation."

"If it works out? You mean, the deal's not closed yet?"

"No. There are still a few contract details to hammer out."

Dad harrumphed. "Ah, yes. I'd be glad to come," he said gruffly. "Very glad."

"Okay," I said. "Good to know."

"Good luck with those contract details," he said. "I'll be looking for that invitation, now. Don't you disappoint me."

"I'll do my best," I promised.

"And whatever happens with your lady friend ..." My

father paused awkwardly. "Call me again sometime. Okay? It was good to hear from you."

"Yeah. I'll do that." My voice felt thick. I coughed to clear it. "Good-bye, Dad."

I hung up the phone and drank some tea to loosen the burning ache in my throat. It was stone cold, but I gulped it down anyway, and stared out my big windows at the impenetrable darkness outside. I was wide awake. Thrumming with an emotion I could not identify.

I was not going to bargain away my life in exchange for the fantasy of control. I didn't want some faceless, agreeable, compatible whoever. I just wanted Nancy.

And if I had to compromise to get her, then compromise I would. If it killed me.

I thought of the ugly, posturing bullshit I'd said, before I left the hotel. She'd seen my worst self. Which meant I had a hell of a job ahead, convincing her to marry me now. But I was a tenacious bastard. So they all told me.

That had to be useful for something besides pissing people off.

Chapter Thirty-Six

Nancy

I stared, unseeing, out the window of my apartment from my place on the futon. It was dark inside but for the faint city glow that sneaked through the window, but I couldn't be bothered to get up and turn on lights. It scared me now, to advertise my presence there. I should probably just sleep, but I was too tired to wrestle the couch down into a bed.

I should have been at the cathedral uptown, where Cantate Domino, my female medieval and Renaissance musical ensemble, was having their big New York concert debut. They were singing the works of Hildegarde Von Bingen. It was a beautiful program, and a very important gig for them. Their first established classical concert series. A big step forward. I should be there to support them.

But I couldn't even get up. Let alone dress, comb my hair, put on my game face, get myself uptown, chat, smile, schmooze.

My ass was weighted down like I was made of lead.

The ensemble understood, of course. Everybody was extremely understanding these days after my near-death episode in the parking lot of the Amory Lodge. They were also treating me like blown glass after seeing me cut Peter and Enid loose.

That had shocked the bejesus out of everyone on my client list.

And Peter and Enid, oh God. They would not let up. My voicemail was full of pleading, wheedling messages. Surprise, surprise—they'd already alienated two new potential managers with those same egregious personality disorders that I'd spent years justifying and excusing.

But it was a no-brainer for me. I was done with that soul-sucking bullshit forever. Maybe it was childish and unprofessional to walk away. It certainly hadn't been a great financial move.

I didn't care. A person learned the lesson, with the requisite pain and suffering, and then she hung on to whatever she'd learned. She made it worthwhile.

At least that was the pep talk I kept trying to give myself.

The events in Boston had laid my pathetic emotional stratagems bare. I'd been scrambling for love all these years, and I only knew this because finally, I'd gotten some. Just a taste. Enough to know what it felt like.

I'd been better off not knowing.

I had earned no love from all my heroic efforts all these years. Love couldn't be earned, or God knows I would have more of it.

Lucia had tried in so many ways to make me understand that, but no one could have protected me from myself. No wonder Lucia had tried to match me up with Liam. She'd wanted me to have a man I could lean on. A man with something significant to bring to the table.

The joke was on me. Liam was plenty solid. Like an outcropping of volcanic granite.

And amazingly, he'd stepped up again, even after our apocalyptic fight. He'd heroically saved me from Snake Eyes. So they told me. I hadn't been conscious to see it. He'd snatched me from the jaws of death, seen me to the hospital, and then, duty fulfilled, he'd shaken the dust off his boots and walked off into the sunset.

Not a word from the man. Not a peep.

I was a miserable mess. I'd been crashing at Nell's place in Williamsburg for the first couple of weeks afterward, but the close quarters were driving us bananas. We were stumbling over each other, and Moxie was stressed and disoriented, too. I loved my sisters, but their intense worry for me was wearing me down.

I'd risked coming back here tonight just for some sweet solitude. Just to enjoy the quiet, even though I was too scared to so much as turn on a lamp.

The doctors said that it would take a while for the anxiety to ease off. The pills they'd prescribed were rattling around in my purse, but I hadn't tried taking them. All I had were my feelings. I didn't want to cut myself loose from those, too.

Besides. I needed to be razor sharp, if Snake Eyes came calling. I'd gotten myself some pepper spray and a stun baton. Maybe I was fooling myself, but damn, I was not going down without a fight if he came after me again.

And Snake Eyes had taken my precious necklace. A fresh insult, and a fresh new disaster. It was a third of that key that Lucia had alluded to. We had not yet even begun to solve the puzzle, and now we never would. So this fear, stress, and uncertainty would never end.

Not until Snake Eyes finally nabbed me.

Ouch. I tried to push the fear away, but I was losing the

knack of stuffing painful thoughts and feelings. They demanded their space now. They would not be denied.

I thought of calling Liam, but something always held me back. He was the one who had walked away, so technically, the ball was in his court. But I was too raw and sad to play games. I just wanted to hold out my heart and say, "Take it. It's yours anyway, you damn idiot. So take it already."

The intercom buzzed, and I jerked upright, my heart in my throat.

My sisters had keys, so it wasn't one of them. And Snake Eyes wouldn't buzz. He would transform into fetid slime, ooze under the crack in the door, and reconstitute himself on the other side.

Which meant it almost had to be one of my clients who'd gotten frustrated with me being incommunicado. Or Peter and Enid, tired of me ignoring their calls.

Fuck 'em. I didn't want to talk. Just as well I'd left the light off. Plausible deniability. I gave the intercom the finger and sat there. Daring it to ring again.

Buzzzzzz, it rang, loud and long and demanding. Persistent bastard.

Buzzzzzz, again. At this point, I was curious. I slunk up next to the window. Leaned out to peek down, ready to lunge back to avoid being seen.

Liam stood on the top of my stoop. My heart thudded painfully hard against my ribs. My legs went rubbery and weak. *Buzzzzz,* he hit the intercom again.

Then he looked up and saw me. I hadn't flinched back fast enough.

He gazed up in silent entreaty. I went to the door, and buzzed him in, then unlocked all the locks, of which there were many. I had added three more to my collection since the Snake Eyes episode.

Dignity, I reminded myself. *Detachment. Hold your ground. You're not going to throw your life away to suit anyone's whim. You've done that long enough.*

A quiet knock sounded. I opened the apartment door.

The sight of him hit me like a blow. So tall. So beautiful. But thinner. He was pale, drawn, his face somber. In the sickly light from the stairwell, I saw fading bruises beneath both eyes. He'd had a broken nose, Eoin had said. Cracked ribs. A dislocated shoulder. Hanging out with me was hard on a guy's health.

I grimly clamped down on the urge to fuss. Fussing was above my pay grade.

My heart raced so hard, I felt woozy and faint. I could think of no coherent greeting for him, so I just stepped back and silently gestured him in.

He shoved the door shut after him, blocking out the light. I was grateful I'd left it off, until memories flooded back of the last time they'd been in this room, in the dark. Making mad love.

He cleared his throat. "Are you all right?"

I blocked all the automatic polite replies at their source. I had nothing to lose, nothing to hide, no reason to lie. "No," I said. "I feel like shit."

He took a step closer. "I'm sorry about what happened between us."

A sound burst out of me, part bitter laugh, part derisive snort. "Not as sorry as me. I can't sleep. I can't eat. I can't concentrate. I'm scared of my own shadow. I'm wrecked, Liam. Don't tell me you're sorry. I don't want to hear it."

"You have to hear it, because I'm not done saying it."

"Oh, yeah?" I sat down on the futon with an undignified thump. "Don't tell me what to do, Knightly. I'm done with your lectures and your bullshit ultimatums."

"I love you," he said roughly.

That cut my tirade off and left me gasping. "H-h-huh?"

"I'm sorry for all the stupid shit I said. I was scared. I was reacting to old stuff that had absolutely nothing to do with you. And I'm so sorry I did that."

I rocked on the couch, my hands over my mouth. "Old stuff," I repeated.

"Yeah. Stuff I never worked through. But after what happened, I had to. I couldn't go on like that. Smothering to death in a box I made for myself. Trying to keep everything under control. It was grow or die. So I grew. I'm trying to, anyhow."

"Um. Okay. Growing how?"

Liam sank down onto his knees. He pried one of my hands off my mouth and kissed it, reverently, slowly. In the silence, it felt like a sacred ceremony.

"I love you, Nancy D'Onofrio," he said.

I was vibrating with emotion, but this thing between us was a maze, a confusion of entrances and exits, full of dead ends and traps and pitfalls. My heart shook at the idea that there might actually be a narrow, winding way through it.

If we could find it together.

"Why didn't you call me?" I asked.

Damn it. I'd blurted out the question I'd sworn I wouldn't ask. It had just sprung up and asked itself without my permission.

He hesitated. "I couldn't for a while. First, I was numb. Then I was scared. Then I was just embarrassed. I'll regret making you wait for the rest of my life."

That startled me into smiling. "Oh, come on. Don't get melodramatic. The rest of your life is a long time." I paused. "I hope," I added delicately.

"Do you?" He slid his arms around my hips, pressing his face to my belly. "I'm glad you feel that way. But no matter how long it is, it'll be too long without you."

Whoa. He'd caught me in a weak moment. He was just waiting for me to cave.

And oh, how I wanted to cave. I ached for it.

I rested my hands on his shoulders, I suppose with a vague notion of pushing him away, but as soon as my body made contact with his, my fingers dug in. He felt leaner, harder than I remembered. His body was taut. Tension thrummed through it.

I couldn't push him away to save my life. I sank down like a wilting flower. I draped myself over him, my face resting on his shoulders, feeling his breath.

"How's your nose?" My voice was muffled against his shirt.

"Healing," he replied. "It's no big deal."

"It was for me," I said. "You saved my life. Again. Thanks."

He lifted his head. "Oh, yeah. Speaking of which." His voice was disapproving. "Why the hell are you here alone? It's not safe. I just came here from your sister's house. Nell and Vivi told me you'd come here."

"Don't start with me," I said. "I've been very good, for the most part. I just needed to be alone tonight. I was in a mood."

He looked dubious. "What mood is that?"

"That question is off limits," I said crisply.

He was silent, pondering that. "Okay. So how did it all go, anyhow?"

"How did what go?"

"The gig. Peter and Enid. The Jericho. Are they mega superstars now?"

"Not one bit of sarcasm out of you, Knightly."

He lifted his hands in quick surrender. "Sorry. I didn't mean to sound sarcastic."

"It went well," I said coolly. "Huge boost for both their careers. Yay, them."

"Ah. Well, good. I'm happy for them. And you."

I smiled at his careful, kid-gloves tone. "That's very big of you, Liam."

"I hope they appreciate you now."

"Hmm," I said. "About that. The truth is, we've parted ways. I no longer manage Peter and Enid."

His stunned silence filled the room. "You did *what?*"

I shrugged, sighing out excess tension. "I had a sort of epiphany," I admitted. "I realized that they didn't deserve the energy I gave them. So I withdrew it."

"Right when they hit the big time," he said, in a wondering voice.

"Yep." My voice was hollow. "Shame about the timing, but hey. There's never a good time. Like a guy I know once told me. Sometimes you just have to put your foot down."

"Funny you should say that," he said. "Myself, I've been working on the concept of compromise."

"Really?" My heart thudded. "And how do you feel about it these days?"

"It's not quite as horrible as I thought," he said. "It hasn't killed me yet. To my continuing surprise."

"Good to know," I said. "I'm really happy for you."

A couple of silent, charged minutes went by, and I gently brushed my fingertips against the bruises under his eyes. He seized my hand, kissed it again.

"So, I called my father," he offered.

That was entirely unexpected. "Did you, now. Why on earth? What came over you?"

I felt him shrug in the darkness. "You know. It was part of the whole compromise thing. I was thinking over the entire arc of my life. If you look at things long enough, you start to see them in a different light."

"I guess that's true," I said. "So? How did your talk with your dad go?"

"It was weird," he admitted. "Stiff. Awkward. Cringey. But we got through it."

"What did you talk about? What did he say?"

He kissed her hand again, and a rush of pleasure rippled through me. "It was a short conversation," he said. "But I asked him if I should send him an invitation to my wedding."

My jaw dropped. I went stiff. "What?"

"Shit," Liam muttered. "Sorry. That came out all wrong. I know it's just a hypothetical thing. Or more like a hopeful, aspirational thing."

"Hy-hypothetical?"

"Yeah. I told him I'd invite him. If I got lucky."

I sat there, dumbfounded. He waited patiently, kissing every knuckle of my hand. Slow, hot, gentle kisses. "Damn it," he murmured. "I did this all backwards, with my usual grace. I meant to tell you first that I'll respect your work and your career, always. That I admire your drive, and dedication, and I won't get in your way, that I'm incredibly proud of your achievements. I should have led with that."

I just shook my head, still speechless.

"I'll spend my life trying not to fuck this up. Trying to be worthy of you. I love you, Nancy."

"I love you, too," I said. "But wait just a goddamn minute."

"For what?" he said. "You're my queen. My goddess. Let me love you forever."

"Liam. One little detail here. You're still bruised from the first time you had to defend me from Snake Eyes, let alone the second time!"

"So Snake Eyes is his name now?"

"As good a name as any. He's out there, and he wants something. I can't give it to him. He'll never stop coming after us. This is mine and my sisters' problem, not yours. Backing away from me is the smart thing to do, Liam. Much better for your health. Being with me puts you in danger."

"I don't care," he said. "That day in the parking lot, I got a good, long look at what life would be like for me if Snake Eyes got you. I couldn't take it. I will not let that happen."

"But he got my necklace," I said, my voice bleak. "It was our only clue. Without it, we'll never solve this puzzle. We'll always be tense, on edge, waiting for the hammer to come down."

"I don't care. I want you. Your problems are now my problems. End of story."

I sniffed back tears. "That's extremely romantic, but it doesn't say much for your judgment, dude."

"Probably not, but is that a yes? Will you marry me?"

"It means that I love you, certainly. But I just don't know if I could handle being engaged again."

"So let's skip the engaged part, and go straight to the married part," he suggested. "Let's run off to Vegas. Tonight. We'll take a red-eye flight. Go to the courthouse to get the paperwork done tomorrow morning, as soon as we get there."

I was laughing, tears filling my nose. "For real?"

"For real. We can get married by an Elvis impersonator. Spend three days on a vibrating bed. Play some blackjack. Drink champagne in a hot tub."

It sounded surreally wonderful. "But what about that invitation to your dad?"

"We'll do another wedding for your sisters and our friends and my dad," he said. "This one is just for us. Our hot, sexy, secret elopement. Makes me hard just thinking about it." He hesitated. "Your schedule permitting, of course," he added. "It can wait. If you've got work commitments."

"Wow, Liam," I said demurely. "That speech sounds extremely rehearsed."

"Is it so obvious? Come on. Give me credit for trying."

"You can have all the credit you want." I slid my arms around his waist. "You're so thin. Have you been eating?"

"Hey. That's my line."

"I have to feed you up. There's this great little Vietnamese place down the block. Great barbecued beef skewers. Killer noodles."

"Do you have noodles here? Spaghetti, linguini? Some tomato sauce, some garlic?"

"Are you kidding? With a name like D'Onofrio?"

"If we make our noodles here, we can get naked while the water boils," he said.

She laughed at him. "You've got yourself a deal."

"That's awesome. I'm thrilled. But you still haven't answered my proposal."

I threw up my hands. "Liam, I love you. You love me. Isn't that miracle enough for now? Can't we just be grateful? Let's not push our luck!"

He looked mutinous. "I want you to be my wife. I want it all signed and sealed."

"Hmm," she murmured. "I thought you were working on the concept of compromise."

"Sure, but let's not overdo it." He touched my face, as carefully as if I were one of Lucia's orchids. "I almost lost you. It would have ripped my heart out. I'll never stop loving you, Nancy. We can push our luck all we want. For the rest of our lives. It's endless. Deeper than the ocean. Wider than the sky. You get me?"

The sweet, hot glow in my chest swelled into something

huge, until my heart was about to burst. There was no more room for fear.

"Yes," I said, reaching for him.

If you want more of the saga of the D'Onofrio stories, don't miss Edge of Secrets, Book 2 of The Edge Trilogy!

Read on for a tantalizing excerpt...

Excerpt: Edge of Secrets

The Edge Series, Book 2
Chapter One

Nell

I'd been waiting for my crush to show up at the café all day, even though I didn't admit it to myself. Then the bell over the café door jingled, and he stepped through. And there he was at last, in my face. Mr. Tall, Dark and Hyper-focused.

I stepped behind the dessert display case, seizing the opportunity ogle him from over the pecan fudge brownies and under the Napoleon pastries. Looking at that man gave me such a rush. It was dumb, childish, embarrassing, inappropriate. I was making my own self cringe. But the rush was impossible to resist. At least right now.

I had to have that little buzz. It was the only thing that even momentarily eased the dull ache in my middle. I'd been carrying that heavy feeling around ever since my world imploded a few weeks ago with my mother's death. Maybe I would be carrying it forever. Always dragging those tight, forced, shallow breaths into that cramped, burning space around my bruised heart. No respite from it, ever.

Chapter One

At least not until I saw Mr. Tall, Dark and Hyper-Focused. The first moment I laid eyes on him for the first time a few weeks ago, I got an effervescent rush through my body. It lasted only the time it took for the guy to order, eat his lunch, pay up, and go, so not very long. But oh, it was such sweet relief. Even for that brief interval.

The sickening awareness of what had happened to Lucia, my adopted mother, was never far from me. The home invasion, the alleged heart attack. Violence, fear, loss, it was always right there. Just pushed a little bit to the back so I could function in the world. More or less. I could dress a salad, pour coffee, bus plates.

But when my crush walked out the door, grief slammed me back down even harder than before, as if to punish me for trying to evade it.

He checked to see if his usual table by the window was free, which it almost always was. Today was no exception. The lunch rush was over by the time he arrived; three-fifteen, regular as clockwork. That gave me a buzzy little hum of hopeful anticipation to carry me along for all the hours of my shift that came before. Yay, me. Win-win.

He took off his jacket, tossed it on the chair, and seated himself. Then he pulled out a laptop, opened it, and set to work with all the grim concentration of a power drill.

For weeks he'd been here, every damn day. And ever since the first day, I'd been working all the lunch shifts, even though I would earn more tips with the dinner shifts, whenever I could schedule them around my teaching schedule.

But no. Broke and busted as I was, that fleeting rush I got from seeing Mr. Hyper-Focused was worth more to me than a pocketful of tips. How freaking silly and sad was that, considering that the man was oblivious to my very existence.

I took my glasses off and swiftly polished them on my

apron. *The better to see you with, my dear.* I perched them back onto my nose and fished the order I'd just taken out of my short-term memory before it disappeared into the churning abyss, and promptly dished up ratatouille for the table of women underneath the aquarium, gawking at my crush all the while. I shot quick, surreptitious glances as I drizzled vinaigrette with a practiced flick of my wrist, and tossed grated beets and roasted pumpkin seeds on their salads.

I loaded the tray and chose a path through the restaurant that brought me right past his table, close enough to smell the detergent his crisp white shirt was washed in. The next pass was to refill the water glasses. That run made me conclude that he had asked his dry-cleaner to put extra starch into his collars and cuffs. Another sneaky run through the tables with the coffee pot garnered me a greedy whiff of his aftershave. Mmm, nice. Woodsy, notes of citrus. And those shoulders. Flaring out, so broad and thick and solid-looking. I wondered what it would feel like to sink my nails into them.

He wasn't movie-star beefcake handsome, not with that rough, angular face, those deep-set, laser-sharp dark eyes, but something about him just got to me. I had studied his features, reviewing them over and over in my daydreams and sexual fantasies.

His face was rugged. Olive skin, that big, bladelike nose with the crooked bump on it, the black, slashing eyebrows set at a sharp upward angle. His cheeks were lean, with grooves flanking his mouth, and he had crinkled lines around his eyes, as if he'd squinted into the desert sun for a long time. His mouth was flat and unsmiling, his black hair was cut short, and it stuck up wildly every which way.

The resulting look worked for me. No way would that guy affect such spiky, messy hair on purpose. He could not be bothered with such petty considerations. He did not give a rat's ass if anyone was looking at him. He didn't care about his hair. For some random reason, that was a turn-on for me. Go figure.

I dared a peek at his computer screen from behind his broad, muscular back. I could make out his prodigious muscle definition even through the fine cotton of his dress shirt. The screen was thick with code. Which was all Greek to me, besides being none of my damn business. I walked away, chin up, resolute. Mature. Ignoring him.

After one last, hungry peek.

Behind the counter, my boss, Norma, looked over from the marinated mushrooms she was grilling with a smile. "He's here again, eh, Nelly?" she said. "Can't get enough of that strip steak sandwich, I see. Before I lose you in a romantic daze, honey, I need to ask a favor."

Oh, God. My crush was that obvious? I grabbed the bread knife and began slicing. "Ask away," I said grimly.

"Easy does it, hon. Don't maim yourself. Couldn't help but notice that you never take your eyes off the fellow. Can't say I really blame you. He's definitely a hottie. Those big, thick shoulders, mmm. If I were twenty-five years younger ... hell, maybe even just fifteen ..." Her voice trailed off, a teasing gleam in her eyes.

I was too mortified to be a good sport today. I just kept slicing bread.

"Workaholic, though," Norma went on in a musing tone. "Always tappity-tapping away, never a glance for the cute little waitress serving him. You're wasted on him sweetheart. Take it from an expert. Leave that guy alone. He'd be good for nothing but a bunch of plate-throwing arguments about emotional availability. And believe me—I know whereof I speak."

"Thanks for the advice." I apportioned the sliced bread into a bunch of baskets. "But I don't need it. I'm not getting anywhere near him, or any other man. Believe me. I have enough drama in my life these days. Any more would break me."

"Whatever you say, honey. Hey, are you free to work an evening shift? Kendra just called in sick. Again. That girl's driving me crazy. Always at death's door."

I gave her an apologetic look. "I'm so sorry, Norma, but I'm teaching a discussion section tonight for the American poetry course."

Norma clucked her tongue. "I was afraid of that. Oh well. We'll be shorthanded, but we'll survive. Maybe I can get Pete to come in, if he's between boyfriends. Go on, get some coffee for that hardworking fellow before he starts feeling put upon. Do you absolutely have to wear those glasses, Nelly?"

I snatched the glasses in question off my nose and polished them again, defensively. "Unless you want me to bump into tables, yes! What's wrong with my glasses?"

"They just make you look so, I don't know. Bookish, I guess."

"Norma, I've got news for you. I *am* bookish! To the marrow of my bones! It's my most defining personality trait!"

"Aww, now, don't get your knickers in a twist. Your eyes are so big and brown and pretty, I just want the world to see them." Norma tucked a hank of curly black hair from behind my ear so that it dangled ticklishly around my chin and proceeded to tug down the front of my apron to show a little more of my chest. "For God's sake, Nelly. Youth is wasted on the young. Go on, scram! Get the man's order!"

I poured out the cup of black coffee that he always wanted and scurried out with my order pad, self-consciously tugging my sunset-tinted apron bib back up over my cleavage, annoyed and agitated. Norma was very old school when it came to directives on mating behavior. She was also an immensely kind woman and a really good boss. I was lucky to have found her, and I knew she meant well, so I couldn't get huffy with her for crossing the line. Besides, I got too fluttery to stay mad when I took Mr. Hyper-Focused's order anyway. God alone knew why. We'd never so much as made eye contact. I could take his lunch order stark naked, and he would never notice.

I placed his coffee on the table. Without shifting his eyes from the screen, he reached for it and took a sip. "Thanks," he said, in that deep, resonant voice that made me go all shivery and stupid. "The usual, please."

"Okay." I concentrated fiercely on keeping my voice from going breathy and high-pitched. "We have three soups today: chicken noodle, French onion, and three bean. Which would you prefer?"

A small frown furrowed his forehead, but he didn't look up. "I don't care. You pick."

"Okay. One bowl of I-don't-care, coming right up." I stared, almost transfixed, at the cowlick at the crown of his head. A wild, spiky vortex. There was raffish stubble on his tense-looking jaw. His starch-stiffened cuffs were turned up, revealing tough, ropy muscles and black hair that lay flat and silky against the golden skin of his forearms.

"Is there a problem?" His voice was distant, but his fingers still tapping that constant, rapid-fire staccato.

"Um, no. Of course not." I fled, flustered, jamming my hip into a nearby table edge.

Ouch. I suppressed yelp of pain. Crap. The bruise that would show up tomorrow would serve as a stern reminder of what happened when one gave in to adolescent urges. Cripes, even Norma had noticed my condition. I'd let this silly crush get way out of hand.

I put the order in and began assembling his lunch. Norma glanced over with professional interest. "The usual, I assume?" she asked.

"Unsurprisingly." I popped a roll into the toaster grill, and scooped an enormous serving of Knorma's Knockout Coleslaw onto a small plate.

"You're ruining me with those portions, hon. Trust me. The fella's not worth it."

"Give it a rest, Norma," I snapped, arranging the thick slices of tomato, radish rosebuds and carrot curlicues onto his plate. I tossed on a handful of alfalfa sprouts, hesitated for the barest instant, and cut a substantial slice of sweet onion. I added it with a flourish, since his breath was neither my responsibility nor my problem. I scooped some oven-roasted rosemary potatoes onto the plate. Then added a few more.

The toaster pinged, and I pulled out the roll, still avoiding Norma's gaze.

"What soup did he want?" Norma inquired.

"He doesn't care. I'll give him the three-bean. It's good today."

"Really? I don't know, hon. Chicken might be safer. You know ... gas?"

I snorted as I ladled his bowl full of soup. "He can learn to express a goddamn preference if he doesn't like it." I hefted the tray, and the soup slopped dangerously near the edges of the bowl.

"Easy does it, Nelly. He's not going anywhere without his lunch."

I gave her a withering look and carried out his soup.

When I brought out the rest of Mr. Hyper-Focused's lunch, the only place to put the sandwich plate was the extreme edge of the table, which looked precarious. He hadn't even touched the soup yet. His big hands chattered ceaselessly on the keyboard. I had to hand it to the guy. Nothing distracted him. It seemed almost pathological.

"That'll be all." His voice was cool and distant.

I backed away, still staring. I'd been summarily dismissed. Now that I had brought his sustenance, like a silent and dutiful handmaiden, the time had come to melt silently and unobtrusively into the walls. God forbid I disturb the grand master at his important work.

His refusal to look at me was really bugging me today. I was getting genuinely pissy about it. I headed back to the kitchen, mentally ticking off the various issues I meant to cover in tonight's discussion section on Emily Dickinson's poetry. The plight of women in nineteenth-century America. Powerlessness. Arid celibacy. Secret, unrequited love. Constraint. Corsets. The life of the imagination. Agonizing sexual frustration.

Things could always be worse. And yet, this reflection did not comfort me.

"Did everything go smoothly?" The smile in Norma's voice drove me nuts.

"Smooth as silk." I loaded ice water on a tray, marched past Norma with my chin up, and tripped over the edge of the plastic mat.

Crash. Glass broke, heads turned, water sloshed and spread, ice cubes rolled.

I took a breath to contemplate the extent of the damage, then got the dustpan and started picking up glass shards and ice cubes. Eyes down, mouth tight.

"Nelly. Honey." Norma put her hands on her substantial hips, her eyes full of dismay. "You have got get out more."

"Norma, I am in no mood for a lecture," I said, through gritted teeth. "My sister was almost murdered by a slobbering maniac. I'm short my rent because of all the lost work afterward. My thesis adviser is on my case night and day to get damn thing finished. I can't get any sleep. And Lucia ... oh, God. Just let me be, okay?"

My face was dissolving. Norma tugged me up to my feet and wrapped me in a big, smothering hug. "Oh, honey, I'm so sorry. What happened to Lucia was so shocking and horrible for you girls. I didn't mean to stress you out. And your sister getting attacked was really scary, but things have worked out, am I right? She's got that big, nice, tough-looking guy looking after her now, and he's down for watching her like a hawk day and night, so things seem to be calming down a bit. I'm sure that if Lucia would want you to have some fun, move on with your life! You know she would!"

I put my glasses back on, sniffling fiercely. "I'm not in the mood for fun, Norma, no matter what Lucia might have wanted. And I don't mean to be rude, but I don't have time for this lecture, either. I need to get dessert for table six, table eight needs their check, and Monica is taking another cigarette break."

"Yes, yes. I'm sorry. Forget I said anything. But truthfully? I'm glad to see you taking a healthy interest in a likely looking man. All in all, that's a good sign."

I grunted something bad-tempered in response to that, and headed out to dump broken glass into the trash. I had to struggle to compose myself to go out on the floor once again. My eyes were red and puffy, but who cared? Mr. Hyper-Focused would never notice. When I refilled his coffee, I asked, "Care for dessert?" I was just throwing it out there, because what the hell. If the sky fell, I would barely notice.

"The usual," he said flatly. Not looking at me.

I hesitated for a moment, then let 'er rip. "Are you sure you don't want to try something new? We have fresh strawberry shortcake on sweet hot butter biscuits today, and the pecan fudge brownies are wonderful, too. Served with whipped cream."

His hands froze over the keyboard. "I'm sure they're all

good. Give me the usual." '*And no back talk*' was the subtext. He was impatient with me. Huh. That alone was more attention that I'd gotten from him thus far in the past several weeks.

I sighed, and went to get him his goddamn apple crumb pie with vanilla ice cream.

As always, when he finished, he closed his laptop, dropped bills on the table that covered the check as well as a very generous tip, and left without a backward look. The guy had the imagination of a cement block. And the manners of a molting snake.

To hell with him. I was embarrassed for myself. Crushing out on a meat-headed, insensible, uncurious, indifferent, soulless, gearhead dweeb.

At least he tipped well, so there was hope for him as a human being.

The rest of the shift was a tired blur. I helped Norma start the dinner prep, and went to the bathroom to freshen up before going uptown to my discussion section. I took off my glasses, leaned close to the mirror, and squinted at myself. A critical onceover.

Norma was right. The round glasses were very eighteenth-century. I think I'd been going for a Brontë sister vibe when I picked them out, but it was not a look that flattered me in the third millennium. And my long, thick unstyled mop of black, curly hair was juvenile and nondescript and dowdy. And very heavy.

I twisted my hair up into a knot, letting curly wisps fall down around my ears and jaw. Marginally better, but I didn't have the technology to make it stay up there. My eyes were my best feature. They were big and dark, with long lashes and thick eyebrows that I had to pluck regularly, or else they did a *coup d'etat* and took over my whole face. A nice mouth, I conceded, if a little large for my jaw. Norma and Monica kept nudging me to wear lipstick, but I always ended up wiping it off whenever I tried it. All that bright red, ka-boom. My lips, taking over my face. It literally scared me.

I should be braver with lipstick. And maybe try contact lenses. And do something to my hair.

Most importantly, I should get my ass moving, or be late to my discussion group.

I splashed water on my face, hefted my heavy shoulder bag, and headed for the downtown bus. Why stress over my looks? What difference did it make? Who cared?

I had more pressing things to worry about ... like staying out of the clutches of our nemesis, who Nancy had named Snake Eyes.

And who knew if I could pull that off.

If you want to find out more about what's in store for Nell D'Onofrio, check out Edge of Secrets!

Also by Shannon McKenna

The Edge Trilogy

Edge of Whispers

Edge of Secrets

Edge of Ruin

The Unredeemables

Master of Lies

Master Of Secrets

Master Of Chaos

The Hellbound Brotherhood Series

Hellion

Headlong

Hellbent

Heedless

Havoc

The Obsidian Files Series

Right Through Me

My Next Breath

In My Skin

Light Me Up

The McClouds & Friends Series

Behind Closed Doors

Standing In The Shadows

Out Of Control

Edge Of Midnight

Extreme Danger

Ultimate Weapon

Fade To Midnight

Blood And Fire

One Wrong Move

Fatal Strike

In For The Kill

Standalones

Return To Me

Hot Night

Meet Shannon McKenna

Shannon McKenna is the NYT and USA TODAY bestselling author of over thirty novels, ranging from sexy contemporary romance to action packed, turbocharged romantic thrillers. She loves tough and heroic alpha males, heroines with the brains and guts to match them, terrifying villains who challenge them to their utmost, adventure, blazing sensuality, and most of all, the redemptive power of true love.

Since she was small she has loved abandoning herself to the magic of a good book, and her fond childhood fantasy was that writing would be just like that but with the added benefit of being able to take credit for the story at the end. The alchemy of writing turned out to be messier than she'd ever dreamed, but whatever, she loves it anyway and hopes that readers enjoy the results of her experiments. She loves to hear from her readers. Contact her by email at her website, http://shannonmckenna.com, or find her on Facebook at https://www.facebook.com/AuthorShannonMckenna/ to keep up with all her news! Follow her on Bookbub to get new release and discount alerts! https://www.bookbub.com/authors/shannon-mckenna

If you'd like to know when new books will come out, and hear about discounts, giveaways and promos, join Shannon's newsletter at http://shannonmckenna.com/connect.php. She has special goodies waiting for you there, exclusive bonus stories that are just for her subscribers, and a free Obsidian Files novella!

She hopes to see you there!